This book is to be returned on or before
~~ ~tamped below.

S

~ 2002

7

SPECIAL MESSAGE TO READERS

This book is published by

THE ULVERSCROFT FOUNDATION,

a registered charity in the U.K., No. 264873

The Foundation was established in 1974 to provide funds to help towards research, diagnosis and treatment of eye diseases. Below are a few examples of contributions made by THE ULVERSCROFT FOUNDATION:

★ A new Children's Assessment Unit
  at Moorfield's Hospital, London.

★ Twin operating theatres at the
  Western Ophthalmic Hospital, London.

★ The Frederick Thorpe Ulverscroft Chair of
  Ophthalmology at the University of Leicester.

★ Eye Laser equipment to various eye hospitals.

If you would like to help further the work of the Foundation by making a donation or leaving a legacy, every contribution, no matter how small, is received with gratitude. Please write for details to:

THE ULVERSCROFT FOUNDATION,
The Green, Bradgate Road, Anstey,
Leicestershire, LE7 7FU. England.
Telephone: (0533) 364325

Love is
a time of enchantment:
in it all days are fair and all fields
green. Youth is blest by it,
old age made benign: the eyes of love see
roses blooming in December,
and sunshine through rain. Verily
is the time of true-love
a time of enchantment—and
Oh! how eager is woman
to be bewitched!

TRIAL FOR LOVE

Rita and Vivian could hardly have been less prepared for the visit of their Uncle Bertolino. Wrapped up in their own worries, the sisters at first had little time to spare for the funny, affectionate little Italian. But he soon became very important and dear to them both. Their new attitude to life, developed almost imperceptibly under the warm encouragement of Uncle Bertolino, prepared the sisters for the enduring partnerships that had before been so elusive.

Books by Doris Howe
in the Ulverscroft Large Print Series:

SOME OTHER DOOR
FOREVER MINE
THE SHORES OF LOVE
I GIVE YOU MY HEART
THREE O'CLOCK
THE WATERS OF TIME
SOMEWHERE MY LOVE
THE EAGER HEART
TRIAL FOR LOVE

DORIS HOWE

TRIAL FOR LOVE

Complete and Unabridged

ULVERSCROFT
Leicester

First published in Great Britain in 1957

First Large Print Edition
published June 1990

British Library CIP Data

Howe, Doris, *1904–*
    Trial for love.—Large print ed.—
    Ulverscroft large print series: romance
    I. Title
    823'.914[F]

    ISBN 0-7089-2221-X

Published by
F. A. Thorpe (Publishing) Ltd.
Anstey, Leicestershire
Set by Rowland Phototypesetting Ltd.
Bury St. Edmunds, Suffolk
Printed and bound in Great Britain by
T. J. Press (Padstow) Ltd., Padstow, Cornwall

For Muriel,
who gave me Uncle Bertolino

1

BERTOLINO CASSIMO rang the doorbell. Benevolently he watched some children playing marbles in front of the next door house. Obviously these buildings were flats. He hummed to himself as he waited. But yes . . . four name plates to the four bells. He pressed the one he wanted again. One name plate was empty.

After some time a middle-aged lady opened the door. Bertolino Cassimo beamed at her. He skipped inside the door, accommodating his bulk with surprising ease.

"Yes?" Miss Jane felt a vague misgiving, as she could never quite make up her mind whether she liked foreigners. This one was very dark, and very fat, and very friendly.

"I ring the bell for my nieces—no? Anna Helena Margharita . . . Vivian Rosa Camilla . . ."

"Oh! You mean the two girls in the

front flat? Of course. Oh, dear . . ." Miss Jane played for time. "I didn't know they had so many names."

"Their mother was, of course, my sister." Bertolino bowed. He appeared to be delighted to give this information.

"We—er, we just call them Rita and Vivian, although of course we knew they had an Italian mother." Miss Jane knew that she could not keep him standing in the hall indefinitely. Obviously he must sit down somewhere soon or he might faint at her feet. She felt quite alarmed at the thought.

"You live with them—yes?" asked Mr. Cassimo expectantly.

"No. We just have a flat in the same building. Actually I'm keeping watch while Rita is out shopping. She's been gone twenty minutes now—I don't think she'll be long before she is back. Did they —did she know you were coming?" Miss Jane was flustered and showed it.

"But no," Bertolino smiled more broadly, his wide, sallow, good humoured face creased in tiny wrinkles. "This is my holiday and I decided to come to see them to surprise them. I come from Italy—by

2

air from Rome . . ." he added importantly. His cheeks puffed out in a way that
decided Miss Jane. She approved *this*
foreigner, whatever the others were like.

"All the way from Rome to London?"
Her voice held awe. "When did you
arrive? But listen, I mustn't keep you
standing here. Please come to our flat and
I'll—I'll make you a drink of some sort,
while you wait for Rita." She couldn't
offer him tea, she decided. Not someone
as robust and volatile as this Italian.
Didn't they always drink wine in Italy?
She preceded him down the corridor,
talking clearly to give Letty time to get the
place tidied. Everything went under the
cushions at such times, she thought
vaguely. "Letty—this is Rita's uncle. He's
flown in from Italy just now."

Bertolino Cassimo bowed from the
waist, before taking Letty's hand. His
keen brown eyes saw what was the trouble
instantly. Darkness was closing in for Miss
Letty, but her manner would not have
given away the secret. She had been hastily
stowing such possessions as should not be
on view, out of sight, and her snowy white
hair had become somewhat ruffled in the

3

process. She could just see the bow and was delighted.

"How do you do?" She indicated a chair. Bertolino waited courteously until both ladies were seated. He set his cane and small black suitcase down at his side, and perched on the most solid chair in the room.

He smiled again impartially. "This is so kind . . . but everywhere I go in England it is so. Poof . . . just ask a policeman and he does more than tell you, he takes you . . . I had no trouble at all in finding this address. London is one big place . . . yes?"

Miss Jane rose. "I promised to give you a drink of something . . ." she whisked out of the room into the kitchen. No wine, no sherry, better be coffee at this time of the morning. Five minutes later she was back, with a tray and three cups of strong coffee. Bertolino bounced up to take the tray from her. Almost reverently he placed it on the small table.

"You are very kind. I see you drink with me?" He appeared to take it as a compliment. He handed a cup to Letty, before passing the second cup to Jane.

4

"You have the red hair . . ." His twinkling brown eyes took all offence from the words, and Jane accepted it as a compliment.

"Past tense," she told him ruefully.

His face became grave. "Not so. I admire red hair. In my country we are all so dark . . ."

"Yes—I've always wanted to visit Italy," Jane said. "I suppose it's a wonderful country."

This was a signal for Bertolino to branch into a voluble description of his home. Furiously he stirred his coffee from time to time.

Jane wondered if he hadn't put enough sugar in it. "You speak English very well . . ."

He beamed. "I do? That is good. I learn it very much—three years I learn. I speak to all the English people who come to my café."

"You have a café?" Letty managed to insert the question, while Jane was drinking.

"But yes. I work very hard, soon I have much money, and now I spend it." He

5

laughed gustily. "It is so . . . one saves to spend."

"Sometimes," Jane admitted grudgingly. "Sometimes one just doesn't save, even to spend."

He was not sure of her meaning, but he beamed again, for obviously she meant well. "I put in a manager, and I come here —to see my nieces . . . my Anna Helena Margharita, and my Vivian Rosa Camilla . . ."

"You see, Letty? They never told us . . ." Jane said, amused and touched. Doubtless neither girl would wish to admit to so many names. "Wait till I get Rita alone . . ."

Bertolino looked puzzled. "Rita is the elder? Where is Vivian now?"

"Yes. Rita is about twenty-three." Jane did not answer the second half of the sentence.

"I have never seen them," Bertolino said simply. "Their mother never returned after her marriage. They are beautiful?"

"Isn't all youth beautiful?" Letty said. "These two girls certainly are. Rita so dark, Vivian fair, and both with those deep blue eyes."

"I see you like them?" he said, glancing round the room. His rotund little figure lapped over the sides of his chair as he sat with his hands clasped on his stomach. "That coffee—it was good . . . almost as good as I make myself."

Jane laughed aloud, glad of the chance to explode her mirth. This dear, funny little man was something of an event in their quiet lives. Nothing ever happened to them now, and even this was stolen thunder, for by rights he should have been in Rita's flat. He talked to them, at times waving his hands to emphasize a point, opening up a fascinating picture of his life in Italy.

Jane and Letty listened entranced.

"You come to Italy and stay with me," he said expansively, and paused as he watched the expression on Letty's face. She was not absolutely sure that she approved of such an invitation. As she said to Jane later: "If he meant it then I don't think it was in very good taste, and if he didn't mean it, he shouldn't have said it. Serve him right if we'd taken him up on it."

But Jane was enjoying the little man so

much that she failed to register Letty's dismay.

"We might, at that," Jane said grandly. "How far can you get on twopence halfpenny?"

"Ah . . . you play the joke," Bertolino breathed. "You have the temperament, eh?"

Jane laughed again. "Something like that. Now I believe that must be your niece Rita coming in the back way. We'll wait a few minutes and give her a chance to get organized." Her glance met Letty's in sudden apprehension. "What sort of weather did you have for your flight?"

As she talked, Bertolino's niece Rita pushed open the back gate. Automatically she counted the four dustbins, one hydrangea (she must do something about that) four galvanized coal bins and the empty clothes lines. All yards were built for utility, but the hydrangea saved this one from ugliness. Who had thought to plant it just there?

She stepped into the kitchen, which when needed was a communal kitchen, for the four luxury flats into which the old house had been converted. Each flat had two bedrooms, sitting-room, kitchenette and bathroom, but this was an extra kitchen where much of the business of the house was conducted. Rita put her loaded shopping basket down on a table, for after a bad night she felt very tired, headachy and depressed. If she could only get into their own flat without being seen she would be something more than thankful.

Hearing footsteps on the stairs she knew herself to be unlucky, and she turned with a bright face to greet the old lady from the first floor front. She pushed the dark hair back from her forehead and tried to rub some colour into her face.

"Good morning Mrs. Page. How are you this morning?"

Mrs. Page smiled. "Quite well, thank you. I heard the doctor come last night."

The sudden attack startled Rita, but she braced herself to meet it. Her dark blue eyes came directly to meet the look in the old lady's. It was useless to pretend.

"Yes—and you must have heard the baby. It was born about four o'clock."

"I know." The old lady nodded and there was genuine sympathy in her warm glance. "How is your sister?"

"I think she's all right." Rita spoke with sudden reserve. The situation had to be met. If only it needn't have been this way. They'd all been expecting it but . . . she bit her lip to stop it trembling. "I'm nervous because there wasn't a chance to get any sleep."

"Yes. Can I do anything? Don't be too proud to ask, will you?"

Tears entered Rita's eyes, and she turned away to hide her sudden loss of poise. "Thank you. You are very kind, but I think we can manage."

"Yes, we all like to manage if we can. Is it a boy?"

"Yes—a boy. I think she hoped it would be a little girl, but it doesn't matter."

"Of course it matters." The vigorous words surprised Rita. "Why do you say that?"

"Because she'll have it adopted . . ."

"Surely not."

"Oh, yes, we feel he ought to be. She's only eighteen and there is so much against keeping a baby here. It will be better in the long run for it to go as quickly as possible." Rita's face hardened, for they could both hear the thin wailing sound as the newly born infant began to cry hungrily. "I'd better go, hadn't I? I've been out nearly half an hour and the nurse is due anyway." She made her escape thankfully, yet knowing that the meeting had been necessary. They would not be able to dodge their neighbours any longer. A pity Vivian hadn't been obliged to meet them herself . . .

"Oh, I'm getting beastly," she thought, as she hurried with her basket to their own ground floor flat. She opened the door, trying to compose her features. The doctor had warned her gravely that Vivian was emotionally ill balanced and she must do what she could to restore the situation.

"Hullo, Vivian . . ." She went through into the bedroom quickly. "I just met Mrs. Page and she asked how you were. They're really a very decent lot, aren't they?" She bit her lips again for she hadn't meant to say that at all. The dwellers in the other flats had been very discreet and something more than kind during this trying situation. She felt she would forever remember it.

Vivian's big eyes followed her about the

room. She seemed unable to talk as Rita bustled about, putting all to rights.

"I think that will be the nurse ringing now—I'll let her in." She rushed to the door and opened it. "Oh?"

Miss Jane stood in the hall outside. "Were you expecting someone else, Rita? The nurse? Well, I'm afraid you are in for a surprise. We've been entertaining someone in our flat who knows you . . ."

"Oh dear . . ." Rita sounded vexed. "I really can't do with anyone today. Why didn't you get rid of them? Couldn't they call tomorrow?"

"Sorry dear, but it's your Uncle Bertolino Cassimo from Italy—your mother's brother." She gave the name with some unction. "He's flown in this morning from Rome . . ."

Her words affected Rita profoundly. She looked completely taken aback. "Oh dear . . ." she breathed. "At such a time . . . Oh, what shall we do?"

Miss Jane spoke sympathetically. "I know. I thought of that. Letty's keeping him busy while I slipped along to prepare you. You'll like him. He's—larger than life somehow. An awfully good sort really. Shall I bring him along?"

"Of course," Rita spoke mechanically. "But what to do? I can't do anything. He'll just have to go to an hotel. Oh, Miss Jane . . . isn't it awful?"

Miss Jane nodded. "Can we do anything? Should we ask him to lunch or something?"

"No—I'll cope. Probably he has some plans." Rita shook her head, and turned to acquaint her sister while Miss Jane hurried back to the flat. Rita followed her, curiosity overwhelming her dismay.

On her entrance Bertolino stood up, bowed, bent to kiss her hand, and then kissed her on both cheeks, all in the most natural way imaginable. "I don't need anyone to tell me, my dear, for you are so like your mother . . ."

The exuberant little man was not smiling now as he watched Rita. "Yes, I am supposed to be very like her," Rita said. "This is a great surprise. Why didn't you write?" If only he had she might have saved this painful moment for all of them, she thought.

"Ah—but it is the surprise . . . I plan him so."

"You must come along to our flat. Did Miss Jane tell you that Vivian is—ill?" She hesitated briefly.

"But no . . ." His sallow face was concerned and serious again. "This I did not know."

"Then come along." Rita was geared up to meet the situation.

Uncle Bertolino picked up his suitcase, bowed and beamed at both ladies. "My grateful thanks for a delightful interlude. Doubtless I will see you again soon."

"Doubtless," Miss Letty said drily.

Miss Jane followed them to the door. "If there is anything we can do to help, Rita . . ."

Rita thanked her quietly. She walked beside her uncle down the long corridor to their own flat. Could anything be more awkward, happening at this particular moment? This must be our year, she thought. Just everything is happening.

Uncle Bertolino glanced round the delightful sitting-room in a pleased, child-like way that showed considerable pleasure. "This is the sort of place where

I would expect to find the two daughters of my dear sister. This so pretty flat."

Rita was touched. Suddenly she came closer to the little man, realizing that he was indeed her dear mother's only brother. Some facial resemblance still lingered in the sallow, fat, good-natured features. Beneath her feeling of worry and doubt grew a sense of relief.

"Uncle Bertolino . . ." She kissed him soundly, much to his pleasure. "I'm glad to see you."

"I thought at first—it was not so?" He blew his nose gustily. "But this, you put it right with a little kiss."

"Sit down while I explain. It isn't that I'm not glad to see you, it's just that I don't want to see anyone just now. You see . . . it's difficult to explain really. Vivian isn't ill. She's just had a baby . . . early today in fact, and we aren't organized . . ."

"A bambino?" He skipped to his feet again, "But this is wonderful . . ."

"Not really," Rita spoke drily. "We've been worried to death. She's eighteen and she isn't married and . . ."

"I understand." He sat down again. "In

15

England this is a crime no doubt. In my country the bambino comes first."

"But it *isn't* right . . ." Rita told him.

"She'll make it right doubtless . . ." Uncle Bertolino got his handkerchief out again. It was a large, white square with his initials in one corner. "It is what may happen while I am in England. I put in a very good manager—to my café, you understand, but I make sure he is not a married man. My daughter she is very good . . . my manager is also very good, but I would not expect they will stay— very good—all the time. This is not in human nature. So I plan . . . and they must marry on my return . . ."

Rita was laughing ruefully at his expressive way of speaking. His small, fat hands were waving in the air, seeming ahead of his voluble explanations.

"I have much money and I want to see you both, so I come to England . . ." he puffed out his cheeks. "And what do I find . . . this thing that troubles you. But you need not feel it will trouble your Uncle Bertolino. I am—what do you say? Not shocked—no, not shocked." He beamed so completely that Rita felt even his clothes must be smiling.

She sprang up and met him half way to the door. "You're a darling. I'm glad you're here. Come along and see Vivian now." She led the way to Vivian's bedroom. Uncle Bertolino was as much at ease here as he had been in the lounge.

Vivian was smiling curiously as she held out a slender hand. Uncle Bertolino kissed it affectionately. Almost at once he turned aside to scrutinize the baby lying in a drawer.

"Excellent baby," was his opinion. "Not like you? Like his papa perhaps?"

Vivian's face hardened. "I hope not."

"What do you call him?" was the next question.

"It's not decided yet. Rita wants me to call him John, after our father, but I don't know."

"Why not indeed? Johnnie?" Uncle Bertolino rolled it on his tongue as if it were an olive.

"Johnnie Bertolino . . ." Rita suggested, and they all laughed hilariously. "That's it."

17

"A great compliment," Uncle Bertolino said gracefully.

"Would it be that?" Vivian asked, with a quiver in her voice.

"Indeed yes. So it is to be Johnnie Bertolino. I like it." Uncle Bertolino stood with his head on one side. "With a name like that he will go far."

Vivian's apprehensive glance came to Rita, who did not reply. "I think we should go now. The nurse is due and Vivian is tired. Instead of sleeping we were talking for hours last night . . ." she bit her lip, not caring to remember all that she had said.

Uncle Bertolino moved ahead of her back to the lounge. He walked with curious softness for so stout a man. He waved to Vivian from the doorway. "I come back—later," he promised.

Rita said: "We only have the two bedrooms . . ."

"I understand. I can go to an hotel. That will be very nice for I can visit you often. There is no room here . . ."

"Are you staying long?" she asked slowly. "That's not meant to be inhospitable. Only there *is* a flat empty here, and if you meant to stay a few weeks it might be worth while taking it."

"Excellent. Excellent. I take it."

Rita felt surprised that he accepted it unseen. "I'll make some dinner now and I can show you the flat later . . . Oh, dear, who's that?" The bell was ringing again. "It will be the nurse."

She hurried to the door to admit the nurse.

"Where is the kitchen?" Uncle Bertolino asked, taking off his excellently cut grey overcoat.

Rita pointed to the door into the kitchen, and forgot him for several minutes.

"Well, dearie, how's the patient now?" The nurse entered cheerfully.

"I expect she's just tired."

"Hasn't she slept?" The nurse was slipping out of her outdoor clothes.

"No." Rita felt ashamed.

"If I were you I'd try to think more kindly about everything that's happened," the nurse advised. "You love your sister don't you?"

"I do." Rita replied somewhat stiffly.

"Then show it." Rita was shut out of the bedroom.

The words snapped off rather shortly, she thought. What to do now? "Oh, yes, I'd better telephone the landlady to see if it's all right if Uncle Bertolino has the top flat."

She went into the hall, where the communal telephone was installed. "We could lend him linen and cutlery and such things," she explained, feeling rather anguished in case the plan was not agreed.

"That will be fine. But he can't have it for longer than six months. I'll want it in the autumn for some relatives," she was told.

"You can have the flat," she hurried back to give the news to Uncle Bertolino. He met her in the kitchen doorway. "She'll want it in the autumn but you can have it until then."

He shook his head briskly. "That will be pleasant—yes. For me so much more pleasant than alone in an hotel."

"You must spend as much time with us as you can," Rita told him. "Have at least one meal a day with us. And we'll lend you half a dozen of everything . . .

20

why . . ." She had passed him and entered the kitchenette. Her eyes flashed in surprise. Uncle Bertolino had been busy during her absence. Something that smelled most appetizing was cooking gently in a frying pan. Coffee was boiling on the stove. A crisp lettuce lay in the cut glass salad bowl . . .

"You like it? I found your basket, and emptied it. This no doubt, you wished for dinner?"

"What a darling you are," Rita hugged his arm enthusiastically. "I forgot— you said you had a café . . . so you can cook."

"I can cook," he agreed, puffing out his cheeks in relief. "This we will eat when the nurse goes."

Obviously Uncle Bertolino was hungry. "As soon as it's ready you tuck in and have it," Rita told him. "Vivian won't want it, so we can eat it all. Come to think of it, I can't remember which day this week we had a properly cooked meal."

"Then it is good I come," Uncle Bertolino said, as he stirred the concoction in the frying pan with terrifying speed. "After the meal I go out and buy a pram for Johnnie Bertolino. Then you can get on with your choirs."

"My what?" Rita was mystified. In spite of a strong accent, he had a remarkably good diction. But this was something else again. "I don't understand you . . ."

It was Uncle Bertolino's turn to look surprised.

"You know—it's a new word to me . . . I don't see what you mean?" she explained. She was already soaking the nappies in soap flakes, stirring them around thoughtfully.

"Ah, yes . . . but I mean all this . . ." He chuckled as he too gazed down at the bowl.

"Oh?" Rita crowed. "You mean my chores? Of course . . ."

"Your chores," he repeated. "You are so busy now, eh?"

Rita scowled into the soap flakes for a minute, until her face cleared. She pushed back a loosened strand of hair with damp fingers. "It could have been worse, I suppose. It could have been twins . . ." At the thought she blanched.

The nurse came to the kitchen door, and

looked surprised when she saw Uncle Bertolino. Rita introduced them hastily.

"How is Johnnie Bertolino?" she asked after a moment.

"Quite strong and healthy by the look of him. I've told your sister what to do . . . but . . ." she gave Rita some instructions. "I'll come in tomorrow about the same time."

"Thank you for everything." Rita followed her to the door, and opened it for her.

She leaned closer before it closed on her. "Sure it's your Uncle Bertolino?" she whispered, flicking a finger behind Rita's shoulder. "He looks like something out of the Tales of Hoffman to me . . ."

"Oh, dear . . ." Rita nodded energetically as the little nurse bustled away down the corridor, her little black bag clanking the wall in her hurry.

Uncle Bertolino was serving the meal, and they ate it peacefully.

"This . . ." Rita said, "is remarkably good. You must let me have the recipe . . ."

After the meal life appeared much more normal again. Rita took their Uncle up to

23

the top flat, carrying an armful of sheets and pillow cases and one freshly laundered tablecloth. Uncle Bertolino had the loose cutlery in one hand and his suitcase in the other. Mrs. Page came out of her flat just as they were passing her door.

Rita introduced them briefly.

"I was just on my way down to see your sister," Mrs. Page said. Her hands were full of flowers and fruit. "If there is anything we can lend you . . ." she added, her calm eyes on Uncle Bertolino.

He beamed, and bowed from the waist down. "My nieces fix me up . . ." he told her gustily. "I stay how many months— maybe three, four . . . maybe longer."

"Delightful. Imagine seeing England for the first time in April," Mrs. Page said enviously. She was obviously impressed by Uncle Bertolino, but Rita was not sure if it was in the right way. "I'll go down and have a word with Vivian while you are up here . . ." Her little round body swayed along the corridor and down the stairs to the ground floor.

Uncle Bertolino nodded approvingly, principally because he hadn't enough breath left to make the announcement he felt fitting.

Rita showed him round the flat, which was smaller than theirs but very comfortable. "You're really very lucky," she told him. "We've been wondering for months who would get this flat. You have a dust bin in the yard too. You must make *our* flat your real home."

Uncle Bertolino was rapidly recovering his breath. His twinkling eyes became serious for a moment. "That is the nicest thing you say to me yet, Rita. I like it. This will be so comfortable and we can pay many visits . . . yes, I like it."

Rita left him and hurried downstairs to her sister. When she went into the bedroom Vivian was lying as the nurse had left her, the flowers from Mrs. Page across the bed. The baby was asleep in the drawer. Vivian's great eyes followed Rita about, as she rapidly tried to tidy the room.

They were talking in whispers so that the child would not waken. "Kind of you to bring the flowers," Rita smiled across at the old woman who sat by the bedside.

"You're not going to leave him in the

drawer, are you?" Mrs. Page asked with some asperity.

"Until we get a cot . . ." Rita could not quite meet her sister's eyes as she spoke.

"I'll get you one this afternoon if you will say the kind you want," Mrs. Page offered. "I'm going shopping."

They accepted the offer, and soon she left them, with Rita's instructions ringing in her ears.

Uncle Bertolino knocked on the door again, before the two girls had a chance to talk.

"Never a dull moment," Rita muttered as she admitted him.

"If you two girls need any help I hope you'll let me know," he said at once, sensing the strain in the atmosphere. "I'm going out now to look around. You want anything?"

Rita shook her head. Evidently the pram was to be a surprise for Vivian, so she did not mention it, but as she followed him to the outer door she told him that Mrs. Page was getting them a cot that afternoon.

"Ah—that is so kind . . ." Uncle Bertolino trotted along the corridor and let himself out through the big double doors.

He waved to Rita before vanishing from sight.

She drew a long breath as she returned to Vivian's room. Now for it. The doctor was the next to arrive, and still the two girls had not had a chance to talk. As soon as she saw him Vivian said:

"I want to keep the baby . . . we're going to call him Johnnie Bertolino . . ."

"Of course you'll keep the baby," he told her, hiding his surprise. "Now get to sleep. Don't worry any more; you've done more than enough of that lately. The child is safe. You'll feel better when you waken up."

"Rita will take it away if I go to sleep."

Rita's startled glance met the doctor's as he straightened. She backed away from him. "I wouldn't . . . she doesn't know what she's saying. I've been feeling resigned to it ever since Uncle Bertolino came . . . I meant to explain . . . but there's not been time . . ."

The doctor tried to cover his surprise. "Go to sleep Vivian. I'll take care of all that. You'll keep your baby." He followed Rita into the lounge and stood with his back to the empty grate. "You know, Rita,

27

we've got something there. She believes that if she closes her eyes you'll spirit the baby away."

"I wouldn't." Rita spoke stiffly. But she felt ashamed and frightened as she tried to explain. "You know me better than that, but one day she may wish she'd listened to me. I was against her keeping him . . . but somehow now . . ."

"You're five years older than Vivian, but she's a mother now, and you can't know the change that has come over her. She wants the child in spite of what she's been through. It's hers and why shouldn't she keep it?" The quick question caught Rita off guard. She tried to collect her wits.

"You must know all the snags in this for an unmarried girl. One day the child may be an embarrassment. Besides, she can't keep it—financially, I mean. She doesn't come into her money until she is twenty-one."

"But you have money . . ."

"Yes."

"And Vivian has a job."

"Of sorts. It doesn't keep her. I've had to make out for her for years, not that I mind in the least . . . but it won't stretch to keep the baby . . . or I thought it wouldn't yesterday. Now it seems different somehow. He's so little. I hadn't realized they were so tiny and helpless."

"I think you are both learning something, Rita. Be kind to her over this matter. She needs it as she never needed anything before in her life. She's stretched to her limit and needs sleep badly. It's up to you, Rita." He left the flat quietly. The baby continued to sleep, for which she was thankful. He had proved the excellent quality of his lungs earlier.

Rita could not bring herself to face Vivian for some time. She finished washing the nappies and pegged them out on the line. The sweet April breezes tossed them playfully back and forth, and she watched them for a moment, feeling quite stunned. There had never been a baby in the flats before. It was something of an event. Johnnie Bertolino . . . as she turned the name over in her mind, the child assumed an individuality he had not previously had. Johnnie Bertolino. Just any baby might be pushed out into the world, to make his way in some other place, to grow up unknown to them, but Johnnie Bertolino was different. He was their very own.

"He's my nephew . . ." she thought, experiencing a rush of feeling, that nearly overwhelmed her.

Slowly she entered the bedroom, her gaze on Vivian's white face. Vivian's big blue eyes held a frightened look, a waiting look, and Rita knew that she had indeed been waiting.

She sat down, her gaze on the sleeping baby. "I feel worn out . . ." she sighed. "But the nappies are drying nicely."

"Did you mean it just now—when you said Mrs. Page could buy a cot?" Vivian whispered.

"Yes. I gave her some money. I didn't know how you really felt about it Vivian. The doctor told me how this had changed your feelings, and Uncle Bertolino . . . made it seem different too. Just now I realized that Johnnie Bertolino is—ours now. I was wrong in my thinking. It's different when they're here, isn't it? I'll help you to bring him up. It'll be a bit tight for a while, but we'll manage. It'll be fun." She spoke wistfully.

"I can work for him," Vivian responded eagerly. "But I can't begin unless you say you'll help me. You know I'm sorry, but unless you forgive me, I can't go on." She started to cry, weak, angry tears that poured down her thin face.

"Of course I forgive you—who said I didn't?" Rita asked belligerently. "We've been awry on this because I'm not a mother so I didn't know how you would feel. I thought you'd want him adopting right away. Lots of girls would. He'll take some explaining. I wish he wasn't so noisy, don't you? I expect it's because he's a boy." In spite of herself she had to put the case honestly. Vivian was needing reassurance and something more, that she felt unable to offer just yet.

"We can meet that later," Vivian said. "Thank you, Rita . . ."

"I must have seemed like a policeman, laying down the law like that . . ." Rita spoke painfully. Her former attitude seemed callous in the extreme.

"It's the first time we've ever been at loggerheads, and I know I was wrong. He's really a lovely baby—look at him, Rita." Together they bent over the drawer where Johnnie Bertolino lay sleeping. There was a ridiculous tuft of very dark hair on top of his head. "Mind you—if I thought he'd ever look like Uncle Bertolino . . ." Vivian was gazing down thoughtfully at her son.

Rita laughed. "He's awfully pleased that you're calling the baby after him though. What do you think of him? Uncle Bertolino, I mean?"

"I like him," Vivian told her. "Queer he arrived today when we were in such a flap."

"He cooks like an angel . . ." Rita whispered, for the baby was stirring in his sleep. "Maybe we're lucky, Vivian . . . in the baby. He's sweet, isn't he? We'll keep him and we'll make a man of him. Do you want him? He's going to yell." She lifted the baby and placed him in Vivian's eager arms. The feel of the soft, warm, fragile bundle was curiously disconcerting. Rita felt a renewed attack of conscience. She watched them for a moment, almost enviously. Out of this turmoil of despair and shame, had come something that was utterly dependent on them both. It was a sobering thought. "I'll help you with him . . ."

Vivian nodded, unable to speak. The exhaustion began to leave her. "I'm beginning to feel sleepy. Goodness, who is it now? The doorbell hasn't stopped ringing today."

Rita left her, to answer the door. Mrs. Page had arrived in a taxi, and the driver was carrying the cot and bedding up the steps from the street for her. She had added two small blue blankets, pillow, and satin eiderdown and slip. As they set it up in the lounge Rita felt pleased for Vivian. They edged the cot into her room carefully.

"Oh . . . glorious . . ." Vivian leaned up, yawning and sleepy, but happiness seemed to be dawning in her fair face. "Oh, isn't it lovely? Look Johnnie Bertolino . . ." She held the child up in her arms. "All for your benefit."

"I got the blankets and things because I knew you'd need them eventually." Mrs. Page was pleased in their pleasure. "You look much better, Vivian. Just take care and you'll be all right now."

Johnnie Bertolino started to cry. Rita

rushed around the room, wondering what to do. "Oh, dear, he's hungry, and nothing is ready. Oh . . ."

"Now don't flap about," Mrs. Page was amused. "He'll keep. I saw your Uncle Bertolino just now. He's on his way . . ." She laughed as if something amused her, but she did not give them an explanation. She followed Rita into the kitchenette where she was putting on the kettle.

The whole flat looked radiant with the flowers Mrs. Page had brought earlier. The grapes were in a dish on a side table. "You two are happier, aren't you?"

Rita glanced across at her. "Yes. Was it so obvious that we weren't—before?"

"Well . . . you've been so unhappy these last few months . . . I guess anyone would feel the same." She watched Rita measuring the feed carefully. After all, it was hard on the girl having these unaccustomed duties thrust on her unwilling shoulders. "I'm seventy-four, Rita. That's quite an age. It lets me say things you might resent from someone younger. And I feel I must say this. You're worried because you feel the situation is all wrong,

34

but you've conquered yourself because you want to help Vivian."

Rita glanced soberly through the window into the yard, where the nappies were blowing gaily on the line. "Isn't it a case of condoning . . . We've always known right from wrong."

"We can't judge the actions of another, child. You sat in judgment and it didn't make you happy. You have to deal with the situation as it is. You're facing it now and that's helping Vivian. It's why you are both happier already. There can never be anything wrong in helping another. No, I wouldn't say you were condoning anything. Your changed attitude has probably saved Vivian."

"Was it as serious as that?" Rita asked slowly. She poured the boiling water on the milk mixture, measuring the ounces carefully.

Mrs. Page nodded. "Yes. She'll be all right now because her mind is content. You know, Rita, you should be proud. She's accepted your word absolutely. She *knows* that without you she would be forced to let the child go. Only you can keep those two with their heads above water. Hadn't you realized that?"

"No, no, I hadn't." Rita looked frightened. "It's a frightful responsibility."

"Not if you take it slowly, one step at a time." Mrs. Page reached up and kissed her, for Rita was tall and slender, while she was a dumpling of a woman. "There, I like you both and I hate to see you so hurt. And probably your Uncle Bertolino will help—you never know." She started to laugh again before going into the lounge. She called to Rita. "Come quickly —don't miss this . . ."

Rita covered the milk mixture and hastened into the lounge. Mrs. Page held up the curtain and Uncle Bertolino saw her and waved. He was coming in at the gate, wheeling an enormous pram. Two small children followed him, sucking candy floss on sticks. There was an air of purpose about Uncle Bertolino as he manoeuvred the pram safely through the gateway.

Tears suddenly began to run down Rita's face. Weakly she stood laughing and crying at the same time. "Oh, the blessed man, the darling man . . ."

Mrs. Page hurried to the door and for a

few minutes all was pandemonium. Johnnie Bertolino decided that he could not wait another minute for his meal and his low wailing increased in force until it filled all their minds.

Vivian began to call out, frightened of the volume of sound her son made. "Rita —quick . . . something must be the matter with him . . ."

Rita rushed back to the kitchenette and secured the milk bottle, wrapping it hastily in a clean towel to keep it warm. "I'm coming. Oh, dear, what's ailing him?" She hurried to the bed. "How can we keep it warm till he finishes it? Oh . . . that's Uncle Bertolino just arriving."

She tested the temperature of the milk against her wrist as the nurse had shown her, and thrust the bottle into Vivian's hand. Vivian thrust the teat into Johnnie Bertolino's mouth and instantly the world was at peace.

"Well . . ." Rita drew a long breath. "So that's all it was. I thought he was dying!"

He smiled, his mouth firmly round the teat. "That's wind . . ." Vivian whispered.

"I'll hold him up in a minute. He's not taken kindly to the idea yet . . ."

"That's the understatement of the week," Rita spoke roundly. She hurried out to greet Uncle Bertolino, who with Mrs. Page's help had managed to get the pram into the lounge. It was full of parcels of every size and shape and description.

Rita sat down suddenly, because her legs would not bear her weight any longer. She put one hand to her head. "This is the queerest day of my whole life . . ."

Uncle Bertolino presented Mrs. Page with a box of chocolates. He gave it to her with quite a flourish. "For you, dear madame . . ."

The old lady was touched and grateful. "That's nice of you. You must come to tea some time. And that reminds me, I must fly. Dominic will soon be home and I have a meal to cook . . ." She thanked him again, before hastening up to her own flat. "He's my grandson . . ."

"She wants me to go to tea—not now?" Uncle Bertolino said to his niece.

"Some time," Rita told him. "She'll plan a date—some time."

"Ah—that is your English way. I understand. Now this and this . . ." Rapidly he emptied the pram of all its contents. "It is the best one I could buy. Even the little Prince had no finer pram than this one. May I . . ." His twinkling eyes indicated Vivian's closed door.

Rita rose to her feet. "We're coming in Vivian . . ." She wondered if all this excitement could be good for her sister, but felt helpless to avert it. Perhaps happiness such as this could not hurt anyone. "Here's Uncle Bertolino, dear . . ."

Vivian was nursing the baby against her shoulder, rubbing his back professionally. Her blue eyes widened in amazement as Uncle Bertolino pushed in the pram.

"Oh . . . oh . . . oh . . ." Vivian was speechless and pleased. "The loveliest pram I've ever seen. Oh, what a beauty."

"It is my gift to my young grand-nephew . . ." Uncle Bertolino breathed benevolently.

"Come here," Vivian said. She put the baby down, and opened both arms to the giver. "There—that's for you . . ." Her kiss was warm. "You are the nicest man I know."

"But of course . . ." He stood, laughing

delightedly in the centre of the room. "I go now. You are tired, no?"

Rita followed him from the room. "I'll make us all a cup of tea, Uncle Bertolino . . ."

An odd look crossed his face. "Tea? But yes . . . your tea is very good, I know."

2

MRS. PAGE wondered how she would tell Dominic when he came in. It was Dominic who insisted that she should take fruit and flowers down to the girls in the lower flat. Only six months before, shortly after they moved in, he had come bounding up the stairs in a fine state of excitement. Dominic, who usually took himself seriously, was completely at sea in more ways than one, Mrs. Page decided.

"Gran—what do you know? I've just seen the girl who's going to be my wife." His queer laugh of excitement had made his grandmother stare at him curiously. Did he mean Rita?

"A bit sudden, isn't it?" she asked.

"Yes. She's a honey. You must have seen her. As fair as an angel, and beautiful too. I just passed her in the hall . . . arms full of parcels. I helped her to unlock her door. When she switched on the light I saw her properly." There was an awed note in Dominic's pleasant voice. "Absolutely gorgeous . . . a real poppet . . ."

"Really!" Mrs. Page was startled. He could only mean Vivian, for Rita was as dark as her sister was fair . . . She was not sure about Vivian, for the girl was evasive and very hard to know. "She's certainly good-looking, but that's not everything."

"I wish you'd get friendly. Looks like two sisters, living together. Imagine, we've been here ten days and I'd not seen her before." Dominic strode about the room like a tamed animal. His dark hair was brushed back from an olive face. Mrs. Page thought he was very handsome but never said so in case it gave him ideas. She had come down from her home in the Lake District to keep house for him. Dominic did not like living in rooms, and his unhappiness had hastened her decision to join him temporarily.

"No wonder you never see them, when you come in so late each night," she pointed out. "Most respectable people are in bed by midnight. If they aren't they should be. But surely you meet lots of girls in your job?"

"Sure." He nodded absently, standing

staring out through the window at the autumn scene. Vivian's beauty must have made a deep impression on him, Mrs. Page decided, with misgivings. It was unlike Dominic, and his usual level-headedness to be so completely bowled over. Of course both sisters had beauty of a very real kind, Mrs. Page granted him that, somewhat uneasily. Wisely she let the matter drop for the time being.

"Nearly Christmas," she said quietly. "Will there be a chance to get up to the cottage do you think?"

He turned back to her quickly. "Sorry, Gran—not a hope. I had a word with the agent today and I can't have even one evening off. Hell, ain't it?"

"It shows you're popular anyway," she said placidly. "And you're doing what you like doing, which is quite something these days."

"But this girl Gran . . . surely you could invite her along one day . . . it's nearly Christmas and party time . . ." Dominic spoke impatiently.

"I'll do what I can," she agreed.

In spite of her gently given invitations, and Dominic's open search, both sisters

43

evaded all overtures of friendship. Dominic was vexed and frustrated as the weeks went by.

"I simply can't believe that we are living in the same house, yet unable to even say good morning . . ." he was quietly fuming on the couch one day, after Christmas. "They just can't be normal . . ."

"Do you really not know why it's so hard to get to know them?" Mrs. Page asked.

"No? Why? I've done my best. Short of knocking at their door and barging in I can't see how I'll ever meet her again."

"I meet Rita occasionally. Hanging out clothes and taking in groceries and that sort of thing."

"That's the elder one—the darker one?"

"Yes. Do you really want to know why you're not meeting Vivian?"

Something in her voice arrested his attention. "Yes. What do you mean, Gran?"

"She's soon going to have a baby." She regretted the words immediately. The light died out of his face. Abruptly he swivelled in his chair so that she could not see the sudden access of colour to his face. "Sure?"

"Certain. It's why they keep to themselves. Vivian is not working now."

"My God!" Dominic bent his head, and she saw it had been a shock to him.

"She's not married. I haven't pried, but you do hear things in flats like these. They are both very unhappy about it."

"You should have told me before."

"I wasn't certain—now I am. You'll have to forget her, Dominic. That lovely face has probably been her downfall."

He went into his room, banging the door after him. He'd get over it, Mrs. Page decided. Now it was all over, and she'd have news for him tonight when he returned. He may even have heard the baby as he passed the ground floor flat. What was it that Rita did that kept her home so much? she pondered. Parcels came for her frequently, and she was always taking other parcels somewhere. It intrigued Mrs. Page, but she dare not ask.

Dominic, tall, slim, twenty-five, and somewhat bad tempered tonight, arrived about eleven o'clock. He always garaged his car at the back of the building, and

45

came in the back way, for he was the only one in the flats who owned a car.

Vivian was drinking a cup of hot chocolate when Dominic garaged his car, and she listened for his eager tread on the stairs. "That's Mrs. Page's grandson. I wonder what he does?"

"I think he's a waiter. Must be if he stays out so late every night. I saw him once in a black dinner jacket and long black cape . . . maybe a bit theatrical but he's handsome."

"I wonder why she doesn't say?" Vivian was more composed now, taking up the threads of her life again. "Probably because we never ask her."

"Oh, I'm tired," Rita sighed. "I hope we can both have a good night." She stretched with both arms above her head. "I wonder what Richard will think of Uncle Bertolino?"

"He's due home tomorrow, isn't he? Richard, I mean?" Vivian's glance showed sudden disquiet.

"Yes . . ." Rita thought about him. After the upheaval of the past few days it would be exceedingly pleasant to have

Richard around again. "Only hope he understands . . ."

"So do I." Vivian agreed fervently. "I've upset things for you, haven't I? I'm so sorry. Makes so many complications somehow." Her loveliness lost its sparkle as she lay thinking.

When Richard arrived the following evening, Rita was delighted to see him, and said so. She drew him lovingly into the lounge, and kissed him.

"Had a good trip, darling? When did you get home?"

"About an hour ago. Couldn't wait to see you. I've missed you . . ." Richard's big frame dominated the room in a most comforting way, she thought. "Jove, you look more beautiful than ever."

His approval was heart warming. "Do I?" Some of it must be artificial, she thought, knowing that her looks had suffered under the pressure of work and anxiety of the past few days. Her magnolia skin had lost some of its bloom; her blue eyes were dark ringed but still sparkling. Knowing that he might call this evening she had made a special effort to appear much as usual. They sat down together on the settee, and for a few minutes Richard kissed her passionately and often. He seemed relieved to be back.

"You're a darling and a honey, and I love you, fit to beat the band . . ." he whispered. "You seem different somehow."

"So do you," she told him. "Older—by at least ten days."

Richard had a thin, thoughtful face. He looked older than his twenty-six years. Rita fitted into the crook of his arm, and felt more at peace than she had since he left on this job for the firm. Richard was a construction engineer and often moved about the country. The separations were always the hardest part to bear, although she knew he enjoyed his job, wherever it took him. He was content to gaze at her for a while, as if the absence had been long.

Suddenly he raised his head. His look came straight to hers. "What's that noise?"

"Vivian has her baby. He's stirring. I meant to tell you at once but . . ."

"Good lord!" He laughed and something in the sound irked her so that she left her place near him. "I didn't know it was quite so imminent."

"Yes, the night before last."

"Everything go off OK?" He was watching her, wondering at her agitation.

"I think so."

"When's the baby going away? You're not keeping him here, of course?"

"That's the point, Richard. Vivian doesn't want to have him adopted. She's going to keep him."

"But I thought it was all settled; she seemed to agree." He was a big man, broad-shouldered and powerful. Rita sometimes felt that his personality overwhelmed hers.

"Yes, it was settled, but when she had him, she felt differently. You can't really blame her can you?"

"Yes, I do blame her. She ought to think for the child . . . It'll be hard on him . . . later."

"Surely it's better for him if he is brought up by his own mother than by someone not really interested in him, or perhaps in a Home?" She sounded perturbed, not sure of her ground. All she knew was that Vivian was determined to keep her child with her.

"And do you think that Vivian is strong enough—morally or physically—to bring up a boy? He won't be a baby for ever, you know." The blunt words whipped the colour into Rita's face.

"I resent that, Richard. You shouldn't have said that. There is nothing wrong with Vivian's morals. I told you how it happened."

He laughed again, a careless laugh that angered her more than anything yet. He was so sure of himself, so sure that he was right, he was not even considering any other point of view.

"Don't you believe me?" she asked, deeply hurt.

"Oh, I believe that you believe what she told you . . ." He spoke good naturedly. "But any man would take it with a pinch of salt."

"What a beastly thing to say." She turned away. "I won't listen to you."

He gripped her shoulders and suddenly drew her close to him. "You'll listen—and you'll remember one thing. You belong to me. What happens to Vivian or anyone else doesn't matter between us. Made up your mind yet about the date for our wedding?" He rubbed his face against her cheek, determined to soften her anger against him. He loved this girl and wanted no interference from the outside world.

"No."

"Why not?"

"I can't leave Vivian yet."

"Why?"

"Because she needs me so much at the moment. Besides . . ."

"Yes? Tell me?"

"I promised I'd help her with the baby until she was at least twenty-one. She gets her own money then." Rita's face flushed, for she felt his sudden displeasure.

"Hell. Do you mean you're going to make me wait three years?"

"We—we needn't wait." She stammered. "We could get married a little later when everything has settled down. In a few months. Vivian will soon be able to get another job, or the old one back. It's not really so long to wait."

Her voice trailed away miserably for she saw that he was out of sympathy with her reasoning.

He held her away, his eyes searching her face curiously. "Just a minute. Let's get this straight, my girl. Are you proposing that Vivian and the child shall be part of our household when we marry?"

"Well—I don't know . . ." She felt flustered, unable to think clearly. "I hadn't thought it out. We just couldn't plan without seeing you first. I did say that I'd see her through . . ."

"Until she was twenty-one?" When she nodded he added grimly: "I've no intention of waiting so long. I've certainly no intention of adopting her brat either. No, Rita, you're too soft with her. You've got to make up your mind between us. Either you come to me as my wife . . . at the latest this June . . . or it's off. I'm not going to have someone else's love child spoiling the first few years of our lives together." He was determined, feeling that she would give way.

She sighed deeply. She had known it would be hard to convince him, but he was even more dogmatic and determined than she had feared. "You haven't seen the baby yet. Please don't shout. I don't want her to be upset yet."

"I've no intention of seeing the baby. What do you think I am? And you're a bit of a surprise yourself. I never thought you'd have condoned wrongdoing. You've always been straight-laced enough with me, heaven knows."

"Oh, Richard . . ." Her voice showed her deep hurt, but he would not relent. His anger was stirring against her.

"At least if I'd put you in her position I'd have married you," he told her bluntly.

"That's enough." Rita's spirit blazed up suddenly. "We'll not discuss it any further tonight. I don't think we can agree."

"I'm darn sure we can't." He watched her closely, pleased with the display of temper. "When Vivian realizes what this is going to cost you she'll climb down. She's a selfish little piece, but it's up to you to be firm with her. I'll call in tomorrow night and see what answer you have for me. But I shan't change my mind, so don't think I shall. Good night. Got a kiss for me?"

She shook her head. "No, I haven't. I don't like what you've said, or the way you've said it. She *is* my sister and I feel you could have shown more respect. You'd better go before I quarrel with you."

He laughed uneasily. Only twice in their acquaintanceship had he seen Rita in a temper and neither time had been very enjoyable. She was a woman who could stand almost anything, until suddenly the lid flew off. It had been interesting seeing how far he could go before he provoked that display, but tonight he had a feeling that he had gone too far. There was in Rita a streak of quiet strength which he respected, and longed to possess. That she might withdraw from their engagement never seriously crossed his mind, but he was determined to show her that he was master of their future together.

He picked up his hat and left the flat.

Uncle Bertolino just happened to be passing through the hall at the exact moment that Richard banged the door after him. The two men eyed one another warily. Richard was so angry that he almost bumped into Uncle Bertolino.

"Sorry," he growled. "Why can't you look where you're going?"

"I was . . . looking," Uncle Bertolino explained mildly . . . So this was Rita's young man? Obviously a young man with a temper. "After you . . ." he added politely.

"After *you* . . ." Richard shouted.

Uncle Bertolino bowed, and slipped through the very small aperture with undue haste. This was no time to argue. It was apparent that Rita had made mincemeat of Richard and he was not enjoying the experience. They reached the gate together. Richard scowled as he caught his mackintosh back from the wind that whipped it up, flapping the coat tails with considerable speed. Suddenly he grinned at Uncle Bertolino.

"Good night. Women are the limit, aren't they?"

Rita bolted the door after Richard. She stood for a moment leaning against it, her hands pressed to her face. She was shaking, for she had tried hard for control. The avalanche of his words struck back to her, and she was appalled at their meaning. There was no chance for her to recover her poise for Vivian called.

"Rita . . . are you there?" She looked up when her sister entered. "Who was that?"

"Richard—he's just gone."

"You told him about . . . ?" Her glance was apprehensive.

"Yes—everything. He doesn't seem to like it too well."

"Oh dear. More trouble." Vivian leaned back, frightened and white. "I suppose I am selfish. You have your own lives to live. You won't want to be troubled with me or the baby. What did he say?"

"Well, he never had much use for children, so it isn't very surprising that he won't want yours when we marry." Rita gave her the gist of what had been said, softening it a little so that she would not be too hurt. "Vivian—you told me the truth about how it happened, didn't you? Richard doesn't seem to believe . . ."

"He can believe what he likes," Vivian said sulkily. "He can go to blazes."

They both thought back to her first frightened confession. Rita waited motionlessly.

"That night—when you thought I stayed at Freda's house . . ." Vivian began.

On the morning of that day Freda and

Vivian met at the stables where they had booked for a horse ride. Vivian loved riding, and went as often as she could. Although it was expensive she managed at least once a week to follow her favourite pursuit.

The two girls cantered towards the Park, carefree and giddy. It was easy to laugh when one was just eighteen.

"I met a boy called Butch last night," Freda was bursting with eagerness to tell her chum the news. "He's oh, so handsome and big . . . and cute somehow. You know what I mean?" She waited for Vivian to draw alongside. The creak of leather accompanied their remarks. Vivian's colour was high, and she was glancing about restlessly.

"Yes. What about him?" she asked absently.

"He wants me to meet him again tonight —says if I'll bring a friend he has a pal and we could go to a club maybe and dance."

Vivian's attention was caught at last. "Dancing." She picked up her ears. "I'd like to go."

"That's what I thought," Freda spoke with satisfaction. "I knew you'd be game.

Well, Butch is lovely, and if his pal is as nice then we'd have a smashing evening." She omitted to say that after the club the arrangement was that they should go on to a party. "Butch has a smashing car. I was out in it last night. Oh . . ."

"What make?"

"A Bentley . . ." At Vivian's incredulous look she added hastily: "Oh, it's his father's actually, but his parents are out of England so he has permission to use it. They must be simply rolling in money. I wish he'd fall for me . . . I could just do with a handsome husband and ten thousand a year to buy my clothes."

Vivian giggled. "I didn't know they came as rich as that nowadays?"

"Well, he's rich. He bought me champagne and chocolates, and tonight we're going to dance the Samba . . ."

"That's kid's stuff," Vivian said scornfully. Her own dancing was graceful and sophisticated for she aspired to be an actress one day.

Freda flushed a little. "Not so. I never learned it anyhow. He's going to show me. His people are from the Argentine."

"Dagos?" Vivian asked with sudden interest.

"Don't be daft. He's as English as we are, only they made their money out there . . . Where shall we meet?"

Walking her horse and hearing the clop clop of its hooves with a singular insistence which she was often to remember, Vivian considered this.

"At Victoria? Usual place?" she asked. "Dance frocks?"

"Oh, yes, of course. I've got a super new dress—black," Freda told her. They gained the Park together and began to trot along the track.

"Mine's blue," Vivian shouted, hair streaming in the breeze. Like a couple of children they started to race their horses along the track. Stones flew from under their hooves as the two animals thundered along, side by side. Vivian excelled in this as in everything she did, and it was she who won the race. "Fun . . ." she said as they settled down to a walking pace. "Gosh, I'm hungry. Did you like the champagne last night?"

Freda wrinkled her pretty nose. "Not

really, but it looks swanky. Tasted sour, I thought."

"Well, I won't have it if I don't like it tonight." Vivian spoke decidedly.

"I didn't like to refuse it," Freda confided.

They spent an hour together, perfecting their plans for the evening ahead.

When Vivian reached home she rushed into the lounge, throwing her hat in one direction, her whip in another.

"Rita—where are you? I'm hungry . . ."

Her sister joined her. "You'll get fat if you go on eating at this rate."

"Isn't it awful," Vivian mourned. "Here I take riding lessons to keep my weight down, then the exercise makes me so hungry I have to eat more. I wish we had tablets to take so that we needn't be tempted by appetizing food. What's for dinner anyhow?"

Rita told her. "And you'd better put your kit away—I won't," she added severely.

"I'm going out with Freda tonight . . ." Vivian told her blithely.

"I hope it's not another of those blind dates."

"No. She knows Butch, and he's bringing a pal for me. We're going dancing."

Rita relaxed. A foursome couldn't be very dangerous. Just lately Vivian had worried her, for her youthful exuberance would brook no interference. One thing she did frown on was the blind date, where girls met boys they did not know, and might never see again.

Vivian had her bath after tea, and emerged from her bedroom looking very glamorous and sophisticated.

"You look about twenty-five," Rita said, laughing, and struck by the beauty of the girlish face and figure.

"Lipstick," Vivian told her. "Gives me confidence. I'm going to show 'em a thing or two tonight. I'm going to dance my partner dizzy." She carolled a happy little song and did a pirouette about the room.

"Well, don't be later than midnight," Rita reminded her temperately.

"Don't ring the Police if I'm later," Vivian warned her darkly. "It'll simply be that I'm staying the night at Freda's if I miss the last bus . . . unless I could get a ride all the way home in that Bentley. Freda says Butch is using his father's Bentley."

Rita agreed, with some misgiving. "I think I'd sooner you stayed with Freda. They sound a bit better off than we are. Do be careful, Viv."

"Oh, don't be such an old stick in the mud, darling. I can take care of myself."

"I know. But this is London . . ."

"And this is *me*." Vivian's lovely face sailed into her line of vision. "Really, Rita, you aren't very complimentary to me, are you?"

Rita relaxed, laughing and relieved. Of course she could trust Vivian completely. Freda was a nice enough girl too, and really these days, one allowed so much freedom . . .

Vivian was gone before she could think it all out. She caught the bus at the end of the street and went to Victoria where Freda awaited her. Both girls were carefully made up and dressed in well-cut clothes.

"I wish I'd got a cape," Freda said discontentedly. "Yours is super."

"Belongs to Rita. She lets me wear it sometimes," Vivian said carelessly.

"Here's Butch now . . ." Freda forgot her complaint. "Gee . . . look at the fellow in the back seat? Wow—isn't he handsome? Yours, no doubt."

"No doubt at all," Vivian agreed regally. She smiled with extreme graciousness when she was ushered into the the car a minute later. Freda sat in the front with Butch and made the introductions with satisfactory bluntness.

"Brickie . . . ?" Vivian looked at her companion. Freda had thought that Butch was handsome but she thought Brickie beat him hollow. They were soon all laughing and talking in the friendly way of youth.

"You're pretty nice," Brickie said gently.

"Thank you." It was after seven o'clock and they decided to have a drink somewhere before going on to the club. It was all very grown up, Vivian decided, secretly thrilled, and she would not have confessed even to Freda that this was her first real drink.

"What'll it be?" she was asked in the

hotel bar, where they all stood a minute later.

"Judging by that Bentley . . ." she began, laughing.

Butch grinned. He was a likeable fellow, looked like a college student, and would probably follow his father abroad in a few years' time. Brickie was different again. Vivian was not quite able to place him, but decided that he was something in the City. They must have lots of money for they talked largely of their plans for the evening.

After two drinks apiece they got back into the Bentley, feeling very lighthearted.

At the club everything was very discreet, Vivian decided. She danced four dances running with Brickie, and decided that she liked him very much. He was tall, powerfully built, good-looking and an excellent dancer.

"You're an awfully good partner," she told him shyly.

"You're a fairy on your feet," he laughed. He was laughing a lot, and although not drunk, was certainly gay.

"I'm glad you haven't to drive that car of Butch's," she told him blithely. Probably Brickie was the oldest man she had been out with—he must be at least twenty-two.

"Do you dye your hair?" was the next question, as they executed a difficult two-step.

"I do not . . ." Vivian blazed up at him in sudden temper. "All my own growing."

"No need to get in a little temper. Come on, let's go back to the table."

Freda and Butch were already at the table. "Let's get out of here," Butch said and his speech was beginning to slur a little. "I'm gonna ring up some friends and we'll have a party at home."

"Oh, I don't think we could . . ." Vivian began uncertainly. She was hot and excited but determined.

"Go on. Don't be a spoil sport. Where's the harm?" Freda asked. If Vivian would not go then she could not either.

"Well . . ."

Butch was lurching across the room towards the telephone kiosk in the hall. Brickie entertained them until his return.

"Asked four of 'em along and I've got plenty of bottles and grub. Come on."

"Where is it?" Vivian asked.

"You'll see . . ." He led the way. "Too quiet here."

Brickie helped her into the long cape, and held her arm as they left the building. Vivian felt very grown up. Brickie was interested in her, she could tell. She liked him too.

Quarter of an hour later they arrived at Butch's home in a quiet square. One of those expensive addresses, Vivian thought, looking up at the bulk of the building in the gloom. His people were away and the house was in darkness. Her head was beginning to ache, and it was after eleven o'clock, but she would not give in. Brickie seemed as much at home here, as Butch who lived here, and together they raced about getting ready for the party.

"I don't think we ought to stay," Vivian whispered to her friend.

"Don't be stuffy," Freda spoke quite fiercely. "They're used to this sort of thing, we're not. I'm in love with Butch and I hope he'll marry me some day. If you go and spoil it all for me I'll . . ." She smiled ravishingly in Butch's direction and went over to help him arrange a trayful of glasses.

The next couple of hours were blurred in Vivian's mind. Several couples arrived but nothing much happened, except that they sat talking and drinking. Whenever her glass was empty someone filled it.

"Hope I'm not mixing my drinks," she said to someone, and was surprised that it was Brickie. Brickie was very attentive and it was flattering, she thought.

Freda didn't seem to be in the room, but it didn't really matter. Only they ought to be going home soon. She glanced at the clock, a small expensive one on the mantelpiece and realized with horror that it was after two o'clock.

She got to her feet shakily. Brickie was there to help her. "Should be going . . ."

"Not yet," he whispered. "Wait for Freda and Butch anyway. We'll take you home in the car." After that he began to make love to her, in a charming way.

Is this the real thing, she thought dazedly? She had another drink, and suddenly the room cleared. With a feeling of surprise she realized that all the others had gone, and they were alone.

"All gone," she said foolishly. "I mus' go too Brickie . . . darling."

"Oh, have another drink . . ." He poured one for each of them and put his arm around her. "The night is yet young . . . let's dance . . ." They tried to dance but collapsed laughing on the floor. "Can't dance . . . can't drink any more . . . can't drive . . ."

Vivian began to laugh helplessly. The room was floating around her, making strange patterns, and suddenly she was in Brickie's arms.

"That night"—Vivian said to Rita soberly—"that night you thought I was at Freda's. But we stayed with Butch and Brickie. I don't know their proper names. I don't even know the address. I didn't realize that we were all getting drunk . . . I don't even know if that was the intention when we went there. We—stayed all night. Next day Butch took us within a street of Freda's house and left us. We—didn't see them again. I didn't want to—I felt so ashamed. All next day it was so hazy and I felt sick. Freda pretended she'd stayed here, and I told you I'd stayed with Freda . . ."

"You knew better than to drink so much," Rita pounced on that.

"But honestly the first two or three didn't affect me. I felt wonderful. Afterwards I must have had eight or nine glasses." Vivian's shame was a painful thing. "Freda's mother is helping her. Why can't you help me, Rita?"

"Because I don't know how—and if I did, I wouldn't, so stop talking about it."

"Maybe if I asked Freda's mother?" Vivian's despair sounded in the low words.

"If you do that, I'm through," Rita spoke harshly. "It can't be right. What is coming over you, Vivian? You must be going mad."

"I'm frightened . . ."

"Well, stay that way." Rita's placid nature was stirred to the depths. She told Vivian exactly what she thought of her conduct. "It isn't that you have the excuse that you were tempted by someone you loved deeply; I think I could have understood that. But this—it's just beastly and disgusting." She was so disturbed that she would not discuss it any longer. Vivian gave her a strange, sad look, before they each went to their separate rooms.

The next evening Vivian picked up the newspaper to scan the headlines. Her sudden scream brought Rita quickly from the kitchen. "Oh, my goodness, Rita, it can't be true. *It can't.*" Vivian was staring in horror at the long report of Freda's death the night before.

Rita read it aloud, while Vivian's cheeks blanched with renewed terror.

"Eighteen—like you. An unpleasant case, it says . . . there is to be an inquest. Oh, dear, Vivian what have you done? They'll have no idea there were two of you . . . Oh, dear God what are we going to do? Does Freda's Mother know—about you?"

"No, I never told Freda . . . I couldn't."

Rita was so distressed that she walked up and down the room, drawing long breaths. How could she best help her sister? There was no purpose in going to Freda's family and perhaps making matters worse. She pondered the question dully, wishing there had been someone more experienced to whom she could turn. What she did now might determine all of Vivian's future. The girl was young and inexperienced and frightened.

"Oh, it's awful . . ." she said, shivering.

"Do you want me to leave here?" Vivian asked quietly.

"Don't be melodramatic. Don't make it worse than it is. Surely it's black enough as it is. I can't understand you, Vivian." Rita was beside herself to speak in this manner to Vivian, for the younger sister was spirited and rebellious enough. She had never been easy to handle, and only the reins of loving care had made it possible for her to live in amity with Rita. They had been alone for five years now, and Rita had thought that when Vivian was eighteen most of her troubles would be over, but this . . . She was so deeply shocked that she could not speak for a while.

"Look . . ." Vivian began awkwardly.

"Oh . . ." Rita looked at her with misgiving. "You're so sweet Vivian, I can't understand it."

The changed tone altered Vivian's hardness. She came towards her sister with a working face.

"I'm not sweet . . . I'm just hateful . . . but I'm sorry. Oh, I'm sorry, Rita."

71

Rita drew her close for a moment, feeling protection and love drive the anger from her heart. Then she put her aside, shaking her head. Nothing was solved and they must work it out somehow.

"What you ask just isn't possible. Freda's death has shown us that. We must think of some other way. You'll have to go through with it, Vivian. I'll help you all I can."

Some strength seemed to go out of Vivian then, a strength that she never regained. The shock aged her, and although she continued to go about her daily tasks as long as she could, she was not able to regain her former stamina.

"You were right, Rita," she whispered. "I see that now. I might have died with Freda—and this will pass, won't it? Some day I may be happy again."

It was a pathetic appeal to the stronger elder sister, one that Rita could not ignore. In those waiting months they grew closer together than had seemed possible. It was only at the end that variance had come, for Rita wanted the child to go from their home. Its presence would complicate their lives still further—be a constant reminder, but she had bowed to Vivian's wishes in the matter.

"You told me all the truth that time, Vivian didn't you?" Rita asked.

"Yes. All of it. I wouldn't want to fool you. Do you believe me?"

"Yes." Rita nodded, and she felt happier. If she had not been able to believe Vivian she felt that nothing would have been worth while any longer. So they must work it out, this problem that had come to spoil their lives. They grew quiet, thinking about all the implications.

"Shall I have to go on paying all my life?" Vivian asked pitifully.

"No—it was a mistake—it's sure to be easier in time."

"What will you say to Richard tomorrow?"

"I don't know. I'll think about it. The way he spoke tonight rather shocked me. I didn't know he could be so downright brutal—oh, not about you, but *to me*. A man that will say as much as that before marriage won't wrap it up after marriage. You know something, Vivian? I believe we're both learning something already. I must have had blinkers on where Richard was concerned."

Vivian smiled faintly. "I hope it won't come to a split between you. I wouldn't like to be responsible for that. You have your own future to think about."

Rita stood up, yawning. "What do you want for supper, Viv?"

"Turkey? Maybe a little chocolate soufflé?" Vivian's mischievous smile peeped forth for the first time, and it heartened Rita. "But I'll settle for brown bread and butter if you haven't those things in the larder. By the way, how are you getting on with your work? Are you held up anywhere? Maybe I could do some reading for you now?"

Rita, who held a Master of Arts degree, was a reader for a famous firm of publishers, and she seldom had less than two or three books to read and criticize during the week. The job helped her to eke out the money which her parents had left, although in itself it was badly paid considering all the work and responsibility involved.

"Oh, I'm not much behindhand, thanks. I'd better do it myself. I can't afford to miss anything. Well, I'll get that brown bread. I'm going to stay up late so I'll make strong coffee. It won't disturb you, will it?"

"No." Vivian lay back consideringly. She reached for her brush and comb and began to prepare her shining fair hair for the night. "The babe isn't really much trouble, is he?"

Rita called back to her from the kitchenette. "They aren't at this stage yet. They've scarcely collected their wits yet. Just wait for a few weeks when they begin to take notice. That'll be the time."

"Yes, that'll be the time," Vivian agreed almost happily. "They make a lot of washing don't they?"

Rita went to answer a knock on their door. Miss Jane stood outside, and she was holding a couple of the hydrangeas from the yard. "How is your sister? Do give her these. I thought they were too nice to waste. And by the way, the plumbers are coming on Monday morning to put in central heating, so if you hear weird sounds in the basement you'll know what it is."

"Central heating? But that'll take years," Rita said, holding the hydrangeas.

"Maybe not so long—months maybe—weeks if we're lucky. Think how nice it will be when finished. We shan't have draughty corridors and stairs. Brr. How I hate the cold weather. Is there anything I can do?" Miss Jane was smiling and friendly. "No, dear, I won't come in tonight."

Rita knew that they must have been wondering about the baby, but they would not ask.

"I'm bringing my nephew to call on you tomorrow. He's quite a pretty baby."

"We'll look forward to that. Good night. Sleep well. You look tired."

"Oh, I am . . ." Rita yawned visibly, and her eyes watered. Miss Jane returned to her sister.

"You know, Letty, we've a lot to be glad about really. At least we haven't got that poor girl's load to carry." Miss Jane spoke slowly and sympathetically. They had been feeling depressed for days because of Letty's failing sight. This waiting period seemed long, with a slowing down of all their normal activities.

"You can always find someone worse than yourself, can't you? What did she say?"

Jane told her the conversation. "Of course I'd heard all about it from Mrs. Page but . . ."

"Aye, it's sad," Letty agreed. She was feeling all round her chair quietly. "Can you see my handkerchief anywhere? It's one of my better ones. I wouldn't like to lose it. I may have dropped it when we were out for our walk this afternoon." A soft colour came into her cheeks, a signal of her distress.

Jane found it for her a moment later. "It wasn't really lost . . . just got under your chair, Letty. No wonder you couldn't find it way back there."

"Thank you." But I'd be lost . . . lost . . . lost . . . without you, she thought, secretly frightened of the darkness that held her in bondage. Jane's steadying hand gripped hers as she started to rise. "Don't fuss me. I'm all right. I can feel. I know where I'm going."

Jane watched her walk to the door, her heart aching for the courage of this beloved sister.

"Uncle Bertolino has been out sight-seeing all day . . ." she said.

"I wondered?" Miss Letty paused. "How did you know?"

"He told me half an hour ago. I met him as he was going up to his flat." Jane looked thoughtful. "He says he wants to give us a meal one day in his flat . . . perhaps when Vivian is better."

"That will be nice. I'm dying to see if he does cook like an angel, as Rita says." Letty sailed off, with her head in the air. She was not absolutely sure that she approved of Jane meeting Uncle Bertolino on the stairs like that.

3

UNCLE BERTOLINO plunged his hands into the flour, hissing with pleasure. It was kind of his niece to give him the freedom of the kitchen. He glanced across at Rita, sensing her unhappiness. The nurse was with Vivian in the bedroom, and Johnnie Bertolino was creating pandemonium in his cot.

Rita sighed. She was bending over the sink. "There are times, Uncle Bertolino," she said distinctly, "when I feel like running away."

"And why not? Surely the good Richard would welcome you in his arms?" Uncle Bertolino approved of Richard, and said so.

Rita was shocked. "You evidently don't understand."

"But I do. I understand Richard's argument completely. What's to stop you marrying him?"

"One reason only—I'm not sure I love him."

79

"Ah-ha . . ." Uncle Bertolino threw his paste on to the board with a flourish. "Now that is something different. Had it been only for Vivian's sake I could have put her in the top flat and you and Richard could have lived down here—which would mean you could care for both—but now you make me to think . . ."

"I make me to think too," Rita sighed. "I make me to think that I don't like all this washing either. Simply ruining my nails."

"But you don't really mind?" Uncle Bertolino suggested, one eye on the enormous size of his pasta. "Now I measure your oven—take your largest tin—so . . . and so . . . and so . . ."

"No, I don't really mind," Rita replied, surprised to find that she didn't. "It's rather fun having a baby around. Are they always so noisy, I wonder?"

Uncle Bertolino's pasta was ready for the oven. Having a good appetite he saw to it that all dishes were sufficient in size to fit the three of them, and leave some over for the next meal.

"I'm not going to let Richard push me around," Rita continued her own line of thought. "I didn't like him laying down the law in that way. If he'll do it now what will it be like after we're married?"

"All men must lay down the law sooner or later," Uncle Bertolino commented drily. "Now I put this to four hundred . . . wait half an hour . . . and there she is." He began to clear away the utensils he had used, with a rapidity that dazzled Rita. "Better not wash up yet—no?"

Rita began to wring out the baby's nightdress, still intent on her own troubles. "I don't see that it's necessary. Marriage should be on a fifty fifty basis— or am I wrong?"

"Not wrong—but not right either," Uncle Bertolino muttered. "It never works out that way. If you want to—not wear the skirt . . . you understand?"

She raised a flushed, indignant face. "Are you meaning that I'm wanting to wear the pants?"

He beamed. "You are so quick to understand. Yes, that is so. I do not approve of the woman wearing the pants."

"I'm not trying to," Rita told him coolly. "But these days you don't have to go through hell just to put up with a man's tantrums . . ."

"I fear you don't love your Richard enough," Uncle Bertolino suggested sadly. "If you can talk this way—before marriage . . . what will it be later on?"

Caught out by his quick-witted reply, Rita had the grace to blush. "Must be all this extra work that's getting me down," she confessed ruefully. "I'll hang these out."

"You need a holiday," Uncle Bertolino said gently. "The winter has been long."

Even the liveliness of the brisk April morning did nothing to comfort her worn spirit. Somehow the issue had come to mean something more than the original argument warranted. Had it been simply Vivian who stood in the way, it would have been easy as Uncle Bertolino said. There was more to it than that, she decided.

The nurse left, and suddenly Johnnie Bertolino was silent again. "What's she do to him?" Rita asked. "I don't think he likes her. You want to check up next time."

"He was hungry," Vivian explained.

"She makes him wait till she's bathed him and that's what riles him. All men are alike really. Or hadn't you noticed? By the way, she left a whole pile of washing again . . ."

"There's no end to it," Rita complained, but as she hung over the baby, her lovely face softened magically. "You're worth it, darling. One day I'll remind you how I slaved for you."

Vivian's leaping apprehension subsided, and she was almost happy again. "You love him too?"

"If it isn't love—it's pretty near it," Rita told her. "He's quite a boy. Uncle Bertolino is making the dinner. Wonderful, isn't it?"

Vivian nodded. "Rita—don't say anything rash tonight when Richard comes, will you? I hate to feel that I'm responsible."

"I won't allow him to be rude to me," Rita said before going to her own room.

She glanced at herself in the mirror. It was the first time all day that she had thought about herself. She brushed the shining dark hair until it clung to her brush. She powdered her pale, magnolia skin, and slipped into a fresh linen suit.

"Will I do—to face the enemy?" she slipped back into Vivian's room.

"You look lovely. I do hope Richard will be reasonable. You're so reliable, Rita . . . I don't know what I'd do without you."

"I feel the same about you, Vivian. Let's not go into it now though. Got to keep my chin up."

Vivian's gaze met hers anxiously. Something in the velvety depths drew Rita closer to the bed. She drew in her breath quickly.

"I haven't given you much cause to trust me, have I?" Vivian whispered.

"It's all been a mistake." Rita was shaken in spite of herself. "It's strange that anything so terrible could bring something into the world as sweet as your Johnnie Bertolino."

"Yes. A father and mother who were so drunk they didn't know what they were doing . . ." She covered her face with both hands. "I wish I hadn't so much time to think."

"Just make one resolution . . ." Rita began.

"That I won't drink anything more? I

know. I've promised myself that—and Johnnie Bertolino too. I hope I'm not a prude but I'll be determined about that in future."

About seven o'clock Richard arrived in his usual confident way. Uncle Bertolino had gone to the ballet, promising to take Rita as soon as she could be relieved of some of her duties. Rita knew that he was leaving the field clear for her, so that she could talk to Richard without interruption.

"Glad to see me, honey?" Richard asked. Was there ever a real doubt in his mind?

"Yes." She sat down, facing him, not as usual on the settee, and he grinned as he saw her motive. Rita had not yet wholly forgiven him. "It's raining, isn't it?"

They were the first words that entered her mind, and she realized that the rain had come on with the spring evening.

"Yes. Mind if I hang up my overcoat?" Richard drawled.

"Oh, I'm sorry . . ." she flushed at the rebuke for she had forgotten that he might be damp. Her mind was so filled with apprehension at the coming interview that

85

she had little thought to spare for anything else. "Put it on a hanger in the hall."

He opened and closed the door, and came back to stand in front of the fire.

"Well?" He smiled down gravely at her. The nicest part of his nature was in his smile, she often thought. There was a genuineness in him that could not be ignored.

She glanced up, and what she read in his deep set eyes brought her to him. Impulsively she pushed her hand through his arm, as he lounged with his hands in his pockets.

"I was a bit hasty last night, Richard . . . Forget it, won't you?"

"I'll forget it. Does it mean that we are now of the same mind?" he drawled.

"Not—exactly, dear. I can't plan ahead yet."

"But you understood me? I can't wait longer than June. I'm no angel, Rita. You know that. We've been engaged for nearly a year now and it's time we got married."

She flushed at the bluntness of his words. Hesitatingly she tried to grope among the explanations that thronged her mind. She tried not to antagonize him for he was in a difficult mood.

"I know how you feel, Richard . . . but you do not seem to understand my side of it. There are others to be considered."

He stopped her abruptly. "You're wrong there. There's just the two of us. You can't take others with you into our life. Why won't you see that?"

She drew a long breath, trying to keep her temper. "I'll marry you a little later . . . perhaps . . ."

"Oh?" He did not look too pleased with this. "What do you mean?"

"What you said last night was a shock."

"The same for me," he reminded her curtly. "We didn't exactly mince words, did we?" He paused. "Do you consider that Vivian would do as much for you?"

"I'm certain of it."

"Then let me talk to her. I'm certain she'll see the sense of my argument. Where is the purpose in you sacrificing yourself?"

"But I'm not. Can't you see I'm not? I'm just—not keen any longer . . ." She spoke miserably, and was almost afraid of the look on his dark face.

"If that's the way you feel . . ."

"Just wait a minute . . ." She held to his arm. "I don't know how I feel."

"Come here . . ." He turned to her, a strange light leaping in his eyes.

She continued to back away from him. "No, Richard—please don't try to sway me that way. I can't bear it. You're not fair. You won't try to understand. This is my life, this is the way it has to be for quite a while yet, and neither you nor anyone else can change it. Bear with me a little longer. I'm certain I'm right." Her voice rose hysterically in spite of a resolution to remain calm.

"Then if you're certain, there isn't anything more to be said," he spoke calmly. His eyes narrowed. "I could make you change your mind."

She drew herself up. "Could you?" Strength seemed to flow back into her slim body.

He hesitated before answering. "Maybe not. But if you let me go this time it's the finish. You're not playing fast and loose with me, Rita."

She bent her head, agitated and frightened. His quiet words did more than anything yet to show her that she was losing him. "I—don't think I can bear it . . ."

"Then be reasonable, darling." His eagerness reached her again. "You're standing in your own light."

"If you'd only wait a little, or if you'd promise me that I could keep them with me for a time. It wouldn't be for ever. Vivian will soon be well enough to work —but you're rushing me . . . you won't wait. Oh, how can you be so hard. I don't believe you love me. I don't believe you love anyone but yourself or you would be willing to consider my point of view. I can't and I won't break my promise to Vivian—and what's more I don't believe I want to. Think that over . . ." She was thoroughly roused now, fighting him to the limit of her strength. "I'm glad I've seen this side of you before it was too late. Marriage with you in this frame of mind could be hell. I don't want it . . . I'm glad, I tell you . . ."

He drew her into his arms by sheer mastery of strength. "You love me . . ."

"I don't. Not any more. The man I loved was someone in my mind. I thought you were gentle and considerate, but you're none of those things. I'm glad I've found out in time. You can't make me change now, Richard—because I don't want to change."

"You'll regret this . . ." he muttered, shaking her.

"I won't."

"When you're an old maid you'll wish you'd listened to sense and reason." He was still shaking her so that her dark hair fell across her face.

"I won't. Do *you* think I'll be an old maid?" She blazed the words at him in sudden fire. He drew back before the expression on her face. "I'll live my life but it *is my* life and I won't be bamboozled by you or anyone else."

"You're self-opinionated." His hands loosed their hold and she drew away from him.

"And what are you?" She spoke contemptuously.

"My lord, Rita, I never thought we'd have quarrelled like this." His hand was on the knob.

"Please go—and don't ever come back . . ." Her voice had lost its strength.

"When you attack Vivian you attack me. I'll never forgive that as long as I live. Now do you understand?"

He looked startled for a moment, until understanding came. He nodded. "All right. Goodbye."

"Goodbye—and I'll send on your ring and other things."

"You needn't trouble," he spoke sarcastically. "Keep it—I shan't need it. I'm through with women."

She waited motionless by the table until she heard him slam the outer door. It seemed to have taken him minutes to get into his heavy coat. When she heard his heavy tread on the path outside she relaxed tremblingly into a chair. One hand went to her hair and straightened it. She felt undone and frightened in spite of the temper that still simmered below the surface. Where had her carefully regulated life gone, she wondered hazily. For several years she had worked to a definite plan, trying to live, and to show Vivian how to live the life her parents had mapped out for them. It had all gone wrong, thrown into the vortex as if there had been no guiding hand, no resolution.

"What's the matter with me?" she asked herself, sitting on by the fire so quietly that Vivian thought she was asleep as she stood holding on to the door of her room. She swayed as she said: "Rita . . . I heard most of that."

"Then you'll know the truth of how I feel about Richard . . ." Rita said harshly.

"Don't you care any longer?"

"I don't really know. Oh, Vivian, you shouldn't have come in here. Suppose you get cold? Get back into bed at once. You haven't even your dressing gown on. What a stupid thing to do."

"But you didn't come when I called you." Vivian slid down into the bed. The rain outside had chilled the atmosphere and she was glad to cuddle into the warm blankets.

"I never heard you; I'm so upset I don't know what I'm doing." Rita felt that it was as well to be as honest with her sister as she could be under the circumstances.

"Poor Rita." Vivian looked up at her appealingly. "It's like a stone in a pool— we don't know where the ripples will end, do we?"

The gentleness of her voice proved to be

Rita's undoing. Waveringly she glanced at her sister, before the tears began to course down her face. "I'm not crying . . ." she gulped while the heaving of her breast denied her lips. She cried so hard and so long that Vivian guessed her secret. She lay looking up at the ceiling not able to speak for a while.

When Rita's despair began to subside, she whispered: "You still love Richard, don't you?"

"I suppose you can't turn it off just as quickly as I thought. It'll get less urgent in time—it's bound to, isn't it?"

"I expect so. I've never been in love—not properly like you and Richard. I've just been stage struck—that sort of thing. Do you remember my pash on Gregory Peck?" Vivian was trying to get them away from the tragic events that had undermined Rita's courage. "I wish it needn't have happened."

"Do *you* think I'm opinionated?" Rita demanded.

"No, dear, you're kind and good and generous, and Richard is fighting mad because he's lost you. Ah, well . . ." They tried to think of other things.

From a small child Vivian had longed to be a film actress but so far the chance had not come her way. She had good deportment, dressed well and she could dance and sing, and for some time had earned extra money as a professional model. This had all stopped during the last year, and she was uncertain that she could regain the small footing she had had in the world she longed to enter.

"Perhaps we ought to move right into London," Rita said, trying to enter into her mood. "But I like it here, and it's only half an hour by Tube."

"Oh, we'd better stay here—it's so handy for you, anyway," Vivian said carelessly. "Did you notice that critic in the paper today, reporting on the new book that's come out? Wasn't it the one you were enthusiastic about? You said if they changed the title it would go with a bang . . ." She began to search for the paragraph she needed in the papers strewn on the bed.

"Yes, that's it." Rita's face kindled as she began to read the review. "You know, it's very rewarding to feel you were right

—all those months ago. Won't the author be thrilled?"

"So will your publishers, I imagine," Vivian said drily. They were safely away from the topic that was so hurtful, and she determined not to return to it. "I wish you'd get on with it and I'm sure I can manage now if you want to go to your desk. You've two or three hours before bedtime."

"Uncle Bertolino has gone to the ballet, so we shan't see him again tonight," Rita told her, sighing. "Good night—do you think the baby will want anything else?"

"No—he'll manage. Go to bed now, dear."

"Another day," Rita whispered. "Sunday . . . I'll go to church . . ." She raised her blind to stand gazing into the quiet spring night. How lovely it would be in the country tonight. If only they could all retract their steps a couple of years. "We seem to be taking all the wrong turnings somehow."

The house was quiet, the wind stilled, only the racing clouds told of the rain that had driven them in fury against the town.

The yard looked white and forlorn and shadowed.

Miss Jane said the following evening: "If you really want to go to church, Rita, I'll sit with Vivian and the baby. I'd enjoy a wee chat with your sister."

"Take Miss Letty with you, then we'll all be happy," Vivian suggested. "I know she likes to go."

Rita went, with Miss Letty leaning gently against her arm. Uncle Bertolino saw them off with a flourish, before skipping back to keep Miss Jane and Vivian company. He had his own personal plans for the next hour or two, and was not quite sure if they would be popular.

Miss Letty pressed Rita's arm gently. "I'm glad we're together, Rita." It was quietly said and could be turned aside if she'd wanted, but Rita accepted it.

"I wonder sometimes if life will ever be the same again," Rita said slowly, as they walked. "I'm only just beginning to realize all that it can mean to both of us—and to the baby too. Nothing we do now can put us back to what we were before. It's that inevitability that is so frightening. It's so

96

final. We've got to go through with our lives . . ."

"Yes, I think I know how you feel. Your pain is partly because what was, has gone forever."

"I feel as if there isn't any real security anywhere . . ." Rita's troubled voice dropped a note. "I don't know if I've got the strength—for what is to come."

"Perhaps Vivian will surprise you," Miss Letty ventured. "After all, the child is hers and she has already surprised us all, by wanting to keep him so passionately. I don't doubt that she too has reckoned up all the penalties, but she is prepared to do what she can for him."

"It's all been so carefully ordered until now," Rita faltered. "I thought we were on top of everything. It's been a shock. Then—you may as well know—Richard won't be coming any more."

Miss Letty drew in a hard breath. "Didn't he understand?"

Rita shook her head. They drew close to the church and entered. She guided Miss Letty into a pew, and together they sat down. The quietness and benediction of those first moments were soothing, and she felt as if the turmoil of spirit was like a clock that was running down. She drew a steadying breath, glancing around her. The lights cast a soft glow along the aisles and the transepts were shadowed.

The choir rose to open the service. The singing was the best part of it, she thought, preparing to enjoy the melody. This evening there was a solo by a famous tenor and she looked forward to that. The service passed over her head, but when the soloist came forward she gripped her hands tightly together. She recognized him with sudden pleasure for she had often heard him.

As his voice swelled out in the little church, ringing with sincerity, she realized that she should not have come in her present emotional condition. She wanted to rush out of the building, to get away from the pain and the beauty and the chaos that his words were evoking within her.

"Oh, heavens . . ." Miss Letty would be astonished if she did that. She knew that she must listen, while every word fell like a hammer on her quivering soul. For her there was no promise, no happiness, no future. The last time she had come here with Vivian, the future had seemed uncomplicated, secure. Ah . . . Vivian . . . she agonized over the sister she loved so deeply.

The words slid away, the soft chords of the organ became muted yet she listened on, hearing their cadence, and meaning, in a haunting fear that paralysed her. She sat with head bent, staring down at her hands. It was the worst moment she had ever experienced and she was dazed with misery and self-reproach. Somewhere she should have found a way of helping Vivian, of preventing her making this mistake.

"I won't listen . . ." she thought. Music weakened resistance, for music was beauty and truth and life. Music has its feet in memory, and memory has the power to hurt unbearably. Memory is the essence of pain, deepening pain only half understood even now, yet so disturbing that the soul could find no real peace. Would the years bring solace?

She stood up to sing the final hymn, because Miss Letty prompted her. Miss Letty was kind but she could not comprehend fully because she was apart, she was not involved. She felt glad of the brief respite when she might return slowly from her mind's wandering.

They returned to the house, with scarcely a word spoken. Miss Letty understood and would not force conversation on her. Miss Jane greeted them cheerily, all had gone well during their absence, and relief made her loquacious. She wondered why Rita appeared to be so depressed but did not comment.

"We've had a simply wonderful time," she said cheerfully. "Your Uncle Bertolino has kept us entertained with stories about his life. It's been fascinating. Italy must be a wonderful country."

"He's a complete darling," Vivian was flushed and sparkling. "I feel to know him so much better now . . . don't you, Miss Jane?"

Miss Jane looked dreamy. "Yes, I do really. He's most interesting. You know, all that sunshine makes me feel I've got to catch the first plane in the morning."

"The food too . . ." Vivian reminded her. "He's made our mouths water. We simply don't know what food is."

"No, we'll not stay," Miss Jane said decidedly, although tempting smells were coming forth from the kitchen, where Uncle Bertolino was installed. It took all her strength of mind to make that decision, as she told Letty later, for Uncle Bertolino could cook. "No, dears, you'll all be wanting to settle down. I'll just see to our fire, and we'll have supper later. Good night, for now."

Uncle Bertolino came to the kitchen door, looking absurd in one of Rita's small aprons. In his hand he brandished a large cooking spoon. His crestfallen air was unmistakable.

"But I insist . . ." he said firmly. "I cook much—enough for all, eh?"

Miss Jane and Miss Letty remained equally firm. Together they returned to their own flat. Uncle Bertolino was almost in tears.

"Put it in a dish and I'll slip along with it . . ." Rita offered comfortingly. "All good cooks have a *right* to be appreciated."

"Ah." This mended the situation. Uncle Bertolino dished up the meal happily. Rita took his offering along to the two ladies, and together they laughed at the situation.

"Nectar and ambrosia . . ." Vivian said, when her tray appeared.

"I've an idea he likes red hair," Rita said inconsequently. "Better than black or gold . . ."

"I see what you mean," Vivian agreed thoughtfully. "Could be . . ."

4

"IF I can't manage that connection then the whole blasted business stops." Rita heard the words distinctly from under her feet. Monday morning, and the plumbers had arrived with unexpected promptitude. Groans were becoming frequent now.

"This coupling . . . Fred, it can't be done . . ."

Vivian looked alarmed. "All that expense goes for nothing if they can't complete it."

Rita shook her head. "Don't worry. They'll find a way. You know, Vivian, if Johnnie Bertolino shows any tendencies to be a plumber you want to have him seen to . . ."

They laughed quietly.

"Give me a three-quarter inch . . . maybe that'll do it . . ."

"I wonder if he knows the new cylinder has arrived," Rita whispered. It stood in the main kitchen, waiting attention. "I

103

expect they saw it as they went through. The radiators are wonderful . . ."

"If they work," Vivian whispered. "There are radiators and radiators . . ."

"Somehow I have confidence that these will." Rita was dusting the room rapidly as they talked. "Has it occurred to you that at any other time of the year we'd have been quite interested—but they had to choose this particular time, when we've something else on our minds."

"Just like a plumber . . . to wait till the spring . . ."

"Now Fred . . ." There was an air of relief in the sepulchral voice below them. "Give me an angle valve . . ."

"All's well," Rita said. "I'd better think about putting the kettle on."

"In a way—I'm glad they're here now," Vivian spoke wistfully. "You'd be busy anyway."

"I don't mind if the roof blows off so long as Johnnie Bertolino doesn't waken before noon." Rita smiled forgivingly as she whisked into the kitchenette to put on the kettle.

A loud bang in the basement made her jump, and wakened Johnnie Bertolino.

The plumber came running up to reassure them. For quarter of an hour all was confusion. Vivian nursed the frightened baby in vain. Mrs. Page came down to enquire what had produced the sudden noise. The plumber's mate vanished with unusual speed.

"I wouldn't know," Rita told her. "Doubtless a T piece didn't slip into a straight coupling or something. I think he'd have mentioned it if the plumber had died, don't you?"

Mrs. Page nodded, and absently accepted a cup of tea from the plumber's pot. "I've been thinking Rita, wouldn't it be rather nice if you and Vivian went up to my cottage in the Lake District for a while?"

"Have a word with Vivian—it's a super idea." Rita was putting out cake and biscuits.

"You can't travel with a baby as young as this one," Vivian said. She looked lovely, with her blonde hair twisted into a new style.

"Of course you can. Just take everything he owns and sort it out when you get there." Mrs. Page knew that she must persuade them for Dominic's sake. "Your Uncle Bertolino must go too; I realize you wouldn't want to leave him on his own."

"I don't know that he'd be lonely," Vivian smiled and a dimple appeared unexpectedly. "It's a good idea though."

"About that," Rita came out of the kitchen. "Uncle Bertolino will be in a seventh heaven. He's always wanted to visit the Lake District. He will want us to travel in a car in comfort."

"Lovely," Vivian stretched like a kitten.

"I shall make six bottles of the milk mixture and every time the baby opens his mouth you must push one in," Rita added. "And there are special nappies now that we can get that will lessen the washing problem for that day anyway."

Rita retired into her work, catching up on the accumulation, and welcoming the chance to work uninterruptedly. Vivian wandered about the flat, sometimes visiting Miss Jane and Miss Letty with whom she loved to chat.

A few days later Mrs. Page said: "I think you two should go up to the Lakes now."

"Are you sure you won't need the cottage yourself?" Rita asked.

"No. Dominic can't leave just now. You know what he does, don't you?"

"No." Vivian glanced up at the speaker. "But we're dying to know."

Mrs. Page laughed. She was secretly very proud of her grandson, and was glad of the chance to air her knowledge. "He's a band leader—you know, conducts an orchestra of his own. He's had it five years but it was only two years ago that he came to London—to make his fortune, he says. He was miserable in rooms and finally I decided to come and look after him. He found us this flat, and so here we are."

"We wondered," Rita acknowledged. "He must be very clever."

"Yes. He is. I think so anyway. He can play the violin and piano too. He composes music too. He makes a recording about every ten days." It was fascinating to tell these things to the girls who were listening intently. "You will have heard his violin?"

"Not often enough," Vivian said thoughtfully.

"You must come up some time, we'd both be very pleased." She slurred away from that quickly for invitations had not been welcomed in the past. "Dominic is working in a show every night and what with rehearsals and recordings he's pretty busy."

"He must be," Vivian was nursing her knees thoughtfully. "He looks like a musician too when you think of it."

"We thought he must be a waiter," Rita said and they all smiled.

"I'll tell him that. It will amuse him."

"They are going up next week," Mrs. Page told Dominic that night as she served his late meal. "That's what you wanted, isn't it? I told them enough to interest them."

"Don't look so serious, Gran. I'll do as much for you some time." He was grinning at her.

She considered him gravely. "I'll be glad when that girl is out of the house."

"Why?"

"Rita's worth two of her—but you're like all the men, you fall for a blonde. You want to take a look at Rita."

"I have . . ."

"She's outshone when Vivian's around

maybe, but she can sparkle on her own account."

"Shall I marry them both?" Dominic asked indolently.

"That isn't funny," she told him, reaching for his cup. "I guess the circumstances are a bit unusual, but they'll be away for a few weeks and we can all get sorted out a bit . . ."

Uncle Bertolino spent an evening with Dominic before going north. He had his own reasons for seeking out the young man. Together they went to the Albert Hall. Dominic came out in a trance.

"I was impressed too," Uncle Bertolino said reverently. "But wonderful. Such music. Such magic . . ."

"Such scope," Dominic put in. He sighed. "You know, sometimes I think I'm on wrong lines. I'm certainly getting into the money, but it's not the most worthwhile thing. I hate jazz sometimes."

"Today everyone wants jazz and jive . . ." Uncle Bertolino displayed his knowledge with pride. Each new word he learned was put into immediate use. "But you—you are the true musician. Your

109

heart is back there—" He nodded over his shoulder to the great building they had just left. People were still streaming around them, as they hurried towards where Dominic's car was garaged.

"Yes. But one has to live."

"Did you ever read about Beethoven?" Uncle Bertolino asked, trotting along beside Dominic's longer, more elegant stride. "Now there was a great man. He starved for his art and today—" he held out both hands expressively. "Today we all know and love his music and revere his memory. Now, if he'd been side-tracked . . ." He waited to see if that could be the right word, for it sounded odd to his unaccustomed ears. "He might have been—how do you say it—just dead?"

"I see what you mean."

Uncle Bertolino beamed on a woman who nearly tripped him up as she stepped off the pavement. His reaction was quick. "Just so. One is dead a long time. It is while one is alive that counts. We go in here? The discussion is good eh?" He followed Dominic who ordered two whiskies and soda.

110

"You've got something there," Dominic brooded. "All this light stuff . . ." Vaguely he waved the waiter away.

"I know. Froth?" Again Uncle Bertolino had pulled off the right word, and his broad back straightened. "Just froth. Not to last. You, my good friend, could make the real music, the kind that will last forever."

"Well, I don't know about that. I keep trying my hand at composing. But I've got to bring in the bread and butter."

"But while you eat the bread and butter, you can be mixing the cake, no?"

Dominic nodded. He liked Uncle Bertolino, and they'd just spent a most enjoyable evening together, but he didn't want to talk about music for the rest of their time together.

"You're going up to the cottage tomorrow . . ." It seemed a safe enough place to begin.

"Ah yes, we leave at eight—that is early, but it is a long way."

"Hope you enjoy it. Are the girls looking forward to it?" Dominic asked casually.

"But yes—all of us."

111

"I may look in later," Dominic said carelessly. "Trying to get a few days off during early May. Do you think you'll get up to Scotland while you're in the north?"

"Hope so." Uncle Bertolino nodded several times. Which one was he after? Neither girl seemed keen on romance at the moment—but that would pass . . . and Dominic was waiting. Uncle Bertolino stared hard into the mirror facing him. The young man was indeed elegant, tall, wearing his long cape with an air. His features might almost be Roman in their aquiline beauty. Certainly a young man to watch, Uncle Bertolino surmised. He smiled suddenly as he realized that Dominic had caught his eye in the mirror. "We go?"

Rita organized the journey so well that they arrived at Ellerwaite with one bottle of milk mixture in hand. She held it aloft triumphantly. Young Johnnie Bertolino was apparently drugged by so much attention, and he slept peacefully while they settled in during the late evening. The car journey had passed without incident. Uncle Bertolino had been a model of discretion, keeping silent at all times when his grandnephew displayed temperament.

The luggage was carried into the cottage, while Vivian held the baby in her arms, not sure where she dare put him down. Wonderingly she watched as each new possession arrived. How could so young a child need so much. Her own suitcases and Rita's appeared insignificant by comparison.

"For me, I bring only my shaving tackle, tooth brush and pyjamas," Uncle Bertolino bounced about excitedly.

The cottage was all Mrs. Page had promised it would be. In the dusk they could not see the beauty of the garden, or the fine old trees about them, but they knew them to be there.

A buxom country woman awaited them. She was smiling and curious. "Now I just thought that would be your taxi. You're overdue, I'm thinking, but not too late. It's a long way, isn't it? You'll be tired. How's the baby stood the journey?" She glanced into Johnnie Bertolino's face curiously. "If you'll follow me I'll show you where you are to sleep."

She followed them into the drawing-room, where Vivian exclaimed in delight over the oaken beams, gay chintz, and polished furniture. A bread cupboard occupied almost the whole of one wall.

"Three hundred years old," Mrs. Lake informed them. "And as good as new." She preceded them up the wide stairs. "These are your bedrooms . . . the other two belong to Mrs. Page and Dominic. I think they said something about coming up later."

"Did they?" Rita asked, surprised. "What a charming house."

Vivian put the baby down on her bed, and glanced about her curiously. The colours everywhere were bright and gay.

"It used to be an Inn about three hundred years ago, but it's completely modernized now, you know. You've got electricity—had you noticed? That wasn't there until this year. They brought it up the Valley and everyone hitched themselves on to the cable as fast as they could."

Rita followed Uncle Bertolino into his single room. "Will you be all right, Uncle Bertolino? They're all small rooms, but at least they're private. I like it, don't you?"

Uncle Bertolino touched the ceiling, bounced on the bed, opened his week-end case, and smiled benevolently, all at the same moment, Rita thought. "I like it. Look . . ." He drew her to the window, to gaze out at the half shrouded view. "Tomorrow we see properly. Tonight Uncle Bertolino makes the meal, for you are tired, no?"

Suddenly Rita was in his arms, leaning her head against his broad shoulder. Tears of tiredness began to steal down her face. "I was so frightened—in case Johnnie Bertolino got a chill, or was sick, or just plain bad tempered . . ." She heaved, trying to steady herself. "I don't know what's the matter with me."

"You're tired," Uncle Bertolino's voice was as soft as the cooing of a dove. Rita felt a sense of surprise that he was so tall. His bulk gave the impression that he was a small man, but he stood taller than herself. She leaned a moment longer, before withdrawing herself from his arms.

Her smile was as tender as his words had been. "Thank you. I do like you, Uncle Bertolino."

He nodded. "I too—like you . . ."

Together they hastened back to Vivian who was undoing Johnnie Bertolino from his cocoon of wraps. The child did not waken, and together they all went down the stairs, leaving him to sleep peacefully on the bed.

Vivian was gay, seeming relieved that the former routine had been broken. Rita realized that they had both needed this holiday badly. They would be able to relax, and perhaps enjoy both Uncle Bertolino and the baby. Until now this had not been possible.

"I wonder if all new babies make such a difference?" she asked, as Vivian helped her to wash up after the meal. They both felt surprised when Uncle Bertolino, who was smoking, told them that he was going up to Scotland the next day.

"But not so soon?" Rita said, dismayed.

"Yes. I go . . . it is my chance to see Edinburgh, while you settle in here. Then when I return we go drives together. You like that, eh?"

"Yes, but . . ."

"You will enjoy a few days alone here, no doubt." Uncle Bertolino spoke firmly.

"We will have the real holiday when I return at the week-end."

Vivian gave him a warm, happy glance. "I understand, Uncle Bertolino. We'll get sorted out—and then you'll help us to enjoy ourselves."

"Something of that," he waved his pipe at them. "I go out now to smell the air, then to bed. Good night, my children."

Rita watched him go, his pipe scenting the cool air as he wove in and out of the garden.

For four days Vivian rested as much as she could, while Rita helped her with the baby. They planned a system and tried hard to keep it, but their awakening love for the tiny baby made it difficult for them.

"He's just been a hungry imp until now . . ." Vivian complained one night. "Just occasionally he gives me a gleam and it's quite startling really . . ."

"Yes, he's wakening up fast," Rita was kneeling beside Vivian, as they bathed the child. "It's awfully bad to tickle them, but I'd love to see him smile."

"Auntie will just have to wait, won't

she, my puffakins . . ." Vivian was growing happier, accepting her rôle of mother in a tranquil way that made Rita rejoice. "At five weeks what can one expect?"

"Italian babies are practically earning their living at that age," Rita said. "At least one would imagine so from what Uncle Bertolino says . . ." They both went off into a gale of laughter that annoyed Johnnie Bertolino. He was already hungry for his supper, and such mirth was unseemly. Rita got to her feet quickly, to bring the bottle that was being kept warm on the stove.

"That lawn is ideal," she said, gazing pensively through the window. "And the weather is taking up at last. We could sit under the tree sometimes. What a marvellous situation it is. So near the village, yet quite secluded."

Rita could see right across the beck to the fields in the distance. They were bright green after the rain of the past few days. Buttercups were beginning to open, and daisies hung their heads limply. The beck was swollen, but rapidly assuming normal proportions. The fells lay like a backdrop against the evening sky. Streaking across the skyline were fantastic colours as the sun set, slipping over the ridge of the world silently.

"Going to be a fine day tomorrow," she told Vivian.

"Hurrah. And Johnnie Bertolino is asleep . . ."

"Uncle Bertolino is coming home tomorrow . . ." Rita read a post card at breakfast, before holding it out to her sister. "Must have had a wonderful time."

"That man always has a wonderful time. I wouldn't put it past him showing the head chef a thing or two . . ." Vivian laughed. She was wearing heavy walking shoes, a tweed skirt and soft warm cardigan. Her colour had returned and she looked both fit and rested, Rita thought, seeing her anew.

"Going somewhere special?" she asked, surprised.

"I. . . Rita, I want to go for a walk this morning . . . would you look after Johnnie Bertolino?"

"We'll come with you, dear . . ." Rita put both elbows on the table in surprise. Until now Vivian had lacked the initiative

119

to strike out on her own. "Just wait till I've rushed around . . ."

"No, Rita . . . Don't be hurt. I want to go alone." Her speedwell blue eyes came to Rita's. There was pain and conflict in them, and some unnamable emotion Rita could not fathom. She hesitated.

"Vivian—it is just a walk—I mean, you won't do anything stupid?"

"I'm not going to commit suicide or anything like that," Vivian promised softly. For a moment the old mischief drove the agony from her eyes. "No, I just want to get away by myself for a few hours. When I come back, I'll be sorted out,—I hope, and we can go on from there."

"All right." Rita saw the wisdom of that. She had gone on the road with Vivian as far as they could travel together, and in her gentle way Vivian was trying to show her this. There were things that only Vivian could decide.

"I'll take the Blea Tarn road—if I like it we'll go there again sometime."

"Then you must take some sandwiches, and here's some chocolate. Nothing like chocolate for sustaining you. And call in somewhere for a cup of coffee—if there is anywhere, I mean." Rita was rushing about finding what she needed. The look in Vivian's eyes almost made her weep, but she knew with sudden clarity, that there was nothing now that anyone could do. Vivian must fight her battle alone today.

"All right." The younger girl took the small paper carrier. "I'll not be later than five if I can help it. Don't worry—will you?" Again that blue look of pain flicked over Rita. She drew a long breath.

"No dear, I won't worry," she said.

Vivian waved from the gate, before turning to the right. She was soon out of sight along the winding road. How lightly and gracefully she walked, Rita thought, turning indoors. The whole long day stretched ahead and Rita wanted to live it usefully. What could she do to pass the time? She wanted to be outdoors as much as possible.

Seizing a gardening fork she crammed an old hat on her dark hair and advanced on one of the flower beds. For some time she worked industriously, the pile of weeds growing higher, the bed growing neater as she worked her way along it. The sun was bright.

At noon she went indoors and prepared a light meal for herself. She was sitting down to it when she heard the latch of the gate click. It was not Vivian, as she half expected but a man's figure that came towards her.

Suddenly she recognized Richard, and the shock sent the colour out of her face.

"So I've found you?" Richard said. "I got your address from Mrs. Page, and having the week-end off thought I'd look you up."

She had forgotten that he was so large, so sure of himself, so masculine.

They were standing in the kitchen doorway, for he had come round to the side after seeing her. When she hesitated, he said: "Aren't you going to ask me in?"

"Yes, of course. Will you have something to eat?"

"Thank you. If it isn't too much trouble." His glance was a little uncertain for she could not pretend to welcome him. She hurried to make more coffee and sandwiches, and cut into the fruit tart which she had been saving for the evening meal. He could manage with that.

"Thank you." He sat down when she indicated that the meal was ready, and did full justice to it. "Methinks I missed a good cook . . ."

"Oh, Richard—please. If you mean to talk to me, let's stick to what we *can* discuss without quarrelling." She glanced at him askance. Her own appetite had fled.

He finished the meal and sat back, lighting a cigarette. "That was good," he told her.

She removed the cups and plates to the sink. "It's lovely under the tree . . ." she said. "We usually spend all the time we can on the lawn."

He flicked a look over her, that was sharp and repellent. "You don't want me to stay in here with you. All right—let's sit on the lawn. Then all your neighbours will be able to see what a swell girl you are."

"I hate you when you talk that way . . ." She winced visibly. She led the way to the deck chairs and sat down abruptly. Richard drew his closer. "Why have you come here today?"

"Want to know?" He was smoking quickly, and as he spoke he threw the cigarette stub as far from him as he could. "Because I want to ask you if you'll be engaged to me again. I want us to get married the way we'd always planned. I'm in love with you. I know I acted like a heel but I was plenty mad that time—and you didn't help much. I've got your ring with me and if you'll say the word it can all be as it was before this trouble hit us."

She sat silently, listening to the words that she had once hoped would liberate her. They did not bring any comfort now. She realized that she was criticizing him, that she sought for a further motive, than the one he had offered.

He leaned towards her earnestly, his voice lowered. "Rita—you once said that I didn't respect you, but I do. Can't you forgive a fellow when he makes a mistake through temper? I admit it all—I'll do anything if you'll say you'll have me."

She looked at him uneasily. Richard's voice was always charming, and she realized that it still had power to fascinate her.

"Haven't you missed me?" he asked gently.

She gulped. "I don't know. Honestly I don't. It's been very hectic . . . and . . ."

"I'd hoped—that keeping away would help my case," he hinted.

"And you were good and mad too," she told him, smiling. She understood him too well to be able to believe everything he cared to say. Richard's powers of persuasion were considerable but she felt as if he were almost a stranger to her. "No, Richard . . ."

"Then you haven't been wanting me . . . the way I feel about you . . ." he suggested.

"Frankly I've not had time to think much about it," Rita answered. "You wouldn't understand." He had not tried to understand, she remembered resentfully.

"Try me . . ."

She shook her head, and looked away from him. "No, I'm sorry. We don't feel the same way about each other. I've changed—and so have you. You'll meet someone else . . ."

He sighed bitterly. "Are you being perverse to put me on the rack a bit?"

How like him to think of that aspect. "No, I wouldn't do that. It's just that you must have killed something in me that night. I haven't any wish to enter your life again. I'm sorry, but that's the way it is."

"Tommyrot." The violent word exploded from him with force. "I made you happy once; I could again."

She considered his words with her head on one side. When she did not answer he said persuasively, "You could let me try. I've been a fool. I realize now you had your side to it. It wasn't just the issue over Vivian either as I thought . . . you resented my manner . . ."

"Yes. I'm glad you see that. I wouldn't care to risk it again. Sorry, Richard . . ." His look flickered before hers. "You've not really had a change of heart; just pretending because you think it would be nice and easy to take me back. Well, I'm not the same person. I've learned things too."

"Blast." He was so angry that she was glad they were outside, and not indoors.

She stood up, ready to dismiss him. She put all the frostiness into her manner that she could muster. "You ought to go now. Nothing to be gained by keeping on at it . . ."

He sighed, beaten. "Just the same, Rita, my love, this isn't the last you'll see of me. I'm not quite the doormat you seem to think. I'll be seeing you. Sure you mean it?"

Her glance was steady. "I do."

He lumbered to his feet, grumbling like a disgruntled schoolboy. In spite of herself Rita felt sorry for him. He'd come a long way to meet such a rebuff. "Well, I'll be getting along. I had to come to see you. Can't blame me for trying, can you?"

A genuine smile flickered across her face. "No, I don't blame you for trying. Goodbye."

"Kiss me?" he drawled, stopping close to her. "For goodbye? Old times sake? Anything you like—but for the love of Harry just kiss me."

She drew back. "No . . ."

"Au revoir . . ." Grumbling audibly he turned aside, making his way to the gate. When he came to the pile of rubbish and weeds which she had carefully garnered in, his foot shot out and he dispersed the mound in all directions.

Rita laughed silently. It was so like

the action of any small boy, showing disappointment.

"So long, Rita, darling . . ." he called softly from the gate. He reached her, on the other side of the hedge and stood on tiptoe. "I'm going up to Alloa for the firm for a few weeks: I'll see you on my return?"

She smiled. "All right, Richard."

The sudden feeling that they could be friends again brought overwhelming relief. Rita waved to him over the hedge, to show him there was no bad feeling on her side. They were not to part in bitterness, in spite of her attitude. He'd get over it— just as she would. When she had time to think . . .

"Oh, lordy, lordy . . ." she raced to the cottage, overwhelmed with anxiety. "I clean forgot Johnnie Bertolino . . . oh . . . oh . . ." Her racing feet carried her up the stairs to Vivian's room, to find the baby sleeping peacefully in the centre of the big bed. Pillows ringed him round, and his cherubic face was smiling.

Wind! Rita leaned against the door casing, punctured with shock. She'd actually forgotten him again. What on earth would Vivian think?

"But I forget him myself sometimes," Vivian told her later. "It's the durnedest feeling to have a baby."

It's why they are given such a big noise inside them, Rita thought, as she went weakly down the stairs again. Without it, they'd be in danger of being overlooked.

Now what was I thinking about before . . . ? Richard, of course. In his way he had tried to make her happy, but it wouldn't work out. She was sure of that, as she brushed up the weeds he had dispersed. She smiled as she tidied the garden again. Nothing to do now until Johnnie Bertolino awakened, or Vivian returned . . . whichever was first. She went indoors and curled up in a window seat with a book.

Johnnie Bertolino won, and she was feeding him when Vivian came in quietly. He tried to turn his head to see her, and they were both deeply moved.

"He does know me," Vivian crooned, throwing aside her cardigan and beret. "Oh, my feet. I've walked miles . . ."

"Everything is ready for a meal," Rita

told her placidly. "Just brew the tea, will you?" They talked casually, while they ate. The evening was closing in, the breeze delightfully cool after the spring warmth of the day. They were glad to sit round the fire, their feet in slippers.

"Richard came . . ." Rita told her sister what had transpired.

"Such a pity. I think he may be the one for you, you know. After all, any man would get mad at such a situation," Vivian told her.

Rita shook her head. "I got mad too— and I haven't forgiven him yet. May be I never will."

"Oh, dear . . ." Vivian looked down at the sleeping child on her lap. Johnnie Bertolino loved to be held in somebody's arms. Was it the extra warmth, or what, she wondered. "We spoil him, don't we?"

Rita shrugged. "What's it matter? They forget it so soon. Once he's on his feet we'll be firm enough. Kindness can't hurt him."

Vivian recaptured the happy look. "I think that too. You know something, Rita? I'm only eighteen after all, and if I'm strong minded, what's happened need not spoil my whole life. Why should it? I've thought it all out. I can't keep on nattering over it, can I? I'm going to concentrate on my career. I want to become rich, and famous, and a wonderful mother for Johnnie Bertolino. If I'm firm I can do it. Do you think I have the ability?"

"Absolutely. I've always thought you had something." The words came sincerely.

"My looks will pass," Vivian accepted her assurance without false modesty. "So I've made up my mind today what I'm going to do. I'll ask Dominic to put me in touch with his Agent and I'm going to work like a beaver. Nothing will be allowed to stop me . . . except looking after the baby of course, and you said you'd help me there? One day, when I'm rich, I'll buy you a cottage up here for your very own, and I'll say 'thank you, Rita, for helping me through the darkest hour of my whole life'."

The soft voice fell away. Rita could not answer. This then was the result of the day spent in silent communion. Vivian had conquered herself. She had laid careful plans for the future, never doubting for an instant that she had both the courage and the ability to carry them to fruition. Rita was touched by the girl's utter simplicity. This and this she would do . . . until she gained the objective she had set herself. There was a strength in Vivian for which she was not wholly prepared.

She bent and touched Johnnie Bertolino's soft, fat hand. "You'll marry some time . . ."

"I doubt it. In any case, not for many years. I feel I have it in me to get what I want from life. I'm a little bit like Uncle Bertolino too, you know. Anyway, I'm determined to try. I feel happier. I'm able to plan." The sad young voice held courage.

"I'm so glad, Vivian. Truly I am."

"I'll make a man of Johnnie Bertolino —with your help, Rita." Always she deferred to the older sister, without whom she would have been bereft. "I'm not going to go around like a drip either. Pulling a long face doesn't help. I'm going to laugh and dance and sing again. Uncle Bertolino said I must. Only you two will know why . . ."

How simple it was, Rita thought. How

simple, and true and real. Vivian was telling her the result of her mind's deep wandering. The hours alone had not been spent in self-pity; instead this was something constructive.

She rose and fetched a book she had been reading earlier in the day. "You can if you will, Vivian. Listen to this and see if it doesn't bear out what you've been feeling. It's something Blake wrote: He spent his entire life trying to 'open the Eternal Worlds, to open the immortal Eyes of Man, inwards into the world of Thought, into Eternity Ever expanding in the bosom of God, the Human Imagination.' But that's not the bit I really wanted. He says something about the lowest state we can be in is that of single vision—that is looking at creation in a purely materialistic point of view. Twofold vision is when we see the Infinite in all things. Threefold vision is that of 'soft Beulah night.'"

"How wonderful." Vivian turned shining eyes towards Rita, as she thumbed through the book. "Let me see it . . ." She sat with it in her hands, reading intently.

"It must be an emotional state—the way we feel now," Rita told her quietly. "You can read for yourself. I've been thinking —this is *our* Beulah land, Vivian. Not just this particular spot, although it comes in to it, but we carry it with us . . . the thing we have found here; this reasoning power, this acceptance, this calm contemplation, this oh . . . I sound frightfully weird, but I know exactly what I mean, if you don't." She was smiling ruefully.

"But I do," Vivian answered thoughtfully. "I do, Rita. Yes, this is our Land of Beulah. Oh, it helps, doesn't it?"

They were each strongly moved, trying to hide their emotion from each other, but finding comfort in the communion of thought.

"If we can only remember to think back to this moment . . . in times of trouble . . ."

"Yes, if only we can remember." Rita's words came slowly. "I suppose it really means that one finds oneself . . . one's real self." It was so easy to talk. It would only be when they were very old that they would know for certainty that they had found their Beulah land. "We can try.

134

Let's hope we have the staying power. I read somewhere, ages ago, that the real meaning of Beulah is to be found in the Hebrew tongue—it means marriage . . .''

Vivian soon put the book down, for the fire was warm, and she was tired with being in the fresh air all day. Suddenly she laughed, and it was a delicious sound after the months of depression. "You know something? I believe Mrs. Page is going to have us for neighbours up here one fine day. I wonder how she'll like that?"

"That child should be in bed," Rita told her, yawning. "This child won't be late either. Oh, Lordy, how the days fly. Uncle Bertolino will be here tomorrow."

"Which will be extremely nice for us," Vivian said, gathering the child up in her arms. "Now the holiday really begins."

She was right, as events proved. Uncle Bertolino arrived with his usual effortless speed. He had had a royal progress in Edinburgh and the Lowlands.

"It was all I ever dreamed," he told them reverently, as they sat near him, listening to his story. "So great—so steeped in history—so . . . fragile . . . No, that's not the word but it is near it. Fragile to me . . ."

"Elusive?" Vivian hazarded.

Uncle Bertolino beamed. "That is it. I found everything, yet I might have found nothing. So it is elusive, yes? And the best part—" his eyes glistened, and he blew his nose as with the blast of a trumpet. "To be sitting here telling you about it. Not many men of my years have such an audience of pretty young girls . . ."

"Just leaning on your every word," Rita kissed him soundly. "We love you, darling, and we're glad you had such a wonderful time. You deserve it. We've been happy too, but we're ready for anything now."

"Then that is good—very good," he told her, but he did not press for more than that.

The following day he hired a car, and they all went to Ullswater, touring round the lovely lake, picnicking on one of the beaches. The day was warm, the sky cloudless.

"We sail down the lake . . ." Uncle Bertolino insisted. Vivian sat with the baby cradled in her arms, listening to the

136

lap of the water against the sides of the boat, but Rita walked up and down the deck with Uncle Bertolino. It was one of the happiest days of her life, she thought soberly. There was such a completely good feeling between them all, almost as if this was a reward . . . but for what? The thought puzzled her. They left the boat at Glenridding, and the car awaited them. "We walk a little way . . ."

It was quiet and pleasant along the country road. "Up there it's Helvellyn . . ." Rita said.

"How clever of you," Uncle Bertolino said, puffing along at her side.

"Not really. I just saw a signpost." Rita laughed at him gently.

It was one of the many outings that Uncle Bertolino arranged for their mutual pleasure. Together they toured the whole of the Lake District, stopping where and when they pleased.

"Of course when you're a millionaire . . ." Vivian said one day. "It does rather simplify things doesn't it?"

"But I am not quite that," Uncle Bertolino beamed at her. He was wearing reading glasses and looked more than ever like some large wicked gnome. "But this money is mine and I spend it where it makes me happiest—and you too, I think."

"It certainly does. Uncle Bertolino, would you be hurt if I asked you a question?" Rita was repairing a lining in one of his sleeves, while he lounged in his shirt sleeves.

"I think—no. You will not ask the question that might hurt?" For the first time the two girls realized that he was slightly apprehensive.

"Oh, don't worry, darling. It's just . . . why didn't you bring your daughter with you to England? I've often wondered. Wouldn't she have enjoyed helping you to spend some of this money?"

Uncle Bertolino took off his glasses, put them on again, and for the first time since they had known him, seemed without words.

"Don't answer if you'd rather not," Vivian said quickly. "Rita shouldn't have asked."

"But it is correct so to do. I wish to answer. It is the right and proper question. I recall I told her about my daughter that first day . . ." He hesitated. "I am happy now—but I was not always so. I work very hard many years, then one day I marry— a widow. It is her daughter I leave behind —not mine. I was married two years only, before my wife died. I thought I die with her . . ." he added simply.

Vivian put her arm round his shoulders in silent sympathy.

He took off his spectacles again. "There was nothing else then for me to do, but make much money. I worked harder than ever in my life. I grew happy again. Now I have much money and I leave behind my daughter because she wish it that way. We are friends yes . . . but she is not just the same as you. She does not like to travel . . . and I had to find you . . ."

"Of course. I understand," Rita acknowledged the explanation with a touch of her hand on his arm.

"So often I think of you—and my dear sister . . . and when you did not send me the usual card at Christmas I knew something was wrong—not right, you understand? So I knew the time was ripe. It was the time . . . I had been waiting for."

"You came at the right moment,

certainly," Rita told him quietly. "Yet that first day I felt absolutely overwhelmed."

"I'm so sorry—about your wife, Uncle Bertolino," Vivian whispered.

He smiled benevolently. "Not to worry. It is past. I know now that I was lucky to have the so great happiness. Not all men have so much—as I had in those two years."

5

LIFE held a dreamlike quality as the days of that enchanted month drew to a close. Every evening Uncle Bertolino sent the two girls out for a stroll, while he kept an attentive ear for Johnnie Bertolino. Every morning that dawned clear, they hired a car and drove to every point of interest they could think about.

"Hills—and trees—and water . . ." Vivian mused. "The same, yet everlastingly different. Look . . ." They were crossing Berker Moor, having taken the steep hill to get there. In the far distance Great Gable, cone shaped and mauve against the azure sky, looked supremely beautiful to their seeking eyes.

"This . . ." pronounced Uncle Bertolino, "is the noblest yet."

A short plume of smoke rose lazily into the air from some building hidden from them. Trees, appearing stunted in the limpid light, grew far off across the grasslands. The long, magnificent slope of country, curved away as far as eye could see into the gathering heat haze.

The noblest yet . . . Rita mused over his words. A trickle of water made music for the ear, while the eye feasted on the scene. "Italy has great beauty . . ." Uncle Bertolino told them. "But an English landscape in the spring cannot be surpassed . . . is it not so?" They had all got out of the car, to gaze about them while they ate sandwiches, and drank coffee from the flasks. Vivian was giving Johnnie Bertolino his bottle, while she mused. Uncle Bertolino tramped up and down, talking to the driver, poking at a dead frog on the road. Rita sat apart, quietly enjoying the moment.

"Dominic and Mrs. Page are coming tomorrow . . ." she said presently to Vivian, who sighed.

"It means the holiday is coming to an end. Well, it's been wonderful, but I don't think it could ever be repeated, do you?"

Dominic was a completely different person in the country from the city. He left his dark suits behind, and appeared at breakfast the first morning, in a polo-necked sweater, shorts and canvas sandals. Uncle Bertolino nodded approvingly, if a little enviously.

"The young dress so sensibly these days," he told Mrs. Page.

After the meal "the young" as they then always referred to themselves in private, played a game of cricket. As they dashed up and down the field opposite the cottage no one would have guessed that only a few weeks before, life had held no savor.

Mrs. Page made a large glass jug full of lemonade and this Uncle Bertolino took out to them when they rested from their labours. Johnnie Bertolino stayed in his bed, out of harm's way.

When Vivian went in to see if he needed anything, Dominic persuaded Rita to walk down the wood with him. "Want to see if the bluebells are out . . ." he told her blithely.

"They are. Soon be over. What a pity these things can't last."

"Oh, we'd not enjoy them much if they did," he told her. It would appear, as they strolled through the bluebells ten minutes later, that Dominic was not as interested in flowers as he had suggested. He was much more interested in questioning Rita.

"Vivian tells me you're an MA?" he said lightly.

"Yes—scared?" She was smiling as she swung along beside him. Dominic was the handsomest man she had ever gone walking with.

"A little. Cambridge?"

She nodded again. "I was there three years."

"I suppose you loved it—they all do." He sounded moody, she thought.

"Why not?" A small boy, with whom they had become friendly on the holiday, suddenly appeared from behind a tree, and apparently shot Dominic dead on sight.

"Bang—you're dead . . . mister . . ."

Dominic scowled. "Not so's you'd notice. Here . . . run and get yourself an ice cream."

"Whoopee . . ." He sped off to the corner shop with the coin clutched in his grimy hand.

"Thought we were going to have him tacked on to us for the rest of the morning," Dominic grumbled.

"He's a good kid," Rita said, laughing at his expression. "He plays excellent Rounders."

"So that's how you've been spending your spare time?" he said, exasperated.

"Occasionally. It rained all the first week . . ."

"You like it up here, don't you, Rita?"

"Very much," she told him heartily. "We've never visited the district before and it's been a wonderful change for us. We've loved it."

They stayed by the mere talking until long past the lunch hour. "We should have brought sandwiches," Dominic was laughing as he held out his hands to draw her to her feet. His dark face changed as she came close to him. "Rita . . ."

She sighed. "I could stay here for ever."

"You're very pretty . . ." he told her, gazing intently at the magnolia skin, the intelligent dark blue eyes, the silken hair.

She dragged her hand away, laughing in a carefree way that irritated him. "Oh, come on, you don't have to be polite."

"I'm not—just truthful . . ." He hurried after her, and as they re-entered the wood he swung his hand to reach hers.

Hand in hand they hurried back the way they had come.

"Dominic likes you, doesn't he?" Vivian said that evening.

"So that's the one he's interested in," Uncle Bertolino told himself as he brooded over Johnnie Bertolino.

The talk, as they grouped themselves about the fire, was all of Vivian's future. In that kindly circle no word was spoken to mar her new found happiness. Vivian was being given a helping hand, and if she would grasp it, she might scale the heights.

"Why is Dominic doing this?" Rita asked herself. She turned to him curiously. "How does it feel to be a success, such as you are now?" she asked.

He smiled, pleased to answer. "At first —wonderful. After a bit you get so you can hardly separate the two parts of your life. This is the longest run I've had. Physically it's pretty hard . . . takes its toll . . ."

Uncle Bertolino nodded. "That is so. I have knowledge of that too. Conductors need clean collars for every performance."

He looked shaken when they all laughed at him. "What did I say that was wrong?"

"Not anything, darling," Rita told him. "Just the way you said it. This week-end will be a real refresher then?"

Dominic lighted a cigarette. "Yes— more than a refresher, who knows?" His eyes met hers and she looked away quickly. "I was growing stale." He added: "How does it happen that Rita is so dark, while Vivian is so fair?"

Vivian supplied the answer. "Our mother was an Italian, and our father English. He was very fair, and I take after him in appearance. Rita is like our mother . . ."

Mrs. Page looked intrigued. She seemed a little tired and had scarcely joined in the conversation round the fire. "It must be a wonderful mixture. Accounts for your wonderful carriage too. You're both so perfectly rounded but so slim and tall . . ."

Rita began to laugh. "Uncle Bertolino . . . no more spaghetti dishes—too fattening. I won't stand for it."

They were all looking at her intently, and she blushed suddenly. Her dark, silken hair was brushed back from her broad brow, and hung in curling tendrils against her neck.

"She's far better looking than I am really," Vivian said generously, "but my being a blonde will be a great help. Everyone goes for a blonde."

"Yes." Mrs. Page glanced at her grandson for confirmation.

"Are your parents both dead?" he asked.

"Father was a solicitor, before he was killed in the war—1944," Rita told him. "Mother died five years ago. Since then we've always sent Uncle Bertolino a card for Christmas—until this year—when he came in person . . ." she added lamely. "We're rather short of relations. Sometimes it does happen that way."

"I'm a lonely orphan—aren't I, Gran?" Dominic said, *sotto voce*.

"Yes—I brought him up from the age of three," Mrs. Page said.

"Look what a good job she made of me." Dominic threw out his chest dramatically. "As fine a specimen of manhood as you can find this side of the Pennines . . . On Porridge . . . I think.

She doesn't approve of my career though, do you, Gran? You think it's a sad waste of time."

"Oh, it's well paid, but it wouldn't appeal to me," the old lady spoke pacifically. "If you like it that's all that matters."

Vivian was hugging her knees thoughtfully. "I'd like to try show business too. What name shall I go under?"

"Think about it," Dominic advised. "Plenty of time. A good, catchy name helps."

Vivian got to her feet, yawning widely. "Thanks for a lovely evening. Do you mind if I go up now? It's been quite a day, hasn't it? And thanks for helping me, Dominic. Oh, isn't it peaceful and sweet here?" She glanced through the uncurtained window into the light night. "Good night, folks."

"Don't you want something to eat—or drink?" Mrs. Page asked. "I was trying to muster up the will to move."

"If you're having a hot drink I'd like one, please. Rita can bring it up when she comes." Vivian trailed away, tired and happy.

"Some of that currant pasty, for me," Dominic said, before vanishing. "I'll be back."

"I'm sure you will." Mrs. Page poured milk into a saucepan. "Dominic is attracted to Vivian, did you know, Rita?"

Rita looked startled. "No—I didn't really know. Are you certain?"

"Life does give us some back-handers, doesn't it?" Mrs. Page reached into the cupboard for the pasty, and cake tin. "We've got to let it take its course, but I thought I'd warn you so that you can help Vivian . . ."

Rita's face burned suddenly. Her blue eyes were suddenly sparkling with anger. She could not trust herself to answer. Just then Dominic returned and he glanced enquiringly from one to the other.

"If it's about my pasty . . ." he insinuated.

"It isn't." Rita picked up a cup of hot milk. "Thank you for this. No, I don't want anything, thank you. I'll give this to Vivian."

"Looks a stunner when she's in a temper, doesn't she?" Dominic said. "What have you been saying to her?"

Mrs. Page looked startled. "Nothing really."

After their return to London, Rita encouraged her sister to make her plans for resuming her career. "I'll do my best for Johnnie Bertolino, and you can plan round him."

Together they visited Dominic's agent, who if not exactly enthusiastic, did hold out hope that one day Vivian might become a star in show business. He advised her what steps to take, and would have been startled had he known how closely she adhered to his guidance.

"If you'll finance me, I'll pay it all back some day," Vivian said earnestly that night. "Besides, I can soon start earning, but I must have those lessons."

"Yes. But don't ask Uncle Bertolino to help you. Let's keep it in the family," Rita advised. "He's done enough for us. Why don't you ring up the Academy now?"

During the following weeks Vivian worked out her schedule, to which she adhered at all times. Singing was second nature to her, and wholeheartedly she studied under a famous vocalist. Dancing lessons occupied three afternoons a week.

She attended concerts to hear all the best singers, under Uncle Bertolino's tutelage. He was delighted with Vivian, and said so often. He would take her to the Opera as often as she could go, for he was as enthusiastic for it as she was. As far as possible Rita helped her with the business side of her work, and about six weeks after returning to London Vivian obtained her first engagement for modelling. She was beside herself with delight.

"I was so afraid I wouldn't get back—now I have—and it's the first step."

Johnnie Bertolino, now settled in a routine which appeared to suit him, was really not much trouble. Every day Uncle Bertolino pushed his pram through the London squares, finding the oases of quietness amid the London traffic, where the baby slept peacefully. It was a great help to Rita who had charge of him during the hours that Vivian was away from the flat.

The daily washing, ironing, bottle washing, mending, bathing, nappie changing, continued without interruption. Rita wondered what they had found to do before Johnnie Bertolino came. Her own life appeared to be slipping into the background, but one day she realized that they were all happy. "That's quite something," she thought, pushing the clothes down into the suds.

They often saw Dominic and his grandmother, but for some reason the friendship between them did not flourish. They were friendly when they met about the house, but Rita held back. She was unable to explain it even to herself.

Dominic was very busy, rehearsing for television, and did not seem to have much spare time. "Wonderful for him," Vivian said enviously. "Wait until I'm so busy I haven't time to say hullo. That'll be the day."

"Oh, he's time for that," Rita smiled in spite of herself. He always made time for a greeting. "He certainly is busy though. So are we—in another way."

Miss Jane and Miss Letty were still waiting for the hospital authorities to send for Miss Letty.

"It's the worst part of it all—waiting," Miss Jane confided to Uncle Bertolino. "I feel so anxious sometimes."

"And you are of the sympathetic

temperament . . . you live it with her," he said gently. "But it will close—end—finish, and she will be well again. Then you will relax and be happy again, eh?"

Miss Jane sighed softly. It was so easy to tell herself those things, and so easy for others to tell her too, but it did not really help this waiting period very much. "An experience of this sort leaves a mark on you."

"All experience does that . . . but some marks are beautiful, no? Better than the clear sheet, perhaps, who knows?" Uncle Bertolino was sitting perched on their best chair, drinking tea elegantly from small, china cups. He often strayed into their flat at this hour of the day. "Like a drug . . . I come again . . . and again . . . to drink your tea . . ."

"Yes. We're used to it," Miss Letty put in unexpectedly. "Tea-drinking, I mean."

"But yes . . ." He nodded to show he understood, which he didn't.

"Anyway, we'll get a taxi one of these days and just go off to hospital . . ."

"*I* will get the taxi . . ." Uncle Bertolino insisted furiously. "I insist. You are my good friends. I could not allow . . . no, you must make me the promise . . ."

Miss Jane was quite startled by his vehemence. When he had gone she said to Letty: "You know Letty . . . for a minute . . . I wouldn't be surprised . . . what I mean, dear, is this, don't you think we should have this room papered next spring?"

Two days later Dominic ran down the front steps just as Rita opened the door to go shopping. "I'll join you if I may?" he said, taking her basket politely.

"I'm only shopping while Uncle Bertolino holds the fort!"

They walked along together towards the shopping centre. Rita bought bread, several vegetables, and some fruit. "Nothing romantic about *my* shopping."

Dominic added a pound of grapes. "For you . . ."

"Thank you." She tucked them into the basket composedly.

"Rita—you're not in a hurry, are you? Come and have a cup of tea with me at the café . . . please. I want to talk to you."

"Do you?" She looked at him

uncertainly. Was he wanting to talk about Vivian? She followed him into the café and he found a table, for it was deserted just now as it was a little early for the usual tea patrons.

"This is very nice," Dominic said, taking off his overcoat. "You are a most evasive person, Rita. I've been wanting to talk to you for weeks but you are simply never there. Why is it?"

She was saved an answer when the waitress came to their table to take an order. Dominic was busy with that for a few minutes.

"Something light," she said. "I'm really not hungry, but I'd love a cup of tea."

They chatted until the light meal was placed before them. Rita poured the tea, her hand shaking slightly in spite of her determination to appear at ease.

"Now." Dominic sat back, regarding her quizzically. "As I was saying . . . you and Vivian never seem to be available these days. Why is that?"

It was a direct question and she realized that he meant to have an answer. "Busy, I think. There has been a lot to do since we returned from the Lakes. Vivian is studying hard, as you know and I have my own work, which keeps me at it most days."

"But you must have some time to yourself?" he suggested. "I began to think you didn't want to know me any more. Most girls can find time to speak to a fellow now and again. Considering our flats are adjoining you'd think we'd meet every day. It's exactly three weeks since I had a word with you . . . and nearly six since you wasted any time on me and . . ."

"That sounds dreadful. I didn't know there was any special reason why you wanted to see me," she said, laughing slightly. She was determined not to take him seriously. "How is Mrs. Page? Is her cold better?"

"It is, thank you. She's just staying in as a precaution. Now, look here, would you like to come to a show with me tomorrow night? I've got tickets."

"You mean—both of us?" Their eyes met for a brief moment, before Dominic's flicked away.

"Naturally. But I've asked Vivian and she can't manage it."

"Oh." She felt hurt that he had not

consulted her first, and she wondered at her own depression. Because Vivian could not accept he was falling back on her company. Was that it? She hated herself for the smallness of the thought. She was not sure either that Uncle Bertolino might feel left out.

"So if you'll take pity on a poor lonely man . . ."

"Lonely?" She spoke quizzically. "A less lonely man than you it would be hard to find. You're always pretty busy, aren't you, Dominic?"

"Don't change the subject. Will you come with me tomorrow night?"

So that it would not become an issue between them she said instantly: "Of course. I'll look forward to that. Evening dress?"

"Yes. I've never seen you in evening dress, have I?"

"I couldn't say. Probably not. Listen to this song, Dominic?" She sat with her dark head on one side listening intently. "If I couldn't do better than that I'd stay off the air."

"Why don't you try—writing a song, I mean? Write one for Vivian. You might make a good team. Vivian is good, you know. My agent says she is going to be tops one day soon."

"Did he?" Rita's face shone. "She is certainly putting all she knows into it. Oh, I do hope she can."

"She might get there sooner if you wrote something for her—something exclusive." Dominic drew his brows together. "You know, you're completely elusive. I never met anyone like you who could put another person off the track. Just where did we begin in this conversation?"

She laughed in spite of herself. "I wouldn't know. Vivian says I'm a flitter . . . my mind flits all over the place instead of applying itself to the person with me. Evidently you have found that out." She glanced at her wristwatch. "I should go. Do you mind? There are a million things to do before Vivian gets home. And I've two books to vet for my publisher."

Dominic rose in a leisurely way, paid the bill, and followed her out to the street. "All right, Rita—you win . . . this time. See you at seven sharp tomorrow night?"

What did he mean by that remark, she

wondered when he left her at the door of their flat.

Early that evening Rita went to get her dress from her bedroom. She had never been able to wear it because they had not been able to attend the ball to which they had both been invited. The shock of Vivian's disclosures had taken away their desire for dancing. She had made some excuse at the time to Richard and so the ball gown had lain in its bed of tissue paper.

She carried the box back to the sitting-room and together the sisters examined the dress. Vivian lifted it reverently from the tissue paper and held it against her.

"Oh, Rita—I'd forgotten it was so beautiful. You must wear it."

"It's so gold it's almost yellow . . ." Rita sounded dubious, but she was pleased with the frock, and sudden colour came into her cheeks as she thought of wearing it.

"You can take it because you are so dark—try it on and let's see if it needs altering."

Rita stepped out of her house dress and

into the ball gown. The transformation was dramatic. Vivian knelt on the ground looking up at her.

Her voice was suddenly husky. "You look beautiful. You've never had anything that suited you more."

"It cost enough." Rita was surveying herself in the large mirror, teetering back and forth on her toes. This was to have been worn at the ball the night they became engaged.

Vivian looked thoughtful. "If Dominic doesn't fall for you in this, he never will."

Rita glanced down at her. "Don't be silly, dear. There is nothing but sound friendship between us. Dominic has his eyes on someone else."

"Really?" Vivian looked dashed. "Who is it?"

"Mrs. Page mentioned it to me when we were up at their cottage." Rita decided not to discuss it with her sister, for she felt that to invade Vivian's hard won tranquillity would not be fair at that juncture. She would know soon enough if Dominic were serious. "He is very fond of someone he met some time ago. She was quite sure about it."

"And I've been thinking all this time that he was falling for you." Vivian looked disappointed.

"Oh, no. Nothing like that. Dominic is just a very kind person, that's all." Rita slipped out of the golden folds and donned her usual clothes.

Miss Letty received a letter the following morning from the hospital authorities telling her that her appointment was for the following day. Would she kindly get to the hospital some time during the afternoon.

"That means today," Miss Jane said, a sudden quaver in her voice. "Oh, dear— and we aren't ready."

"Of course we're ready," Miss Letty was much the calmer of the two. "All you have to do is lift that parcel off the chair into the suitcase. I'll change from the skin out and you can bring me a change to the hospital one day. Don't let's fuss."

Miss Jane was already through the door. "No, but I must let Uncle Bertolino know in case he has anything else planned. He wants to take you to the hospital." She

hurried along to the top flat. Uncle Bertolino threw open the door with a flourish.

He came out in his shirt sleeves. "This
is such pleasure. But you have news? You
come within? No, I understand . . ."

Miss Jane went a little pink because he
understood almost too well. "Letty has to
go to hospital this afternoon . . ."

"That is good. I take you both there—
at two? Yes." Uncle Bertolino was rolling
down his sleeves at lightning speed.

"But weren't you going to Kew . . .?"

"Tomorrow—not today," he denied,
waving both hands to show how little it
signified. "Today we go to hospital.
Tomorrow we go to Kew."

Miss Jane was trembling. "I'm scared
now it's actually here . . ." She spoke to
Mrs. Page who had come out on to the
landing, having overheard part of the
conversation from her room.

"I couldn't help overhearing, Miss Jane.
You must feel worried, but it'll be all
right. Think of the future, when she'll be
all right again. Sight is so precious."

Miss Jane straightened slowly. She had
dashed along with the pipe cleaners still
curling her hair. They looked like small

stiff butterflies clinging to her head. "Yes, I must think about that—only . . ."

Uncle Bertolino vanished. "I go . . ."

Mrs. Page grinned at Miss Jane. "I go too, darling. Try not to worry. Just think —it's over, for both of you . . . this long winter of waiting. It must have got you down sometimes. Tomorrow the operation will be over—and in a week or two Miss Letty will be bossing you around in that gentle way of hers."

Miss Jane hurried back to her sister, who was sitting with the letter gripped in her hands. The delicate pink and white of her apple blossom complexion was suffused with colour.

"Tell me again—what it says, Jane . . ."

Miss Jane read it again, and from the calm instructions they derived fresh courage. This was an everyday occurrence. Miss Letty was merely one of thousands who took the operation. She leaned back in her chair, pleased and confident.

"I'm glad it's come. High time too, in my opinion. I've been very patient."

Miss Jane laughed ruefully.

When Rita heard the news she came

along to their flat. "I'm really glad the waiting is over. You've been so good about it. Uncle Bertolino is taking you, isn't he?"

She arranged to make the midday meal for the plumbers, who were still toiling somewhere in the basement. "They must be getting to the end of things . . ." Letty said.

"What are Yorkshire elbows?" Miss Jane demanded. "They've been talking about them several times. Quite intriguing. I don't think that the big plumber is the right shape for his job either, do you?"

Rita left them, feeling cheered. Miss Jane was already reaching for the suitcase.

"Now let's see, Letty . . ."

The departure was a small triumph. Uncle Bertolino managed to be in several places at once. Even Dominic came down with Mrs. Page to help to give the ladies a send off. Miss Letty's soft colour was high, but she was more composed than Miss Jane. They emerged from their flat behind Uncle Bertolino, who carried the suitcase importantly.

Vivian had a small bunch of freesias tied

up with yellow ribbon, and she pressed them in to Miss Letty's hands as she bent to kiss her goodbye.

"Why . . . delightful . . ."

Rita had brought a bag of fruit, grapes, pears, and oranges, because Miss Letty preferred them to other things. Mrs. Page had tied dates and figs together with a box of paper handkerchiefs into one small, secure package.

"You can open them at the hospital, dear," she said, holding the shawl closer about her for she felt there might be a draught in the hall, and her flu hadn't entirely gone yet.

Dominic, not to be outdone, brought writing paper. "Pretty useful at times . . ."

Miss Letty was gently amused. "At my age I don't write many love letters . . ."

Rita rushed back into their flat for a carrier. "There, you might drop them otherwise . . ."

Uncle Bertolino offered his arm with a flourish. No one, but Miss Letty, overheard what he said, but her gallant head went up, and she stared straight ahead as they walked together to the door. Dominic was ahead of them to open it. He bowed deeply. Miss Jane almost tripped up in the excitement.

"Now, mind . . ." Letty warned.

She turned towards them as they crowded into the vestibule. "Thank you all—and bless you. I'll be seeing you . . ." She walked forward with confidence.

The words sobered them all. Rita felt as if her spine chilled, and she shivered. It meant so much the way Miss Letty said it.

"The taxi is waiting . . ." Dominic hurried forward to open the car door. Uncle Bertolino guided Miss Letty down the path and helped her in to the car. Miss Jane sat beside her sister. Uncle Bertolino hopped in to the front seat beside the driver. Dominic slammed the door shut and stood back, saluting.

Miss Jane and Miss Letty leaned forward, waving energetically. They were laughing at something Uncle Bertolino said as they drove off.

A small triumph, Rita thought. One had not the right to feel sad in the face of such courage.

"Miss Jane has promised to come straight up to have tea with me," Mrs.

Page said, as they parted. "I thought it would be less lonely for her that way. She won't enjoy going back to an empty flat."

They dispersed a moment later. Miss Letty had her own brand of courage, and right now not one of them could help her.

"Perhaps we do help—by being interested," Rita thought soberly. "Uncle Bertolino is certainly helping."

Vivian went out to one of her endless classes, leaving Johnnie Bertolino cooing in his cot. Later Miss Jane returned to the house, alone and went up to Mrs. Page's flat. The house was quiet, for even the plumbers had gone home, short of yet more vital equipment.

"Probably Yorkshire elbows," Rita thought. "Now how can I go out with Dominic this evening feeling like this? Doesn't seem human, somehow."

"But you must go," Uncle Bertolino settled it when he returned later. "Yes, I think so."

Vivian returned from her dancing class, carrying a spray of mimosa. "Lovely, isn't it? I'm going to put it on Miss Jane's doorstep." She went off happily to leave the golden spray where Miss Jane could not fail to find it, when she returned from drinking tea with Mrs. Page.

Uncle Bertolino smiled approvingly. He made some almond truffles for Vivian that evening.

"I suppose I'll have to get ready now," Rita said, after their light tea. "I honestly wish I hadn't promised to go. I suppose you wouldn't change your mind and take my place?" She spoke to Vivian who was changing Johnnie Bertolino.

Vivian shook her bright head. "I would not. Why you accepted I can't think. Of course we didn't know about Miss Letty then."

If it had been Richard with whom she was going to spend the evening, Rita knew that she would have felt wildly excited. I don't know how I feel, she thought wretchedly.

Dominic was in evening kit, with the long black cape over his arm. She smiled across at him when he called.

"You look lovely," he said. "Don't wait up, Vivian. We'll be late. We're going to paint the town a lovely shade of vermilion."

"I'm ready for anything," Rita said.

"Don't say it with that air of bravado, or I'll change my mind and come with you," Vivian followed them to the door.

Rita settled into Dominic's car. He pressed the self-starter. "Taken me weeks to manoeuvre you into this. I'm not the type to rush things."

"I'm sorry Vivian couldn't come . . ." She spoke sincerely.

"Oh, sure . . . yes, of course." He laughed as he backed the car. "Well, I thought we'd have dinner first then go to this Cabaret show and later dance till we're tired. That suit you?"

"Very well."

They followed the pattern of the evening. Rita discarded her loose cloak, and Dominic slipped her satin purse into one of his pockets.

"You'll not need that—I hope," he told her. "May I say how wonderful you look in that gown?" Dominic broke a fairly long silence to tell her this.

She laughed. "I wondered why you were so quiet, Dominic. Obviously you were stunned by the grandeur. Am I then such a little brown mouse?"

"No." He hesitated. "No, I wouldn't call you that." They had finished their meal and he was smoking a cigarette. "Let's go. I don't want you to miss the Cabaret turns. They're sensational in my opinion."

They went quickly, and finally when they were seated at a special table on the edge of the dance floor, Rita realized that they were enjoying each other's company very much. For half an hour they watched various Cabaret turns, before the dancing started.

"Come along," Dominic said urgently. "Let's dance." He stood up and she went into his arms. Instantly she felt the magic of the evening accelerate. Neither spoke as he led the way across the now crowded floor. Rita was a good dancer but somewhat out of practice.

"I'm a little rusty on the new tunes," she told him. "Don't expect the impossible."

"I won't." There was a warmth and support in his arms that she felt exhilarating and new. Richard had been a fairly good dancer, but not so good as Dominic. She found herself comparing the two men.

Dominic did not speak much, whereas Richard had been full of conversation, often keeping her laughing through a whole foxtrot. "That's to keep you from noticing that my feet haven't got rhythm," he would say, and she wondered if there were not some atom of truth buried in the lightly spoken words. Richard always had an excuse for anything he did wrong.

Dominic's dancing was flawless, if a little careful. Rita began to enjoy it as they became accustomed to each other's steps. The floor was smooth, the orchestra a particularly good one . . .

"And the night is yet young . . ." Dominic said, as if he had followed her thought.

"Oh, it's wonderful to be dancing again," she said, smiling.

"Yes, for me too. I haven't been off the chain for months . . ."

He ordered drinks when they sat down again at their table. "Champagne?" Rita said.

"Yes. Celebrating . . ."

"Just what?" she demanded curiously.

"My birthday if you must know. I'm

twenty-seven." Dominic poured her a glass. "To us . . ."

She raised the glass to her lips. "To you . . ."

"To *us* . . ." he insisted, not drinking.

"All right." She nodded smiling at his persistence. "To us—and Many Happy Returns. How nice of you to ask me to the celebrations."

He frowned. "Sometimes I wonder about you, Rita. Is it that you simply have no idea of your own attraction?"

She laughed indulgently. "All women want to be attractive."

"To men, you mean?"

"I suppose so, but to everyone, themselves included." The answer was honest.

"Yes, I see. That is—all decent women anyway."

"I don't know any of the other sort—do you?"

He smiled at her. "No, come to think of it, I don't."

"Let's dance again." The music was starting once more and Rita's feet were already itching to get onto the dance floor. She wanted to get away from Dominic's questions but it was not to be. As he put his arm about her waist he said: "What's become of that fellow who used to haunt your flat at one time?"

"You mean Richard?" In spite of herself she stiffened in his arms.

"Yes. I thought you were engaged to him?"

"I was—but not any longer."

"Good." It was said with such an air of relish that she laughed. "Personally I never could stand the chap. I take it that you are not losing any sleep over him?" It was said quietly and her face clouded.

"I did—but . . ."

"He just didn't measure up—is that it?" Their talk had become engrossing in spite of her determination. She told him of the quarrel between herself and Richard during Vivian's illness. She shivered as she recalled those difficult days, when the world had seemed full of trouble. "Don't think of it. I was a fool to remind you. Come—we're here to enjoy ourselves. Care to come with me to a magic island . . . ?"

The music was changing to a slow, nostalgic waltz. The whole tempo quietened as if at a signal. Dominic drew her closer. The lights were lowered, the colours changing mysteriously and the whole room took on a different form. Rita felt the rhythm and beat surge through her own blood, felt the slow sound of feet moving impatiently over the polished floor. The whole room was swaying to that haunting melody, the recurring beat. The moment of awareness was fully charged for her as she realized that she had fallen a little in love with Dominic. Her rush of feeling for him caught her up in a glad, mad whirl of excitement and happiness. She closed her eyes, feeling with every sense within her, the responsive force of this wonderful moment, as she remained suspended in time.

For that one moment there was no sense of shock or outrage, such as was to come later. It was completely fitting. Had she loved him all the time, and yet not known? She glanced up at him, her whole face alight with the feeling within her. Caught on the rebound? Was it real? She did not know. Dominic was humming the melody under his breath, his hand held hers, and she sensed that he was as happy as she was.

"Let it last . . . let it last for ever . . ." she prayed soundlessly.

6

UNCLE BERTOLINO had every appearance of enjoying himself. Mrs. Page had recovered from her bout of influenza and was entertaining him as she had promised. Uncle Bertolino was a sympathetic listener, and Mrs. Page found herself telling him much more than she intended, much more than she had ever told anyone else, if it came to that.

She looked somewhat wildly around the room, wondering why she'd said that. "Of course, you understand—that's all in the past. I never refer to it in any case, in front of Dominic."

"I understand." Uncle Bertolino looked thoughtfully at his clasped fingers. "You must often have been worried . . . but you made a good job of him."

"I think so myself," she agreed eagerly. "He's good to me, and that means a lot. I can't tell him now that his mother's still alive, can I? You are a man of the world —tell me I have done the right thing."

Uncle Bertolino waited a moment most effectively. "You did the right thing. What good would it do? Let well alone . . . that's as true now as the day I first said it."

She laughed indulgently, feeling that he'd slipped up there, but not quite sure where. "I'm so glad you agree with me. Dominic is sensitive . . ."

"What Dominic doesn't know will keep him safe," Uncle Bertolino said abruptly.

Mrs. Page looked startled. To hear it summed up just like that would have startled a younger body than she was, she thought. Already she was regretting her confidence. After all Uncle Bertolino was a foreigner, and you never knew with foreigners. Still, he'd be going back to Italy and he'd forget all about it, no doubt.

"My lips are sealed . . ." he said, as if he read her uneasiness.

"Thank you." The old lady felt tired. What had come over her to tell him all that. It was past history now and best forgotten. "Oh . . . oh, here's Dominic. Sometimes he does come in after rehearsal."

"Then I will go," Uncle Bertolino

beamed on the young man as he entered the room. "I am just to go. Your grandmother gives me the excellent tea."

"Vivian's going to have a spot in my next television show," Dominic said. He was in a good mood, and wanted Uncle Bertolino to know whom he had to thank for this concession. "I had a word with the powers that be and I think it'll come off next week sometime. This could be her big chance. She's in a seventh heaven, of course."

Mrs. Page looked at him adoringly. Dominic was handsome, no doubt about that. He was kind too, which was even more important. He certainly didn't take after his father. Her hand shook as she poured him a cup of tea. It was years since she'd thought about that.

Uncle Bertolino wound up the afternoon expertly. His face was like a thunderstorm as he ran agilely up to his top floor flat. "Bah . . . I don't think properly in the English . . ."

He began to think in Italian, and soon felt much better.

In the bottom flat, Rita was parcelling a book in thick brown paper. One eye was on the clock, for she must catch this post. Vivian was dancing round the room, young Johnnie Bertolino in her arms.

"It's my big chance, Rita. You'll come, won't you? Oh, isn't it wonderful? Dominic has arranged it for me . . . I'm going to take the chance with both hands."

"When is it to be?" Rita asked. She was sealing the package with red wax.

"I think—Friday, but it may be later. Tra la la . . ." She bounced the baby up and down.

"He'll be sick any minute . . ."

"Oh, darling. Your mum's going to be famous . . ." Vivian tried to calm down.

"Vivian, I'm thinking of going away for the week-end. I'd be back in plenty of time for your date." What excuse could she possibly make, she wondered.

Vivian stood still. "With Uncle Bertolino?"

"No. Alone. I just want a change somehow. Don't be hurt, will you? My mind is as feckless as your feet, and if I don't do something about it soon I'll blow a gasket." She spoke explosively.

"Not ill?" Vivian asked. "You've

been quiet lately, now I come to think of it."

"I'm not ill. I just want a week-end away. What's wrong with that? Uncle Bertolino will keep you company."

"Of course." Vivian's defencelessness always caught at Rita's heart. The tide of her affairs could only be kept high, when Rita was solidly behind her.

"Don't look like that," she said. "I'm only going away for three days. I've got to think something out . . ."

"Not about Johnnie Bertolino . . . ?"

Rita saw her agitation. She picked the baby out of her arms and kissed him soundly. "Not Johnnie Bertolino," she agreed quietly. "I love the little rascal."

Vivian drew a breath of relief. "Give him back to me—you're going to miss the post. Of course I understand, Rita. Don't be long."

"I think I'll go to that place we used to visit when we were children . . . can you remember the name?"

"I'll think about it," Vivian promised. "Where it always rained, you mean?"

Rita smiled at her as she slipped out of the room. "It won't matter—but it shouldn't at this time of the year, surely."

Two days later she proceeded to the village of her dreams. It was good to be here, good to know that she had this breathing space in which to determine her future plan of action. As she ate the excellent meal in the hotel, she tried not to think of the problem, but it was impossible, for it filled her whole mind and being.

"Richard—and Dominic . . . Richard or Dominic . . . ?"

That night she slept as if she had died, and then the following morning wakened early, to find the room filled with sunshine. The gay chintz curtains could not keep out the cheery beams. Rita shivered as she slipped into her bathing suit, for it was cold before the world warmed up. Putting on her coat she made her way noiselessly downstairs and out on to the promenade.

Only the woman who cleaned the steps of the hotel, gave her greeting. "Nice morning, Miss."

"It is indeed." Rita smiled and went on her way. Movement brought warmth back to her and she walked briskly towards the sea, across the damp sand. This bay was safe, and she had no fear of the water. She took off her coat, and placed it on the sands, before walking to the edge of the sea. Brrr. It was cold. Very cold.

She ran in, with her arms wide, and soon plunged into the waves. For ten minutes she enjoyed the sheer exhilaration of swimming against the lazy waves. When she turned towards the land again, she saw that someone else was cleaving through the water, not far away.

Whoever it was, waved, and she waved back heedlessly, before striking out towards the beach. The stranger came on.

"Wait . . ."

She turned to watch, and something in the dark, brisk turn of the head, made her feel oddly faint.

"It couldn't be Dominic," she told herself. She swallowed sea water suddenly and almost made herself sick. Spluttering and completely disorganized, she awaited him.

"Hullo . . ." His powerful overarm stroke brought him quickly towards her. "Didn't you recognize me just now when I waved to you?"

"No. I thought . . . I mean I just waved as one does to a stranger." She was glad they met out here, where she could turn and tread water, where he could not read her embarrassment.

"I'm no stranger." He was smiling. "Good morning, Rita. How are you?"

"Good morning, Dominic. What brings you out here?"

"The lovely morning, hot sun, a liking for swimming . . . and you."

"Really?" She did not know what to make of his mood. "When did you arrive?"

"An hour ago."

Her eyebrows went up. "Really?"

"Yes. You shouldn't have gone off like that—just slipping away, without even Miss Jane knowing where you had gone. I got your address from Vivian."

Rita swam rapidly away, finally reaching the shore, where her towel was waiting. Quickly she rubbed herself as dry as she could, before slipping into the coat. She shivered.

"I'm going back to the hotel now, Dominic, to get dressed." Why couldn't she think of something scintillating to say to him? Why had she to be prosaic when she wanted to be witty and amusing? Why did she feel so dumb?

"I'll come with you then." He strolled along by her side, his smooth olive body moving lightly. Evidently he had come out just as he was, not caring who might see him. "Glad to see me?"

"I—suppose so, but I thought you were always busy, Dominic? How comes it that you can get time off just now?"

"Oh, that—I had forty-eight hours leave and decided I needed a change. Too far to go up to the Lakes so when Vivian said you'd come here, I thought I'd join you."

So that was it? Rita felt disappointment drowning her. She was quiet as they walked back to the hotel. Possibly Vivian had been worried about her, and so he had come to play chaperon for the two days of his holiday. How he must love her, she thought, to go to so much trouble to make her mind easy.

She parted from him a minute later, with a cool nod. No plan had been made for them to meet again, but she was not surprised when he was seated at her own table. He rose as she approached, and drew out her chair with something of a flourish. Rita bit her lip. She was dressed in a pink cotton dress with white sandals on her feet. It was a colour that suited her dark hair, and she saw the look of admiration that was in Dominic's eyes before he handed her the menu.

"Do you eat large breakfasts?" he asked.

"Yes . . . after swimming," she studied the menu, embarrassed in spite of herself. Dominic was not thinking about her, she reminded herself. "I'll have grapefruit, then bacon, with toast and coffee. That should keep me alive . . ."

"Until mid-morning . . . you're having coffee with me at the Blue Grotto—did you know?"

She shook her head.

"I've my car here, and I'm taking you for a run this morning. Vivian told me about the Blue Grotto and I simply must go there."

She laughed, as she tackled her grapefruit. "It's a place we used to revel in when we were children, but really I think Vivian must have forgotten . . ." She frowned suddenly. He must have talked a

186

lot with Vivian to know so much about the place.

He did not press her to finish the sentence, and they talked lightly during the meal. She found that it was easy to spar with him. His sophistication was not the deep down affair she had thought it. He waited for her replies in a way that confused her a little. She felt as if she were getting to know him all over again. Many of her previous thoughts about him had been wrong. There was a simplicity about him that took her right back to the weekend in the Lakes when they had all been together in his cottage. They spent the whole of the day together. Rita wondered dazedly how it could happen.

As she got ready to go with him in the car to the Blue Grotto, she thought: "I'll have today. At least no one can take from me what I have had . . ." It was a rebellious thought, but her mood held rebellion, and she felt ready for anything as she joined him some minutes later. Her white coat was warm, and she tied a scarf about her dark hair.

"You are one of the few women who can wear a scarf successfully," Dominic told her. "Usually I loathe the things—look too much like bags."

"I look exactly like a peasant woman from Normandy—and I don't care," she told him.

"You look exactly like a Queen in disguise . . ."

Rita laughed in spite of herself. The rebellious mood vanished, and she determined to enjoy the hours ahead. Dominic drove well and rather fast, but she enjoyed it. Dark curls left the shelter of the head scarf and sprang out in the wind. They walked for nearly a mile when they came to the Blue Grotto, chatting easily, and pleasantly.

Dominic bought her the coffee he had promised. They sat drinking it, with the beautiful bay spread at their feet.

"We're really quite high up here," Rita said thoughtfully.

"Yes, I noticed the slight rise almost all the way here. Wonderful, isn't it?" Dominic was contentedly smoking, seemingly at peace with his world.

"Yet only a few miles away there is the valley where they mine for coal—an ugly place . . . not beautiful like this."

"Perhaps it was beautiful—once. Perhaps if you could see under the slag heaps it is still beautiful." Dominic glanced at her. "There could be coal under here." He pointed below them.

"Then I hope no one discovers it," she said hastily. "I'd hate this place to be carved up. After all, there must be beauty as well as utility. We couldn't live without both."

He nodded, his eyes narrowing. "I agree. When once we've sacrificed beauty to the other thing, then we're on the downward track—as a country I mean."

"Beauty means a great deal to you, doesn't it?" she demanded.

"Doesn't it to all of us? But after all—what is beauty? It is in the eye of the beholder. What is beautiful to one chap may not be so to another. All a question of personal taste. Now if you asked me the type of feminine beauty I like best . . ." He glanced at her quizzically for a moment.

Rita felt that she could not bear to hear his taste in this direction. Would he give her a complete portrait of Vivian, she wondered, dulled by the sudden pain that flowed over her. She managed to flash him a vivid smile.

"I don't ask—for I think nothing could be more dull. Don't you think we ought to go? The waitress is hovering. Quite probably they are waiting to get the tables ready for lunches?" She rose with determination as she spoke. She scarcely saw the brilliant sunlit bay, the grass green and vividly clear beneath their feet, the steep cliffs outlined against the skyline. Dominic did not speak as he followed her to the entrance of the tea gardens.

There was a knitting of his thick brows that made her tremble in spite of herself. Was he offended, she wondered? Her sudden termination of the conversation had not been in very good taste. They re-entered the car in silence. Dominic reversed until they were on the edge of the cliffs, with only a light wooden partition between them and the drop to the ocean below.

Suddenly he grinned at Rita. "If I thought there was no future for us I'd take the plunge right now."

Was he joking, she thought, her gaze coming to his in sudden anxiety. For a moment his dark glance held hers masterfully, before he relaxed.

"As there definitely is a future in it, I see no reason to make all that trouble for someone, do you?" He laughed suddenly, and the car shot forward. "Are you always going to be cross with me?" he pleaded.

In spite of herself Rita's lips twitched and they both burst into laughter. She must not take Dominic too seriously. This was his holiday, and he was merely entertaining her to keep himself from being bored. After all, most men liked to take a pretty woman about with them, and she was Vivian's sister.

Calmly she gazed out as the car sped into the crisp morning. She drew a long breath and leaned back in the car seat. For a moment she closed her eyes. If only this ride could go on for ever and for ever. Wasn't that Dominic's wish in reverse? She opened her eyes quickly, to find him glancing sideways at her.

"Tired?" There was a quiet note in his voice that unnerved her.

"No—not really. Just thinking."

"I would like to know what goes on in that head of yours. Quite a lot of thoughts that you will never let anyone else see. Vivian said she was worried about you, for you had never gone off like this on your own before."

"There always has to be a first time, hasn't there?" She felt breathless.

"Not usually—not with someone as pretty as you are."

"Do you think I'm as pretty as Vivian?" In spite of herself the question slipped out.

He considered gravely. It took him a minute to answer. "If you want my considered opinion I think you're streets ahead of Vivian . . . in a different class altogether."

"But Vivian is absolutely lovely," she cried. "And I'm not . . ."

"No, you're not in her class, as I've just said. You can't really be judged against each other. She's tops as far as I'm concerned, and I expect nothing will stop her now. I like her pluck; she means to get somewhere pretty soon."

"You'll help her?" she whispered, her lips dry.

"Yes. She'll get her chance. Glad?"

"You know I am." She could not define his expression, and she looked away, wretchedly aware of her own smallness. Of course she must be glad that he was going to help Vivian to her happiness, to her future career. There was all life ahead of her yet. Ahead of me also, she thought . . . and realized how distant were the lonely years ahead.

That evening they danced to the strains of the small orchestra. Dominic looked at his best in evening dress, Rita thought. She had brought one silk dress that must do for all informal occasions. The blue of the silk exactly matched her eyes, deepening them to startling beauty. Her dark, shining head was close to Dominic's shoulder as they whirled round the small, but pleasant ballroom.

"It's been a wonderful day . . ." Dominic spoke softly. "Thank you . . ."

"Yet what have we done?" she demanded. "A ride in your car, lunch together, a walk along the cliffs this afternoon, now dancing. That's really quite ordinary."

"Think so?" His arm seemed to draw her closer. "Life can never be ordinary when you spend it with the right person . . ."

"No . . ." she whispered, and she suddenly glanced straight up into his dark face.

"Let me tell you . . ." His voice was as breathless as her own.

For a moment she was sorely tempted. Only the training of years saved her then from making what she felt would be a terrible blunder. "No, Dominic. I think we are both a bit bewitched tonight. Let's just be happy—as we are now, and leave everything else. Tomorrow . . ."

"Yes?" He was guiding her towards the door which led on to a small iron balcony. Quickly he whisked her outside and closed the door after them. It was a perfect night, with only the sky and stars and sea to keep them company. The strains of music followed them from the ballroom behind. Rita glanced about her quickly, but could see no one. She felt trapped and frightened, unsure of the whole situation. If only she could have turned to Dominic in utter surrender, if only she could have watched his brilliant dark eyes light up with love for her. It was not to be, and she knew that she must hold him away when her heart longed to draw him close.

She drew the soft folds of her stole closer, glad of the extra warmth, for she was suddenly shivering. To ease the sudden tension between them Dominic drew out his silver cigarette case, and offered her one. She shook her head, then relented. It would be something to do, something to employ her trembling hands. As he held the match to light her cigarette, he saw her shiver involuntarily. "Cold?"

"No, not really. Just nerves."

"So long as you aren't afraid of me . . ." He laughed, as if amused at her.

"Why should I be?" she challenged.

"No reason, but you are the world's most elusive woman. I wonder just how long it has taken me to manoeuvre you into this position—where you are alone with me, and I have your exclusive attention. Those flats are too public for my liking."

"I didn't know you were manoeuvring," she told him honestly. "I've been living a very busy life—and so have you. There *are* other things than romance, you know." They both watched as her restless fingers pressed the spent ash against the iron railings. "Look what I'm doing—"

She bent and rubbed the paintwork clean again.

"Not more important things, Rita. You must admit that. We've got to sort this out . . ."

"That's the reason I came here in the first place," she spoke vexedly. "I'm just flapping about mentally, and I thought I'd have a real stocktaking. You've scotched that."

He laughed, not displeased with her words. It was obvious that he would figure largely in any stocktaking that was to be done.

"Look, Rita . . . be nice to me."

"I wish I could be," she told him honestly.

"You like me . . . more than that perhaps . . ." He was drawing her nearer with gentle arms.

"Could be. But I'm not certain. I told you—about Richard? If he hadn't been there I'd have been in love with you, Dominic. But I've enough sense left to know I can't be in love with two men. It's just not done. But which one? I just don't know."

"You thought I was in love with Vivian, didn't you?" he asked after a minute.

She waited tensely. "Weren't you?" Full knowledge on that point might help her to settle the score with herself, she thought miserably.

"No. I was—infatuated for a while. It went no further than that. When I saw your kindness to her I realized you were a very special person."

She stood silently, trying to believe him. His fascinating voice held danger for her.

"Couldn't you care for me?" Dominic asked so gently against her ear. "I'm very much in love with you, darling."

"It's sweet of you, Dominic—but I wish you hadn't come here. Don't press me now. If you do we may both regret it later. I can't make promises in this state of mind. I think I do love you really, but I'm trying to be sensible. Uncle Bertolino says one must be sensible even where one loves."

"Blast Uncle Bertolino . . ." Dominic was suddenly furious. "What's he got to do with it?"

"He was talking to me the other night," Rita spoke uncertainly. Was it something that Uncle Bertolino had said that had made her even more wretchedly undecided than she had been?

"Some girls like to keep two strings to their bow . . ." Dominic sounded annoyed.

"I'm not one of them. I'd be quite satisfied with one string, if I knew which one. I know I'm very flattered—who wouldn't be, under the circumstances, but that doesn't mean I'm in love with either of you."

"Where's Richard now?" he said. "Your efficiency expert in the engineering trade?"

The sneer made her so angry that she could have smacked him. "I won't talk to you."

"Well, he's not around . . ." He meant to get to the reason if he could.

"He's in Alloa for the firm for several weeks, that's why. Aren't you believing what I have told you, Dominic? I'm normally a truthful person."

"I know." He sounded downhearted, and she forgave him.

"Perhaps I'll never know . . ." she said, feeling her way. If Dominic really loved her surely he would find a way to convince her?

"That's morbid. You've got to make up your mind. Surely you're not going into a convent just because you've too many suitors?" Dominic was disturbed or he'd scarcely have spoken quite so rudely, she thought. "You'd have a wonderful life with me—had you thought of that? Music, fun and dancing. Something big in your life all the time . . ." he paused. "Instead of greasy overalls and your husband away from home all the time."

"Richard doesn't wear overalls," she pointed out coldly. "He's not that sort of an engineer."

"You stick up for him . . ." he said moodily.

"Only because he isn't here to defend himself. I'd do the same for you if you were being attacked." She moved as far away from him as she could. "It doesn't mean more than that."

"Blast him . . ." Dominic was so irritated that he could not think.

"Well, I wish you'd let me alone until I could get it thought out . . . *I* didn't invite you down here."

"I was so certain . . ." he began, smoking furiously.

"I had to tell you the truth when you pressed for it, hadn't I? I'm sorry." She watched him secretly, attracted by his distinguished air and good looks. He was a handsome man. Beside him Richard looked—ordinary? No, not quite that, but certainly not as good looking. She saw that he was confused, his carefully made plan of campaign all astray. Poor Dominic, longing to take her in his arms . . . she sighed gently.

"Then there isn't anything more to say, is there?" The words came on a slow breath. "Quite sure you know what you're doing? I'm not the type to hang on indefinitely."

What man is, she thought soberly. "If I knew my own mind I'd tell you."

"Then I've been imagining that you liked me . . ." He could not finish the sentence for the rush of feeling that swept him. She rushed to help him generously.

"It—wasn't imagination. I know there is a strong attraction between us. There is no doubt about that. But that's not all there is to it. I've got to be sure. Attraction isn't everything."

"It could lead to—everything . . ." he suggested.

"Yes, but I'm not ready, Dominic. The future counts . . ."

"You're wrong there. Only the present matters. There may be no future."

She laughed. "That's morbid." She understood his mood only too well and felt sympathy for him. They were both gazing out into the star-filled sky. How soft the breeze was. This was high summer and they were both feeling a desolation that only came with winter. Why couldn't she go into his arms, tell him how truly she loved him, and just be at peace? It would be wonderful to have Dominic's approval and love. Why did she hesitate on the brink?

"Well, as I'm not the type to throw you over my shoulder and bludgeon you into obedience, there's nothing more to be said, is there?" His voice sounded cold.

Her eyes filled with tears. She wished the pain would stop. Dominic could only see it from his side. Had he sympathized with her indecision at that moment she would have turned to him in utter surrender. When I'm old it won't matter, she thought.

"Let's go in. I don't think I want to dance any more, do you?"

"Just a minute Rita." He put his hands on her shoulders and drew her to him with a sweeping action. Gravely he searched her face, seeing the brimming eyes, the sincerity of genuine distress. "All right . . ." He drew her closer, and she felt his strong attraction. It was almost her undoing. She longed to put both arms round his neck and feel his approval. Her lack of response caused his arms to fall away. Mechanically he drew aside to allow her to pass him. "Can't be helped."

He followed her back to the brightly lighted ballroom. Only then were they conscious of the music, the soft, appealing strains of a waltz tune. For them everything had been shut out by their deep emotion.

"I haven't been playing with you, Dominic—you believe that?" she asked.

"Yes, I know," he sighed. "Have this one with me . . ." She slipped into his arms for their goodbye waltz. Together they glided round the floor, close in each others arms. The magic had gone for both of them.

They reached the hall door. "Thank you. Good night, Dominic." She slipped away, leaving him gazing after her. As she mounted the stairs she felt dissatisfied and lonely. It had taken all her moral strength to withstand his pleading, but she had convinced him.

Dominic returned to London the following morning at an early hour. He left a message for her at the Reception desk.

"I'm not giving up . . ." she read, as she waited for breakfast. "You'd better make up your mind soon though. Not very complimentary to me, are you, sweet love?"

Not very complimentary to either of her suitors, Rita thought somewhat wildly. Just who was responsible for this state of bewilderment? Uncle Bertolino had been at his most grave as he warned her to be very sure of her own mind.

"It is for life . . . you know? . . . for now . . . and the wrong man stays the wrong man . . ." What on earth did he mean?

She had no appetite for the food that was placed before her. Yesterday Dominic said gaily: "Do you eat large breakfasts, Rita?"

How could she continue to meet him daily, as it was natural they would, both living in the flats? Resolutely she tried to turn her thoughts to other things. She spent the day on the beach, feeling completely undone. She mentally added up all the things in Dominic's favour, and all in Richard's favour, and managed to make them exactly equal. Now all the things against them? The scales were tipped heavily against Richard there, she thought. She could not easily forgive him for his jibes against Vivian. Dominic had been kinder. But Dominic had once thought himself in love with Vivian, and so he would perhaps be more sympathetic—or at least, would judge less hastily.

"Brr . . . men . . ."

She returned to London the following day, and was enchanted with her reception. Vivian was pleased and relieved to see her. Uncle Bertolino kissed her on both cheeks with more than usual gusto, Johnnie Bertolino managed to rear his head up, and smile his toothless smile in her direction. Tears came into her eyes. This was her family. This was genuine and kind and real.

"Did you have a nice week-end, darling? You certainly look better. I felt a bit worried after I'd given Dominic your address; Uncle Bertolino said I shouldn't have . . ." Vivian was dressed ready for her dancing class, and looked about twelve.

"Oh, it was all right, but I wanted to be on my own really." Rita was tickling Johnnie Bertolino until he chuckled aloud.

"That's all right then. I'm working like a slave this week, Rita. My spot on Dominic's programme is tomorrow night and he says I'll probably stop the show. Isn't he kind? Oh I can hardly believe it's happening to me." She did a few impromptu steps and clapped her hands for Johnnie Bertolino's benefit. "You're all coming to the show. He's managed to get tickets. I only wish Miss Letty were here to see it, but we can tell her."

"I'd be in a flat spin if I had to face it," Rita told her, marvelling.

"That is because your talents lie in gentler soil," Uncle Bertolino said unexpectedly. "Vivian has this gift and must use it."

Rita would have welcomed a spate of books for reading, from her publisher, but nothing appeared the next day, so she attacked the flat cleaning with goodwill.

Miss Jane went to the hospital to see her sister and brought back welcome news. "She'll be home tomorrow . . . and it's a success. That was what I was scared about," she admitted to Rita. "If it hadn't been . . ."

"But it is. It was a miracle operation thirty years ago, now it's done every day."

"It's still a miracle," Miss Jane said gently.

"Yes." Rita acknowledged the correction. No matter how many times the operation were performed it could only bring thankfulness and hope to all concerned.

"She has to be careful for ages yet, of course . . . but she's really funny. So happy and hilarious now it's over. I'm killing myself trying to get the flat ready for her . . ."

Rita laughed at her. "You darling. She'll not care if there should be a bit of dust. She'll just be glad she can see it."

Vivian returned, in a whirl of parcels, throwing the flat into chaos. Uncle Bertolino took Johnnie Bertolino out for another walk. Miss Jane was going to be baby-sitter that evening, while they all went to the show.

"Everything must be perfect," Vivian explained, flying round. "I don't want to have anything on my mind, and nothing must come down, or break . . . you know what I mean. I've been experimenting with my make-up and I don't think it will run . . ."

"Won't there be an expert at the studio for that?" Rita asked.

"Yes, but I've been getting my skin conditioned. Oh, Rita, I can't believe it . . ."

"You're lucky. Still young and lovely enough to grasp every opportunity. I know it will be a great success."

"For Dominic's sake too. I'd hate to let him down. How do I look?"

Rita walked round her critically. "You look stunning. Never seen you lovelier. Everything—charm, looks, deportment, ability, the lot."

Vivian laughed excitedly. "You say the nicest things. Seriously though, I need bolstering. Then I'll do?"

"You'll do," Rita said dryly. "Very much so."

They all went together in Dominic's car. Mrs. Page, Rita and Uncle Bertolino sat at the back, while Vivian sat with the driver, to receive last minute instructions.

"Although there isn't a single thing to add," Dominic was smiling as he turned to see they were comfortable. "She knows it all—from here to there—and now it's up to her."

His dark gaze sought Rita's for a moment, but did not linger. She was dressed in her favourite ice blue and looked very cool and assured.

At the studio, Dominic showed them to their seats, before vanishing with Vivian behind the scenes. All was bustle and stir about them, Mrs. Page had a hectic spot of colour on each cheek, but Rita felt as if this was happening to everyone but herself. She glanced at Uncle Bertolino and smiled.

Several other guests were added to the limited number of seats available, and she realized that it was quite a distinguished audience. She was intrigued by the big cameras, the rich lighting effects and all the paraphernalia of the bustling studio.

The musicians could be heard tuning up in a room to one side of the stage, and suddenly it was time to begin the show. Someone addressed them briefly before the light flashed on, and they were on the air.

The gleaming curtains parted, and Dominic could be seen standing in front of his orchestra. How handsome and assured he looked, Rita thought, her eyes straining so hard that they watered. Each man in the orchestra was in evening dress. Dominic bowed, tapped the rostrum with his baton, and the show began.

Mrs. Page gripped Rita's hand. "It's the first time for the full show on TV for him too," she said.

Rita nodded, watching with all her heart. Pride struggled within her. This was quite a moment for them all. What a pity Miss Jane and Miss Letty could not be here, but Mrs. Page had explained that no more could be invited. How was Miss Jane faring with Johnnie Bertolino?

Then it was Vivian's turn, and they turned their whole attention on the girl who danced lightly on to the stage. How slight and young she looked, Rita thought.

Her shining hair had been arranged in a new way, the lovely dress rippled as she moved assuredly to her position, near Dominic. They all saw how she smiled up at him in that moment of silence before she began her song.

For a few moments Rita felt so completely taken aback that she could scarcely comprehend what was happening.

Vivian hummed the first opening bars of a catchy tune, before starting to sing. She seemed to smile straight out across the auditorium at Rita, as she swayed and sang, keeping wonderful time with the orchestra muted behind her. Dominic was half turned to her, a smile on his face as he kept the orchestra to a slow, monotonous beat, undertoning what Vivian's small sweet voice was singing.

"Goodness," Mrs. Page whispered, horrified. "It's about spinach . . ."

Rita sat appalled, her backbone seeming to turn cold. It couldn't be true. This was the silly little song she had made up years ago to inveigle Vivian into eating her spinach. There had been no real tune then, just something that was made up to suit the moment, but now there was a definite swing, a monotonous, ever recurring beat that was oddly tantalizing. She sat well back in her chair. The theme had been developed and expanded and oh, that tune was one to catch at the heart beats . . .

Incredulously she listened, and when it was over, the thrill of applause liberated her. Mrs. Page was excited and pleased.

"Listen . . . it's a success. It's something new. You couldn't imagine anyone as young and sweet as Vivian singing drooling love songs. Oh, Rita . . . it's wonderful. I'm so happy I could cry."

Uncle Bertolino beamed and clapped until she had to restrain him.

Rita could not speak. The applause died away, and Vivian prepared to sing again. How unaffected she was, taking this chance with both hands in a way that delighted the watchers. Again she sang a sentimental little song, not one of Rita's composing this time, but one they had known all their lives. It too went over to a roar of applause, and before Vivian slipped away, she knew that she was a success. Dominic turned back to his orchestra, tapped lightly and went on to conduct the major part of the arranged programme.

"Vivian's spot—was worth while," Rita whispered, finding her voice.

"It certainly was. I'll bet everyone is humming that first song of hers tomorrow."

"Magnificent." Uncle Bertolino boomed.

After the show Dominic came to see them, smiling and assured. He was tired, Rita could see, but intent on taking them out to celebrate.

Vivian had changed and presently when she was ready, she joined them. She gripped Rita's arm excitedly. "Weren't you surprised, darling? I was. Dominic wanted it to be a surprise for you. I was humming it once when he overheard me and wanted to know all about it. He concocted the theme. Oh, it went well, didn't it?"

Dominic nodded. "At least it was original, if a bit slight. Had there been more time I might have made a bigger job of it. You want to start writing lyrics, Rita. There's money in it. There is a ready market, if they were all as good as this one."

"You were so clever, matching it to the right rhythm that way," Mrs. Page said lovingly.

"You write 'em and I'll sing 'em," Vivian said ecstatically. She was happy tonight and carried them all before her youthful eagerness. Dominic was in good mood too for there was nothing but praise for his own part in the programme.

"Nothing to it when everything is carefully arranged beforehand. That's the secret. Good organization behind the scenes. That's why I made Vivian rehearse every action and word. Can't do too much of that sort of thing." His olive skin was flushed. "Weren't you surprised Rita?"

"Petrified," she admitted. "Spinach—of all things. I ask you . . ."

Dominic laughed. He was excited by the success of the show. "This could mean plenty in the future." In an aside, while the others were talking, he said to Rita. "I did it for your sake, darling. I knew it would please you if I helped Vivian."

"But she's good too?" she spoke jealously. Vivian had been excellent, she thought.

"Naturally. I could scarcely have put someone on my programme who wouldn't measure up. I'm not exactly Father Christmas," Dominic said curtly.

Uncle Bertolino was humming the theme. "I can't manage the words, but it was good, very good. Somehow, it has a familiarity . . . I hum it so . . ." They accompanied him lightly, laughing at their own absurdity. "Yes, somewhere, I hear something like it . . ."

"Oh, you often get similarities," Dominic said carelessly, but he flashed a look of spite at Uncle Bertolino for spoiling his pleasure.

"Ah yes . . . similarities . . ." Uncle Bertolino beamed on them all in a benevolent way and decided to let the matter drop.

Mrs. Page and Rita laughed so much during the remainder of the evening that they pleaded to be allowed time to eat. Rita was secretly pleased that it went off so well for she had rather dreaded a tête-à-tête with Dominic. He showed no disposition for this however.

Time flew by, while great plans were made for the future.

"Oh . . ." Vivian wailed around midnight. "My dear Miss Jane and Johnnie Bertolino . . ."

"We go," Uncle Bertolino said, rising magnificently, and bowing to each of the ladies in turn. Dominic watched him.

"Funny old stick—your Uncle Bertolino . . ."

Rita rushed to his defence immediately. "He's a darling . . ."

Dominic smiled frostily. "You always rise to it, don't you?"

She flushed. Her dark head came up proudly. "Only when I have cause . . ."

"I can scarcely wait till I see what the critics say," Vivian told them, her feet dancing as they left the hotel.

"But you must wait," Uncle Bertolino followed them at top speed. Dominic brought his car round, and they all got in tiredly. Rita found herself in the front seat.

She gripped both hands together.

"Thank you for all you have done for Vivian . . . for both of us."

"I didn't do it for thanks." He looked pleased however. "If I were you I'd go ahead and write lyrics; you definitely have a flair for that sort of thing."

"Really?"

"Yes, both you and Vivian have something out of the ordinary. Maybe you get it from Uncle Bertolino?" He laughed jeeringly. "Vivian has sought expression consciously, but you have not."

"I lack ambition perhaps?" Rita said. "What else can it be?"

"I don't think we can go into that tonight," he said lightly. "Should we make a date for tomorrow to thresh it out to your satisfaction?"

She felt that he was mocking her, and she glanced up into his face. There was nothing mocking in his expression, and she felt sorry as she read the message in his eyes. Success had come to him tonight —perhaps to all of them in lesser degree —but had it brought happiness? Only time would tell them that.

Tiredly they said good night to each other a few minutes later.

216

"Go straight to bed, and I'll bring you a hot drink," Rita said briskly to Vivian who was trying to stifle her yawns. "You must sleep the clock round. Good night Uncle Bertolino—Mrs. Page."

Vivian came to her, and caught both hands into hers. There was sweetness and maturity in the look she bestowed on her sister "Dear Rita . . ." she said, and that was all.

They parted a moment later. Rita went into her room, drawing aside the curtains, to lay her aching head against the cold of the window pane. In that gentle clasp and that loving look, had lain all of the past with its responsibility, and all of the future, with its uncertainty.

Rita drew a long, deepening breath. They could go on from here, for they had tried to straighten what was crooked.

The following day Vivian bought all the daily papers and some weekly ones, and was gratified to find two small paragraphs about herself, among all the attention that Dominic's orchestra had received. Vivian's part had not been neglected, and she could scarcely have expected more praise for a completely unknown singer.

"Small, clear voice—remarkably good reach for so young a soprano—excellent diction—should go far—" She sang the words to herself blithely. "I'm on my way, Rita."

Mrs. Page brought down two newspapers which Dominic had given her, as she thought they may not have seen them. "Dominic is *very* pleased," she said importantly.

"Who wouldn't be?" Rita asked, as they sat for an hour chatting. Uncle Bertolino had taken Johnnie Bertolino for his daily airing. Miss Jane and Miss Letty had arrived home that morning. Miss Letty was resting, but the operation had been a complete success.

"I have to be careful for a long time yet, but I can see, and that's the important thing," she told her visitors.

"Can you see just as well as before?" Vivian asked her. The flat was a bower of flowers, tastefully arranged by Miss Jane.

"Everything in front of me. I need glasses all the time, but I expect to be able to read and sew as before. Wonderful, isn't it? It's just heaven to see where I'm going again." Miss Letty was bright and happy and excited. She had already bought wool for a cardigan. "I'm getting Jane to fill in my coupons for another week or two, then I'll take over myself."

"Completely organized already," Rita said admiringly. "Your fingers always have to keep busy, haven't they?" Her heart ached a little for their happiness, for there was still a long way to go. Miss Letty must rest for a long time yet.

Miss Jane came buzzing into the room. "Mrs. Page has asked us to go up to her cottage in the Lake District when Letty can manage it. Won't that be something? I've already started packing our wee bits . . . but we won't be going this week . . . or will we?" She glanced at Letty enquiringly.

"I'd better get back!" Rita flew back along the hall. "I've had an idea, Vivian. Why not ring your agent? He may have news."

Vivian went to the telephone, and held a long, and somewhat involved conversation with someone at the other end.

"He's quite pleased," she told Rita. "It's wonderful to have everyone approving of me for a change. He's sorting things out. He's had two offers already, but he'll think what is best to be done. I'm not too keen on leaving London . . ."

"Did I hear you say something about a fan?" Rita asked. She was sorting through the mending bag, in search of some black material.

"Oh, yes, I nearly forgot. I've evidently got me a 'fan'. Someone who wishes to meet me. Isn't it exciting? I asked him not to send him round here. All that sort of thing can come later."

"You sound so wise, Vivian." Rita smiled at her. "You're restless, aren't you? What do you want to do tonight?"

"I wonder if Uncle Bertolino would baby-sit while we went to the pictures? Dominic is working so we can't go dancing." Vivian wandered over to the radiogram and put on a couple of records. "Isn't this haunting?" Humming the tune she began to sway up and down the long room. On her feet were low heeled bronze slippers, soft and shapely. Her lavender dress fell in soft folds about her slender figure. Her fair hair was caught back in a pony's tail, tied with lavender ribbon.

Rita laughed. "You look about twelve."

"Do I? That's an idea. I might do an act pretending to be very young, then half way through change to my real age. That would knock 'em . . ."

Rita folded her sewing, for she longed for a cup of tea. Uncle Bertolino would soon be home too, and he was rapidly becoming Anglicized in his liking for the tea-time ritual. Just as she rose the outer bell rang, then the smaller one that was for their flat.

"That can't be Uncle Bertolino," Vivian said absently.

"I'll see," Rita tidied her hair automatically. Usually their friends came to the inner door—this was someone who did not know their flat. She walked up the hall, hearing her steps resound in a way she had not previously noticed. It couldn't be the butcher either because he always came round to the back.

She opened the door enquiringly. A tall, broad-shouldered young man stood on the top step. She smiled at him, wondering who he was. Twenty-two perhaps, brown, the outdoor type . . .

"Yes?" She spoke first as he looked past her.

"I . . . wondered if . . . Vivian would see me?"

What a deep voice he had, she thought. Musical too. It was strange for him to ask for Vivian in that way, but of course she was adopting it for professional uses too.

Suddenly she realized that he must be the fan mentioned by the agent. "Are you one of her fans?"

"Er . . . yes. I got her address from the agent today. Will you ask her to see me, please?"

"Certainly. Wait here. Who shall I say?" Rita was intrigued in spite of herself. This handsome young man must be very determined if he had managed to extract her address from the agent. He had not lost much time either.

He hesitated obviously. "I—don't think my name would convey much to her . . ."

"All right." Rita left him, and returned to the flat. She left the door ajar.

As long as her life lasted she would never be able to forget the look on Vivian's shocked face, as she half clung to the radiogram. Evidently she had heard them talking. The man's deep, cultured voice would carry further than Rita's lighter one.

Only the weight of the radiogram kept Vivian upright. "Close the door . . ."

Rita turned back and closed it automatically. "What's the matter?"

Vivian's face looked thinner even in those few moments. Some of the bloom was brushed aside. She was so white, and her eyes so large that Rita hurried to her.

"Don't faint . . ." she spoke sharply. "What is it, Vivian?"

"Don't let him in here," Vivian said in an exhausted voice.

"Then you know who it is?"

"Yes."

Suddenly Rita knew too. "Oh, no . . ." They looked at one another in panic. "What to do?"

"Keep him out of here. I can't bear to see him again. I don't want him to know what's happened. Oh, God . . . and Uncle Bertolino may come in any time with the baby . . . Oh . . . Rita, help me. Help me. Get rid of him. Tell him anything. Tell him I'm dead." She was numbed by shock and sheer terror. Rita stared at her irresolutely.

What excuse could she make? Presently, when Vivian appeared to be unable to add to her plea, she returned to the hall. The young man was still waiting, hat in hand. What could she say? Her face felt cold.

"I'm afraid you can't see my sister just now."

"If only I could have a word with her," he began eagerly. "Tell her . . ." Rita cut across his words without formality.

"Sorry—she's entertaining friends. It's not convenient." It was the first excuse that came to mind. She hoped it would have the necessary effect. He would surely hesitate to barge in if others were present. "You must have heard the radiogram," she added coldly.

"Yes, I see." She wondered if he believed her. If only she could get him away before Uncle Bertolino and the baby returned she would be thankful. "I'll call later on . . ."

"Vivian will be out of town for the next few weeks." Her manner was so cold that he flushed to his hairline.

"All right. Thank you . . . good day."

He did not believe her, Rita knew, and he had not enjoyed the rebuff. His face was grim as he opened the outer door and ran hastily down the steps to the street. So that was Johnnie Bertolino's father. Suddenly her face suffused with colour. She wanted to call him back, to curse him violently to eternity and back for the evil he had wrought. She was trembling with the force of her sudden spurt of anger. The young hooligan . . .

She returned to the flat, gripping her ice-cold hands together. If she felt this way, how much worse must it be for Vivian.

Vivian was seated on the floor, where she had sunk down in despair. The terrible look of fear and suffering lingered in her face. She glanced up at her sister.

"He knows where I live."

"Yes—the agent gave him this address."

"To think that my poor little effort last night—has brought this . . ." Vivian's low voice held desperation. "What shall I do?"

"I don't know. Thank heavens the baby wasn't in . . . that would have been the last straw." She was nearly as upset as Vivian. "I told him you'd be out of town for a few weeks, but I don't know that he believed me."

"He won't. He'll bide his time, you'll see."

"Wouldn't it be better if you did meet?" Rita hazarded but at Vivian's violent reaction she stopped, recalling her own violence as she watched him go. This was not the time for finesse—or recriminations. Vivian needed help. "Oh, lord . . ."

Vivian got to her feet tiredly. All the elasticity of youth had left her slender body. "I tell you—if I have to meet him, I'll commit suicide."

"Don't be silly," Rita said roundly. She wanted to say how ridiculous it was to be so dramatic, but the words would not come. Vivian meant it, for she could not bear any more.

"I think we'd better ask someone what we should do—Uncle Bertolino perhaps . . ." She was seeking inspiration. "No, not Dominic—he'd never understand. He'd just kick him out."

"And a good thing too," Vivian said.

Suddenly the tears began to course down her face. She covered her face with both hands in despair, and stood in the middle of the room alone and defenceless, sobbing heartbrokenly.

Rita felt her heart turn over with pity and love, but she stood absolutely still. There was nothing anyone could do.

"I can't bear it." Vivian spoke hoarsely after a while. "Just when I was getting somewhere, for this to happen. I'd never thought that seeing me on TV would bring such developments. I wanted to make something of my life. I wanted to get on, for the baby's sake as well. Yet this has to happen. What'll I do if he finds out about the baby?"

"I don't know." Rita sighed. "I wish I were older and could advise you."

"I'll never let him have him."

"Probably he'll not want him," Rita hazarded.

"He'll not get him anyway."

They were both quiet. Rita tried to think of something that would comfort Vivian, but it was difficult. She sighed. "It was sheer bad luck—but you can get over even this, if you will, Vivian. You remember—that 'soft Beulah night' when you pledged yourself?"

It needed only the reminder, for such

had been their emotion at the time, that even the words recalled that evening when life had been simplified by their awareness and understanding. Vivian had been strong then, challenging the future. They stood silently, remembering the starlit sky, the soft, warm breezes, and within doors the heaped fire, and their own awakening happiness.

"This is one of the times when we have to remember . . ." Rita prompted.

Vivian raised her head, the tears still marking her pale face. The smile that dawned in her eyes was infinitely sad and lovely. Strength seemed to flow back into her body.

"Thanks for reminding me, Rita."

How prosaic the words, yet how deep their scope. Rita drew a long breath of relief. They could both hear Johnnie Bertolino returning. Uncle Bertolino negotiated the pram triumphantly. "There are all those nappies to wash yet, Vivian . . . and a thousand other things to do. I think we'll have a cup of tea first, then we should ask Uncle Bertolino perhaps? We don't need to submit to blackmail or anything of that kind. Not that I think . . ."

Vivian lost her colour again. "Could that happen?"

"I wouldn't know, but it's as well to be prepared. For some reason he's come back into your life. By the way, he said his name wouldn't convey much to you."

"It wouldn't." Vivian admitted wrily. "I've thought since how clever they were. We just knew them as Brickie and Butch . . . obviously they didn't want to use their real names. Cunning, wasn't it? What beasts men are, aren't they?"

"Some," Rita admitted, thinking of Dominic and his gentleness. "Anyway, I don't see that we need despair. Uncle Bertolino will understand without you having to explain too much."

Vivian was drawing comfort from all she said, and some of the first shock was leaving her. "I'm thankful now that it all came out when it did—not that we could have concealed anyone as noisy as Johnnie Bertolino, bless him. Listen, he's getting ready to bellow . . . Oh, isn't life hellish?"

She hurried into the hall, and lifted her small son from the pram. Her whole manner changed as she nursed the baby, and comforted him. She carried him into the kitchen where Rita was preparing the tea.

"Isn't he lovely, Rita?"

It was a cry from the heart, for she needed reassurance and help. Rita turned and kissed the baby soundly on his forehead. "He's a honey but he's hungry, and I don't think he can wait much longer. You know something, Viv? He's like— Brickie . . ."

"Oh, dear, I'd hoped he wasn't. I don't want him to be like anyone but our side . . ." The words showed that she had considered the question before. Rita stood with her dark head on one side considering them impartially.

"In my opinion he's more like his father than his mother."

Vivian reached for the bottle of milk that had been warmed. She was fuming, all her fear gone, and Rita smiled. "He'll alter . . . he's got to . . ."

"I wonder what he thought of your success on TV?"

Vivian was cuddling the child in one arm, and holding the bottle to his lips. "I wonder." She pushed the small, helpless hands aside. "Don't be in such a hurry. I never knew such a lad for his food . . ."

Rita continued to make banana sandwiches. Life was just haywire . . .

Uncle Bertolino sat down in the lounge, got out his glasses, and prepared to read the paper.

7

UNCLE BERTOLINO said musingly: "What have you got to lose? Nothing at all. You should hear what he has to say. This may be important to him. It may not be what you think. May not be—blackmail, you say? What makes you think of that?"

The tea things were strewn about them, for Vivian had allowed him to have his beloved tea in peace, before telling him of what had happened. "That was Rita's idea, but it is a possibility." She was staring over his head, through the long, wide window. "We thought we'd better tell you, because there is a chance that he will come again soon."

"That will be so," Uncle Bertolino said gravely. "Yet you don't wish this meeting?"

"No." She looked at him distastefully. "Would you?"

Uncle Bertolino did not speak at once.

"I know it's shirking it, but couldn't you and Rita see him for me?"

"No." Uncle Bertolino pounced on that at once. He shook his head several times. "No, he would not talk so much—if another man were there. Had you thought of that?"

"I can't take it on, Vivian. I don't mind helping you out, but it's only fair that you should see it through." Rita sounded unusually firm.

Vivian coloured nervously. "I don't wish to see him again—ever."

"But if he calls?" Uncle Bertolino persisted. "I think we should have a plan. Yes? Rita will answer the door . . . I will sit with Johnnie Bertolino . . . you will see this man."

"No." Vivian stood up violently. "No. No. No."

"Then Rita will stay with you . . ." he suggested.

"Don't be so emphatic, Vivian. We're trying to help you. We're on your side," Rita told her.

"I don't want to run away from it really, but I just hate to think of it all the same. Oh, I wish it hadn't been necessary.

Perhaps he won't come," she added hopefully.

"He'll come," Uncle Bertolino opined. He sighed gustily, and rubbed one hand over his black, shiny hair. "I hope . . ."

"That's not very kind of you," Vivian told him restlessly.

Soon Uncle Bertolino went up to his own flat to prepare for his evening at the Opera.

"I love the Opera . . . and this young man will not come again tonight, no?"

"I shouldn't think so," Rita told him. "I must have frozen him . . . anyway, I'll be around, and it *has* to be faced."

Vivian put the child to bed without trouble. "He's been out a lot today, so he's sleepy. That's one blessing, anyway. He shouldn't awaken now till seven tomorrow —with luck."

"He had an ounce more than usual too," Rita told her. "I thought it might help."

They smiled as their glances met. Vivian pushed the nappies and soiled clothes into the washer, with some energy. "He'll not come tonight—but it shook me . . ."

Later they settled down to read, quietly glad that the day was ending peaceably.

Vivian did not turn any of the pages of her magazine, and Rita wondered what were her secret thoughts. They could not be very happy ones.

About half past eight, the doorbell rang. Having got so far through the evening they had felt able to relax. He would not come now. Vivian sprang up nervously.

"Uncle Bertolino is out . . ." she wailed.

"This is it," Rita breathed in concern. "Oh, dear . . ." She stood considering what to do. They could ignore the bell but it might bring worse upon them. Miss Jane was sure to answer it for them. "We've got to meet the challenge. After all, it may not be him. I'll see and if it is, I'll ask him to wait before bringing him in."

"Oh . . ." Vivian sank back into her chair nervelessly. "Suppose Johnnie Bertolino wakens?"

"He won't . . . don't be so worried." Rita straightened her shoulders and walked quietly to the door to answer the second impatient peal of the bell. The next hour would probably be the worst of their whole lives, but it would end somehow . . .

"It'll all be over and done with by the time Uncle Bertolino gets home . . ." she said. "Think of it that way. It won't be so long . . ."

It was the man they expected.

The young man raised his hat. He did not look quite so grim this time, she thought.

"I wondered—would you mind asking Vivian if she would see me tonight. I know it's rather late to pay a formal call, but if she's going off tomorrow I might miss her."

"Oh." Rita considered him carefully. "Do you mind waiting a moment?"

She left him standing in the hall, while she went to see if Vivian were ready. The room was tidy, the fire still good.

"You'll stay, won't you?" Vivian whispered.

Rita promised. "I'll not leave you for even a second. It's best to get it over with." She returned and invited the man into their lounge. His hat was in his hands and he looked uncomfortable as he followed her. Rita stood aside, and closed the door after him.

His gaze rested on Vivian, who made no

effort to rise from the chair. Rita knew that she was unable to rise, that the effort would have been more than could be expected from her at this moment.

Neither smiled, or uttered a greeting. Rita said, to break the tension, "I'd like you to know that whatever you say, has to be said with me here. I'm not leaving no matter what happens."

"Fair enough." The deep voice sounded strange to them both.

Vivian was unable to break the silence. She was waiting for him to make the first move. All vivacity had been drained out of her by fear.

He stood erect just inside the door, still twisting his hat between nervous fingers.

"Won't you sit down?" Rita said. He took up so much room that she would be glad to see him sit down, she thought. He strode to a chair.

"Thank you." He glanced at her briefly, before turning his attention again to Vivian. "How are you, Vivian?"

The gentleness of his voice surprised them both. Vivian swallowed twice before she could answer. "I'm all right. Why have you come?"

"I'd have come long ago—but didn't have your address."

"Yes, it was sheer bad luck that you found me . . ." She grimaced nervously, and glanced away.

"I wouldn't call it bad luck exactly," he continued, "I've been searching for months."

"Why?" The word came bluntly. Vivian wanted no prevarication or evasion.

"To see if there was anything I could do to help."

"There isn't, thank you." She got to her feet. "If that's all you came to say then it's said and you can go. I don't want to see you again."

"Just a minute." He did not stir, and his attention did not waver for a moment. "Please hear me out, Vivian. If you don't it means I must come again—and you wouldn't want that?"

She wavered, and finally sat down again. "Well?"

"Forget about me," Rita said, somewhat wildly. She felt her position in that moment more keenly than she would have thought possible.

He smiled briefly, but she knew that the

238

words had scarcely registered. Between him and Vivian there was a growing tension that could not be ignored and could not be eased save by complete frankness.

"Thank you," he put his hat down on the floor beside him. "Listen, Vivian, apologies don't mean very much, but I want to tell you I'm sorry about what happened."

The words held a hard ring, but there was no doubting their sincerity. Vivian acknowledged them by a slight inclination of the head. Rita realized that she could not have answered just then had her life been forfeit.

"I wish you'd believe that."

"I think she does—we both do," Rita put into the well of silence that seemed to be smothering him. She didn't know how to help them, or if it were right to do so.

"I didn't worry much for a couple of months . . ." he said. "It was something of a lark . . . but when we heard about Freda's death . . . that changed things."

"I'm sure it did," Rita said. They would be hardened criminals had they not been moved by the tragedy of that young girl's death. And he was not that, not a criminal it spite of what had occurred. "By the way, what is your name?"

"Benet . . . but Vivian knew that?" he said in some surprise.

"I didn't," she defended herself suddenly. "I only heard you called Brickie . . ."

"I see." He nodded as if he agreed. "Well, after Freda died I realized that perhaps it wasn't such a lark after all. I called on her mother and tried to get your address but the family was so upset, and she didn't have it anyway . . . so that was that."

"Did you tell her . . .?" Vivian breathed.

"No. If they knew anything about you they heard it from Freda—not from me. I knew you lived somewhere near London —but it was a pretty wide search."

"What happened to Butch?" Vivian asked after a minute.

"He went abroad."

"Oh? Why didn't you go with him?"

"I thought I'd better stay for a while." The reply was evasive, Rita thought. "I don't know that he wanted me around

240

anyway. He was pretty sick of himself, and of me. We hadn't meant it to end that way."

Vivian gave him a strange look. "A couple of complete cads," she said. "You knew what you were doing."

Rita looked at him sharply, wondering how he would take this. His look was meeting Vivian's coldly. "I don't know that you were so blameless yourselves. When a couple of girls allow that sort of petting, what can they expect?"

The bluntness of the accusation took their breath away. Vivian gasped painfully.

"Of all the cheek . . ." she breathed.

So that was it, Rita thought. With the candour of youth they were not sparing each other. Theirs had been the mistake of youth and high spirits. Vivian had been too young to know what she was doing, and Benet was not one of her usual boy friends. He had been older and had probably not realized Vivian's immaturity.

"She was just eighteen," Rita put in. "She was not used to drinking—or petting either, if it comes to that."

"She put up a pretty good show. How was I to know?"

This was worse than anything yet, Rita thought, trying to find safe ground in the morass of feeling between them all. Vivian was speechless, her face white and haunted.

"I think you've said enough," Rita began, troubled. "What can be gained by going over things like this. It's not fair to place the blame anywhere but on yourself."

"I'm not trying to do that. I take the full blame. As Vivian said, I knew what I was doing. Why in hell, didn't you call a halt Vivian? I'm not all beast."

Vivian got to her feet and moved swiftly to the other end of the room. When she answered her voice held a thin rasp of feeling. "Because you had me sozzled long before I realized what was happening. You both gave us plenty to drink . . ."

"And we were drunk ourselves . . ." Benet said. "Had you never thought of that?"

"Frankly—no." The reply held sarcasm.

"Well, it's true. We'd been drinking long before we met you—and we had plenty after."

"Now that you've explained to your own complete satisfaction, don't you think you'd better go?" Vivian demanded passionately. "Leave me some shred of pride."

"I'm not going yet. You've got me wrong. I'm not trying to whitewash either myself or Butch. He's not here to answer for himself—but I am. He can't do anything about Freda—but I'm asking you—will you marry me, and let's straighten the mess as best we can."

So that was it, Rita marvelled. His voice was low, but so deep that they heard perfectly. There was no mistaking his meaning.

Vivian appeared to be thunderstruck. She glanced across at Rita for help, seeming unable to find any answer. Her slender body trembled under the feeling that shook her spirit.

Finally she said: "The answer is: *No . . . No . . . No . . .*"

"Think it over," he said. "I don't want you to answer in the heat of the moment."

"Do you suppose I'd ever give such an offer another thought?" she demanded hotly. "You must be made of stone. Don't you realize what all this has meant to me . . ." Too late she realized her slip, and she went faint with recurring shock. "Oh, Rita . . ."

Rita went to her quickly. "Sit down, dear. He's just going. There needn't be any more of this. Of course you needn't go on with it." She was talking to give Vivian time to recover.

Benet stood up, towering over them in the lovely room. The nightmare scene continued into deeper channels than any they could have imagined.

"Please go now," Vivian said, hiding her face in both hands.

"No." He came and knelt down by her chair, not touching her, but so near that she felt his warmth and strength. "Let's have it. What happened?"

The crisp words were not what they had expected. They seemed, however, to give Vivian strength. Rita watched them both apprehensively. What was said now would have a bearing on the future. There was a sensitiveness in Benet which kept her silent. They must go about this matter in their own way; she could not interfere. Thinking objectively could never get to the underlying truth. Was it that Benet had made a mistake too?

"I had a baby—and he died . . ." Vivian said. Her low voiced slurred on the words.

The room was completely silent for a while. So silent that Rita heard the traffic passing along the highway at the end of the street.

Benet drew a long, free breath. "God . . ." His hand clenched on the chair arm until the knuckles stood out like cords. He was deeply moved, apprehensive too, but almost as if he had been expecting something of the kind. Rita felt her throat constricting until she could scarcely breathe.

She rushed to aid her sister. "That was over three months ago."

"I meant to keep him," Vivian explained, as if he had a right to know these things. "I wasn't going to allow him to be adopted. Tell him, Rita . . ."

Briefly Rita told Benet what had occurred, leaving out the fact that Johnnie Bertolino lay asleep in Vivian's bedroom. The lie had shaken her, but it must be that

Vivian feared he would take the child from her.

"I wanted him—when he came," Vivian said passionately. "At first I didn't but later it was different." She covered her face again with both hands.

They were too young to realize the significance of her words. They were still too close to it to be able to see the form that was emerging, like a Phoenix from the dead, drear ashes of that lost passion. Rita was on the edge of understanding but Vivian acted instinctively, like a tiger at bay. What would he make of it?

Benet continued to kneel. His face had drained of colour and he looked as he would when he grew old. Rita saw him then as he truly was, young, masterful, ashamed, proud, sensitive, unbelievably moved by Vivian's revelation.

"I'll go . . ." Rita said hoarsely, feeling the silence unbearable.

Vivian grasped her hand. She was crying quietly. "No . . . not yet . . ."

Benet noticed her, and spoke apologetically. "I'm sorry it's to be this way. You must be feeling awful."

Rita signified her dismay, but she did

not move when Vivian continued to hold nervously to her hand.

"It was worse than I knew," Benet said presently, as if he had been thinking it out. "I wish he'd lived."

They did not answer.

"When Freda died—I tried hard to find you . . ." he continued doggedly. "I suppose the shock brought me to my senses."

Rita thought back to that morning when Vivian returned from her riding lesson. Surely that was her last carefree day of youth. It was that morning that the two girls had made their plans for the evening date.

"No wonder you both hate the sight of me."

Vivian blew her nose, and stopped crying. She sat up, determined to end the situation.

"You've heard it all now, so you can go. I don't want to see you again. Do you understand?"

"I'm not going, Vivian, now I know. We've got to come to some agreement."

"No . . ."

"I say yes. Can't you see that?" He turned to Rita as if to seek her aid.

"Frankly—no. Nothing has changed."

"But it has. Now I know the full facts and that changes it all for me. I'm sorry. I want to make things right if I can."

"Why should you worry? It's all over and done with. There are no feelings involved except mine—and Rita's . . . and we'll get over it. We were—until you forced your way in here and opened it all up again. No, Benet, I'm independent of you. I have my career—and I've no wish to see you again. Please believe that. Just leave me in peace, will you?"

He got to his feet and roamed round the room. Rita felt irritated and insecure. They had so little knowledge of this man, and what they knew was not to his credit. In spite of his emotion he was the unknown quantity.

Suddenly he came back to Vivian, as if he had made up his mind. "I'll go now— because none of us are thinking straight any longer . . . but make no mistake, it's not finished with. I'm coming back."

"You can save yourself the trouble," Vivian said.

"One thing—you believe what I've said?" he demanded, reaching for his hat.

"Yes," Vivian said.

He smiled for the first time, seeming to relax, and Rita realized that it had taken courage above the ordinary to face them together as he had done tonight. He could so easily have taken the easier way out and just let the situation alone. Something of this must have been in Vivian's mind for she answered the smile.

"Why don't you join Butch abroad?" she said.

"How can I now I know?"

The answer surprised both sisters.

"If Butch had been wise before Freda's death—maybe it'd never have happened."

"As if either of you cared a button . . ." Vivian said coldly.

"Well—he did, after it happened. He couldn't settle after he knew . . . Well, I'm off. Good night—and thanks for your forbearance." He smiled at Rita, but did not offer to shake hands with either of them.

He was actually at the door when Johnnie Bertolino uttered his hunger cry. The long, frantic wail could not be mistaken, or ignored. Vivian stood up nervously, then sank back into her chair, betrayed by her own instinctive response.

Benet stepped back into the room. "What's that?" He closed the door with a slam.

Rita would not tell him a lie, at the child's expense. She hurried from the room, leaving the two together.

Benet came and stood in front of Vivian. "You lied to me . . . he didn't die."

They waited until Rita returned, carrying the wide-awake Johnnie Bertolino. "Take him. I'll get his feed . . ."

Vivian accepted the child. Tears were running down her face. Johnnie Bertolino opened his mouth to tell her in the only way he knew, that he was mighty hungry, when he caught sight of Benet, standing directly in front of him. He smiled delightfully, his toothless gums showing pink and wide. There was even a tiny chuckle for this tall man, who knelt suddenly in front of him.

"He's begun to do that now," Vivian said, interested in spite of herself.

Benet was seemingly unable to answer. Gravely he noticed the dark eyes, like his own. The clean, sweet smell of a loved child. The ridiculous tuft of dark hair on top of his head. Tentatively he put one finger out and the child grasped it.

Benet said, not looking at her: "You'd no right to try to deceive me."

Vivian was speechless. Thankfully she heard Rita returning. "This may be enough, if not we'll have to make some more. He's got an awful appetite," she explained.

Vivian cuddled the child, and gave him the bottle of milk. Benet moved away, drumming his fingers ceaselessly against a small table.

"Now we're in a fine mess," Rita said her thoughts aloud.

"What's his name?" Benet asked presently.

"Johnnie Bertolino," Vivian spoke softly, for the child was falling asleep in her arms, half the bottle left. "I'll take him back to bed." She was glad to escape for a while.

When she returned Benet had gone. She drew a breath of keen relief. Her anxious glance came to her sister's at once. "Phew

. . . I'm glad he's gone. It must have been ghastly for you. I'm sorry."

"Not to worry." Rita went through into the kitchenette. Now that it was over she saw that it might be the best thing that could have happened. Both Benet and Vivian would be put in their places, by their sense of responsibility concerning young Johnnie Bertolino. She glanced at the clock surprised to find that it was after eleven o'clock. The minutes had ticked by relentlessly while the storm of feeling had washed over them. She carried a tray back to the lounge.

When Uncle Bertolino joined them they told him what had transpired. He listened attentively.

"Nothing to eat—but I'm thirsty," Vivian said. The fire was dying, the heat in the room starting to wane. None of them felt able to end the day. "What am I going to do?"

"I don't know," Rita's reply was low. "I suppose you couldn't consider his offer?"

"Of marriage? Goodness, no. Why should I?"

"For Johnnie Bertolino's sake. It is the right thing to do." Uncle Bertolino spoke sternly. "You must think now of the child's future, as well as your own."

"I don't know that it would be right. Making another mistake doesn't necessarily straighten out what has happened. I don't have to marry him. If I've managed as far as this I can go a bit further. Surely you don't think I should?" Her startled blue gaze came to Uncle Bertolino suddenly.

He nodded twice and they looked at him amazed. "This I would do, yes."

"I'm quite as much in a spin as you are. I don't know. I think I would in your place." Rita switched to Uncle Bertolino's viewpoint suddenly.

A spot of colour burned in Vivian's cheeks. "Oh, be careful. You know how much I think about what you say. Don't advise me wrongly." It was an appeal, but Rita hardened her heart.

"If he comes again—which he will— clinch it. I would." She yawned. "Johnnie Bertolino rather settled things tonight, didn't he?"

Uncle Bertolino watched them, not sure if the matter were closed. They were so calm . . . only half Italian after all.

"Must take after his father," Vivian muttered vexedly. "I thought I was getting away with it. Oh, Christmas . . ."

Uncle Bertolino smiled politely and bid them good night. He seemed displeased or disappointed.

When he had gone, Rita glanced across at her. "No one else on your mind?" she asked lightly.

"No—not so's you'd notice." Vivian trailed off, calling out good night. Rita sat on, trying to justify her advice to herself. It looked as if it had to be. She heard the car sliding into the garage, heard the soft closing of the doors as Dominic put the car to bed.

If Vivian married Benet—and if she married Dominic—and if Uncle Bertolino . . . Thought stopped there. "I've no right to plan things. Vivian may feel as bewildered as I do. I can't push her; it's never right to play God . . ."

Draggingly she went to Vivian's bedroom door and knocked. Vivian was sitting up in bed with her hands behind her bright head. Rita stood just inside the door, speaking in whispers so that Johnnie Bertolino would not object.

"I was wrong just now. It's not for me to advise you, one way or the other. You must do what seems right to you. Don't go on with it, Vivian. You've got as far as this alone . . ."

Vivian gave her a grave, troubled smile. She didn't answer at once and Rita went on:

"I realize that it wouldn't do. Your future happiness means more to me than anything else. Stand still until you know what is best to be done."

"Johnnie Bertolino?" Vivian whispered.

"He's not the only baby in that position. We can manage. Why sacrifice your happiness? I don't think it can be right to marry a man unless you love him."

"I see. I don't feel to know anything any more. But thanks, anyway, Rita. By the way, how are you getting along?" She asked the question mischievously. "Your two beaux, I mean."

"We'll leave that for another day," Rita answered. "Good night."

Benet called again, as they felt he would.

"It is a certainty," Uncle Bertolino had listened to the full story with marked attention. "Any man, having seen his own son, would do this. Why not?"

"You take his side," Vivian accused.

"Well, I don't. He's not having Johnnie Bertolino. I'd sooner let you take him back to Italy with you, where he would be safe."

"This I would not do," Uncle Bertolino forgot to smile. "Such a plan would be stupid . . . not good, no. I am not pleased, Vivian."

"I'm worried . . ."

When the doorbell rang again Rita answered it.

"I have to come during the evening," Benet explained. "I'm busy most days. Is it too early? I can call later, but I must see Vivian."

She left him standing as she had previously. Uncle Bertolino stood his ground and was introduced. It was a lovely sunny evening, and the windows were wide open. Some of the former happiness seemed to be leaving them, Rita thought. Uncle Bertolino threw down his newspaper and shook hands with Benet. He also offered him a cigarette, while they waited for Vivian.

Rita looked on with some dismay. This wasn't the way Benet should be received. When she heard them laughing she lost her temper. Uncle Bertolino had no right to be so interfering. He should not encourage Benet in this way. She was seething quietly. She picked up a saucepan to wash it and stood staring at it critically.

"What are you laughing at?" she spoke coldly to Uncle Bertolino, when he followed her out of the lounge. She turned and threw the saucepan at his head, so angry that she could not control herself. "What are you laughing at?"

"It was my little joke . . ." He was still chuckling. "I always make it. Ah, now I know you love me, little one. You have the temperament eh!" He caught the saucepan expertly.

"Yes, I'll see him," Vivian had said coldly, and added: "Alone . . . What's come over you Rita? You might easily have hit him."

"Aren't you afraid any more?" Rita demanded wrathfully. It was all right for Uncle Bertolino—he wouldn't have the mistakes to live with.

"With you and Uncle Bertolino in the

257

flat—no?" Vivian hurried into the lounge. "What is it this time, Benet?"

She took a seat near the open window. The breeze was pleasant. She felt worn out with her own rioting thoughts. She was wearing a cotton washing frock in blue linen, with sandals on her slender feet. Benet watched her secretly.

"Well?" She sounded impatient. She could hear Uncle Bertolino humming to himself in the kitchen, the clatter of the tea things as Rita washed them, and the sounds were curiously comforting.

Benet smiled. He was more at ease than when Rita had been with them. It was easier to talk to Vivian alone. "Glad to see me?"

"No, why should I be?"

"Johnnie Bertolino not on view to-night?"

"His bedtime is six o'clock—every night."

He was disappointed, but she would not relent. "What did you come to say?"

"Will you listen sympathetically?"

"I'll try—but don't expect the impossible." She looked away studiously.

"Will you marry me as soon as I can make arrangements?"

"Why?"

"Well—it fixes it for Johnnie Bertolino . . . and I can offer you a fairly decent sort of life. I believe we could be happy."

"What makes you think that?"

He seemed taken aback by the question. "You're not the sort of girl I took you for originally. Johnnie Bertolino wasn't the only shock I got last night."

"If you are suggesting that I threw myself at you . . ." she began hotly.

"I'm not. Climb down. Don't pick on everything I say. We both stepped off with the wrong foot. Maybe we had to meet— I wouldn't know."

"What makes you think I'd consider marrying you?" she asked curiously.

"Because you love Johnnie Bertolino . . . but it is only a hope, not a certainty in my mind."

"I don't trust you. I never could. How would you get over that?"

"I thought of that too. Not much we can do about that. When you get to know me better you may feel differently." It was his turn to stare out of the window, while

Vivian measured him carefully. Her agitation was increasing.

"Marriage wouldn't have a chance," she spoke slowly.

"Maybe it would. You can't be sure. Any marriage has to be tried for . . . I like you."

"I wish I could say the same. I also wish I could see into your mind for the real motive."

"It's none of the obvious reasons." His gaze met hers searchingly. "You wouldn't believe me . . ."

"I might. Try me."

"Put it this way—I'm just glad to find you alive. You've been on my conscience for months. Butch thinks of himself as a murderer. Indirectly he caused Freda's death. We're just luckier. Nowhere in the world is far enough away for him to get from himself."

The words were so low that she scarcely heard them, yet they registered in her memory. Benet held her look with sudden mastery, and she knew that she believed him. Johnnie Bertolino was not the only factor here. This was his way of telling her that he regretted what had been.

She drew a long breath. "I don't know what to do . . ."

"Marry me . . . and we'll consider it an engagement only for three months until you get used to the idea." He saw her hesitation. "If you give me three months' grace I'll naturally make the most of them."

"What happens if I hate the sight of you in three months' time? Would you promise to let me divorce you?"

"No. There'll be no talk of a divorce for us. If we go through with this we must work it out within the framework of a decent marriage. That's the one promise I will never make to you."

In spite of herself, she liked the spirited reply. It told her better than anything yet that he was serious in his desire for marriage. Impulsively she said: "All right —marriage. You give me three months in which to get to know you—and make your life a misery?"

"Do you want to do that?" He spoke softly.

"No." She glanced away uncertainly. "I'm not vindictive. I'll try to forgive and forget—if you will too."

"I promise I'll do all I can to help you. I'll make the arrangements as soon as possible. You'll want a few guests to be at the wedding, of course."

"Uncle Bertolino, Rita, Miss Jane and Miss Letty, Mrs. Page and Dominic . . . that's about all. I wouldn't feel married if they didn't witness it."

Vivian rose to terminate the interview. She held out her hand graciously. It was a small gesture of returning confidence, and Benet accepted it as such.

"Thank you, Vivian."

She looked at him unhappily. "Make what plans you wish . . ."

"I'll let you know as soon as I can. My parents will be at the ceremony . . ."

For the first time she considered his side of the affair. He had parents—possibly brothers and sisters? He shook his head when she asked him.

"I'm the only one."

Vivian's face grew sad. "I feel so grieved for them, won't they be terribly upset when you tell them all this? I shall dread meeting them."

"I shall tell them tonight. They're not

going to like it, but it has to be. They'll think I've gone haywire."

"Will it—spoil anything in the future for you?" she asked presently.

"No—I'm already well into my career. I'm a chartered accountant in my father's firm." Their sadness was almost a physical thing. These matters had to be discussed, but they would try to forget them as soon as possible.

"I only hope Johnnie Bertolino won't hurt us this way one day . . ." she said.

"That's up to us, isn't it?" For the first time they were identified together. "I'll do my best, Vivian—that's a promise."

She gave a sad smile, her hand in his. "Thank you, Benet. What about *my* career? Will you mind if I continue with it?"

"As if you cared what I thought." He laughed grimly at the thought. Their politeness covered depths that they dared not penetrate. "Well, I'll go. Thank you for being so understanding. I'll see you in a couple of days. Sorry you must meet my parents, but I'm afraid they'll insist. Good night."

Vivian followed him to the door, before returning thoughtfully to the kitchen.

"You two can come forth. Goodness—a few more interviews of this nature and you'd have spring-cleaned."

Rita had filled in the time to good advantage. Uncle Bertolino was making a risotto in the frying pan. "Bella . . . bella . . ." he said smacking his lips, and waving his hands in the air.

"Listen—I'm going to marry Benet pretty soon. I want you all to come to the wedding. We've talked it out and that seems about the best way."

Rita went quite white with the shock, in spite of half expecting it. Uncle Bertolino nodded approvingly. "It is good so. I like Benet. Yes, you are so wise."

Vivian looked at him sceptically. "Really? I'm thinking it's a case of where fools rush in."

"You said you wouldn't do anything impulsive," Rita reminded her stiffly. "You might have given us all a chance to get used to the idea."

"I think I've done very well," Vivian told her sturdily. "Bound to straighten out."

Uncle Bertolino stirred something in the frying pan, watching both the girls with considerable interest. He chuckled, and turned it into a cough when Rita looked at him balefully.

"Pepper . . ." he explained mildly. "My throat, not so good."

"You shouldn't use so much seasoning," Vivian came over to see what he was doing.

"A little of everything—bella . . . bella . . ." He sniffed the aroma appreciatively.

"You don't love him," Rita continued inexorably.

"No . . . but I like him," Vivian had a far away look in her blue eyes. "Some of the things he said. You said he was a real man, Uncle Bertolino, and I think he is— or he will be. He made mistakes, but so did I. Anyway, that's what we plan to do," she added calmly. "It will be best for Johnnie Bertolino. We don't want him to suffer."

"Well . . ." Rita was bereft of words.

"She . . ." Uncle Bertolino puzzled over the right approach. "She—gets on with it, no? Such good sense, such wisdom. This is real thinking. I compliment you, little one."

Both girls stared. Vivian's attitude softened suddenly and she turned to her sister gripping both elbows. Surely Uncle Bertolino had suggested this line of thought originally? Or had he—she was confused.

"Listen—I'm out on the limb alone this time, darling. You can't do anything—more than you have, I mean. It's best this way. I don't know why I feel so sure, but I do. It's the way Benet feels too. If I didn't think we could make a go of it I'd never have agreed. He said we must find our feet within the framework of marriage, and work out our lives decently. He must take it all quite seriously, mustn't he?"

Rita was still bewildered. In her code you didn't marry a man unless you loved him. But how did you know if you loved him? How could you be sure that any feeling would last. Even violence was transient. She could not understand Vivian.

"Didn't you like him at all?" Vivian asked, after a minute. "Uncle Bertolino did."

Uncle Bertolino continued stirring. Rita

wondered if he would eventually scrape through the pan bottom.

"It's an old pan," she told him coldly. "I don't know, Vivian. I suppose so—superficially. It's hard to be quite fair in the circumstances. One is naturally prejudiced."

"Yes, I imagine so." Vivian sighed. "Well, I feel relieved somehow. It settles things for Johnnie Bertolino and that means everything to me right now. After all this, I wonder if I'll be able to concentrate on what the agent is planning for me. I'm to do two more TV sketches . . . and I had thought of going into repertory for a season . . ."

"I give up . . . Everything seems to happen to you, Vivian. Or do you make it happen?"

"By the way," Vivian continued calmly. "It won't be a real marriage at first. For the first three months we've agreed to stay separate. It gives us a chance to get to know each other properly. I'm going to give that man the biggest run for his money that man ever had. He'll not know where he is when I'm through with him."

Uncle Bertolino sneezed violently into

the sink. "Bella . . . bella . . ." he gasped. "You cannot think how . . . how entertaining you are . . ."

"It isn't funny," Rita said, but for some reason she too began to laugh.

"He'll get to know me—oh, boy, he'll get to know me," Vivian spoke with keen satisfaction.

8

THE postman who called at the flats was always the happiest man on any London round. He was certainly the most welcome of any caller during the day. Gaily he rang a tattoo on the four bells, waited for a minute before slapping the letter through the broad letterbox.

Rita or Vivian usually reached the door before he ran down the steps. It was Vivian this morning who smiled and waved. He turned back in his stride.

"How's Johnnie Bertolino?"

"Fine—just fine. He's on solids now."

The postman nodded approvingly. "Good thing too. I checked up—our first was fourteen pounds at this age . . ." It was not the first time they'd compared notes.

"Johnnie Bertolino is a bit overweight," Vivian said. "But you can't rule their appetites completely. He seems to need more than some babies. I brought a few almond truffles for yours . . . can you take them now?"

The postman could, and did, and he waved again as he hurried up the path next door.

Vivian bent to pick up the letters. Uncle Bertolino, Miss Letty, Rita, Mrs. Page, herself. Quite a good bag. She placed them on the hall table, and carried her own and Rita's into the flat. The postman's energetic ringing was already bringing results. Steps could be heard, doors closed discreetly, Vivian smiled as she examined her letters.

"Rita—another one from Richard . . ."

"Oh . . ." Rita came from her room. "That man."

"Do you get one every day?" Vivian enquired curiously. "Seems to me there are an awful lot from him, considering you aren't in the least interested in him."

"Well, ever since he came up to the Lakes that time, he's kept in touch," Rita admitted. "I think it's why I can't get him out of my mind."

"Naturally," Vivian said. "That's the idea."

"He encloses simply lovely handkerchiefs, scent sachets, dainty cards, chocolates, scarves, gloves, artificial flowers, nylons . . . the lot," Rita said gloomily.

"You don't hand round the chocolates," Vivian pointed out.

"Oh, I stopped those—told him they were too fattening. Honestly, Vivian, don't you find Uncle Bertolino's dishes a bit too much? Last night I burped nearly as much as Johnnie Bertolino does."

"Don't change the subject," Vivian said. "Although I couldn't agree more. It's the only thing that will make me resigned to him going back to Italy. But about these things from Richard. He's courting you all over again, isn't he?"

Rita's magnolia skin turned a delightful pink. "I've tried everything I know," she wailed. "Answering coldly, not answering at all, forbidding him to write again, but still they come . . . and he'll be home this week. Oh dear, what can a girl do?"

"Marry the brute and stop it that way," Vivian advised.

"That's it—it would stop it most effectively, and between ourselves I'm quite enjoying it," Rita confessed.

"Both your swains seem on the generous

side," Vivian reflected. "How do you do it?"

"Must be my sweet nature," Rita told her sourly. She opened the bulky envelope. A small pair of baby socks came out with the tissue paper. Rita turned red. "Of all the nerve . . ."

Vivian sat down, laughing uproariously. "Oh, dear . . ."

Rita read the letter hastily. "It's all right —they're for Johnnie Bertolino . . . for a minute I felt quite . . . rattled."

Vivian picked up the socks tenderly. "Rather nice of him to send them for Johnnie Bertolino after being so mean about him at the beginning."

"He's just getting round us," Rita said.

"Well, isn't that what we all have to do when we're sorry about something?" Vivian asked in the same gentle voice. "Richard was provoked . . . he reacted that way. In the future the same set of circumstances might never arise. I think he's asking you to forgive him, Rita. He isn't the only one who felt mixed up at that time."

"No, he isn't," Rita admitted. "Oh,

dear, what to do? I wish I could make up my mind swiftly as you do."

Vivian rose. "I'll take these then? It's up to you, Rita. Don't let anything he said about me stop you doing what you know is right. Some of the things he said were probably true—even if they all weren't."

Miss Jane and Miss Letty always read their mail at the breakfast table, because they never rose "all that early" as Miss Jane pointed out, because there was no need. Now that they were both retired, they enjoyed the freedom of stretching the hours to the full.

"Just the usual pools coupons to fill in," Miss Jane moaned, and she poured herself another cup of tea to bolster her disappointment. "I never seem lucky, do I?"

"Neither do I. Honestly, Jane, do you *really* expect you'll win on the Pools one day?" Miss Letty handed her the bill for a new pair of stepladders. "Mine's worse —we're out of pocket on that."

"We-el . . ." Miss Jane spoke thoughtfully. "I *did* hope once . . . but not any more. If you can fill in the coupons all these years and not get a sausage then I think there must be something wrong with either the system—or with us."

"It's us," Miss Letty said decisively. "Time we made a change of some sort. *I'll* do them for the next month and see what that brings."

Miss Jane smiled politely. "Are you suggesting, Letty, that I'm not good at it? Considering you've been the one to have most say in the final decisions I think that is in slightly bad taste. If you remember on two occasions we changed the sequence . . ."

Miss Letty waved that away hurriedly. "That was a mistake. If only I'd kept quiet we could have had over forty pounds. Oh . . . that's quite a sum. It would more than pay for the stepladder anyway. Well, is that all? No luck this morning then. Perhaps tomorrow? . . ."

"Yes, probably something to cheer us up tomorrow," Jane agreed.

Miss Letty smiled as she looked through the window. "Isn't that fleecy white cloud beautiful, Jane?"

Jane saw it with renewed eyes, and suddenly her own filled with tears. "Beautiful," she said, and added flippantly: "Or as Uncle Bertolino Cassimo would say . . . Bella . . . bella . . ."

"The postman must be better . . . it's the dark, little fellow this week," Miss Letty said. "I saw him talking to Vivian. Was it an ulcer?"

Miss Jane shrugged. "I think so—but he's got over it evidently. This modern age . . ."

Uncle Bertolino hummed to himself all the time he was reading his stepdaughter's letter. Once a week she wrote to him, and once a week he answered. This time the news in her letter made him stop humming somewhat abruptly. Something was going wrong, obviously.

"He's gone away . . ." Rosa wrote in her spidery hand. "And I'm glad. I couldn't stand the man. There's a lot of money missing—just how much is not known, but it was the takings of one whole week. I think some of the best silver is missing too. He had the lists. Really, you shouldn't have trusted him the way you did. I could have managed much better alone. Now, when are you coming home? Are you having a good time? Please write and tell me what I must do. I

275

hope you are well. Your loving, Rosa . . ."

The news shook Uncle Bertolino profoundly. If he were wrong in that, he could be wrong in other things, he thought deeply . . . in Italian, because it was easier that way, he told himself. Disciplined thought was his pet fetish. Rosa would manage. Obviously . . . because the worst was already past. Bah. Forget the scoundrel. A little money would not matter.

The news kept him quiet most of the morning as he tidied his small flat. He had much with which to occupy his mind.

He sat down to compose a suitable reply, one that would tell Rosa everything —and nothing.

"Not yet can I return, for my work here is not finished." He wrote. "But I will be with you in one month. Do not take any action; the money will doubtless be spent. See to the customers and do not talk to the neighbours. Be discreet in the matter . . . Keep well.

Your loving, Bertolino Cassimo."

Uncle Bertolino sealed the letter gravely.

Until this morning there had been all the time in the world—or at least, he corrected the thought, all the time that was left of this glorious summer. Now he felt rushed, and slightly harassed, and that was not good. One needed to work with deliberation and finesse in these things. English women had not the warm temperament of his own Latin country-women.

He placed his hat on his head, put the letter in his pocket, and sallied forth. At Miss Jane's flat he paused and knocked. He beamed when the door opened. "I go to post—you have something ready? No?" He smiled with a show of splendid teeth at Miss Jane as he raised his hat and went.

"Who was that?" Miss Letty called.

"Uncle Bertolino," Jane answered flatly, and went on to finish tidying her room.

Miss Letty, on her knees brushing the hearth, suddenly went still. She stared down at the cream tiles with misgiving. A spider dropped down from the ceiling and landed beside her. Automatically she put out her hand and despatched it to another world.

Horrified, she called to Jane . . . "Oh, Jane . . . I've killed a spider . . ."

Her sister came to the door hurriedly. "I thought some disaster had happened. What's wrong about that?"

"Well, I hate to kill a spider. Always did. They haven't much to look forward to . . ." She sounded shaken.

"Something in that. They'll have their own angle certainly. Don't worry, Letty. It'll all come right. I've been thinking—are we getting anything new for Vivian's wedding?"

They both gazed round their small and pleasant home. Reality had slipped away from them for a moment, but Jane's words brought things back into focus.

"She'll look a picture," Miss Letty said. "Violet velvet, long sleeves, with tiny buttons up to the elbows. Her hat matches . . . and she's such pretty feet . . ."

"She'll look wonderful," Miss Jane agreed. "Anyway, we can't compete. Rita will be in blue. Nice of them to show us their dresses yesterday, wasn't it? I think we'll be all right in our new suits."

"We'll not let them down," Miss Letty agreed, feeling less shaken than she had.

Rita was looking critically at her dress as it hung outside the wardrobe. It was something special, and the accessories had cost the earth, but who cared at such a time? Richard was due to call that day, for he had returned from Scotland. Would he be at the wedding? Rita scarcely thought so. Richard had not the charming ease of manner that Dominic possessed. Whatever Dominic felt, he never showed it, which was pleasant in one way, but might lead to trouble occasionally.

Uncle Bertolino arrived back at the flat with Richard. They met as they both tried to enter the gate together, Uncle Bertolino raised his hat politely and gave way.

"You first," Richard said, in his deep voice. Curious old blighter, he thought.

Uncle Bertolino skipped in lightly. "You seek someone?"

"Yes." Richard did not tell him who, but Uncle Bertolino guessed. He took out his key, and signified that Richard should follow him.

"I go to tell Rita . . ." Uncle Bertolino enjoyed the joke, more than Richard.

"So you're Uncle Bertolino. I might

have guessed. Rita mentioned you in her letters."

Uncle Bertolino beamed as he led the way. "So kind. Come in here. You would have a glass of something?" When Richard nodded, he hastened to a small cabinet in which he kept a few bottles for just such events as this one. He poured a drink and brought it to Richard. "You like that? Very special . . ."

"You not drinking?" Richard was thawing rapidly.

"I don't in the morning . . . my stomach, she's not as strong as she looks." Uncle Bertolino tapped his stomach mysteriously. "I don't believe in overdoing it . . ." He was triumphant as the phrase rolled off his lips.

Richard laughed good naturedly. "Neither do I, if it comes to that. Can't afford to in my job."

"And your job is engineering?" Uncle Bertolino said, and added when Richard looked surprised: "My niece tell me. Now you have the cigarette while I find if Rita is in. She must shop each morning, but she may be back."

"I'm back," Rita entered on the words.

"I overheard you, and guessed it must be Richard." She was taken aback to see them so cosily ensconced. Richard rose to his feet as she entered and came towards her.

Uncle Bertolino saw that he was forgotten, and regretfully closed the door after him. He peeped through the window at Johnnie Bertolino who was sleeping in his pram in the yard. Vivian was out at one of her classes. The flat was quiet. It really couldn't be better, Uncle Bertolino thought. It just couldn't be better.

"Hullo, Anna Helena Margharita . . ." Richard said softly.

"That's what I'd call the wrong approach. Hullo, Richard." They shook hands briefly.

"I quite like your Uncle Bertolino. A nice old boy . . ."

"He's not really that old," she corrected nervously. "My mother would have been about forty-eight, so probably he's only around fifty. He's a darling, anyway. I don't think age counts these days, do you?"

Richard followed her to the window. "Glad to see me, Rita?"

She stood with her back to him. "Yes."

"Now . . ." The bare word pleased him. "That's something." He took her hands and drew her round so that she faced him. Smilingly he searched the delicate, lovely face and eyes for some sign that only she could give. "You've been thinking about me?"

"I could scarcely not do so. Really, Richard, you must have spent a small fortune on gifts for me. Why did you do it?"

He laughed drily. "Can't you guess? I had to keep me in your mind, in case some other fellow came along. I couldn't be here but I hit on that . . ."

"You've been away a long time . . ." she ruminated. Her hands were still in his but she had not responded to him yet.

"Did it feel so long?" he whispered.

"Oh—I didn't mean that. But I mean, your firm, it was as long as, longer than other trips surely?" Her tongue tripped slightly over the words.

"Yes. Six weeks . . . a lifetime. Only the thought that I'd lose my job kept me up there. You know why? Because I thought I might need that job if . . . you'd have me. Will you, Rita?"

She drew her hands away gently.

"There's no one else?" he suggested after a moment.

"No . . . no."

"That doesn't sound too certain. That fashion plate, Dominic, I suppose?" His tone held a spurt of bitterness.

She laughed. "He called *you* an engineering efficiency expert."

"So you've been discussing me with him?" The fury in his voice reminded her of old times.

"No, not really. But when he asked me to marry him I had to confess about you and he was a bit rattled . . . as you are now." Her dark blue eyes lifted to his suddenly.

"And are you going to marry him?" he asked stiffly.

"No." The tantalizing word stood alone, and they both contemplated it thoughtfully.

"Why not?"

"I've decided I don't love him enough."

"Then have you decided who you do love?"

Silence. Rita found that she could not reply.

"If it should be me, I'd be very grateful to know it," Richard said humbly. "I'm mad about you. We've been engaged, and you know the worst of me. I've been a heel but I think I'm cured. I realize that marriage is a fifty-fifty business, if two persons mean to keep their own individuality. I've given it a lot of thought."

"Is that why you sent those socks for Johnnie Bertolino?" she demanded.

"I thought you might forgive me about Johnnie Bertolino. You can adopt him if you want to. I won't interfere."

"No," she looked at him, and the dimples began to appear in a fascinating way. "No. I've been thinking too. You were right that time. I'll tell you—it's all going to be solved without us. He's Vivian's responsibility really. Vivian is going to be married. Uncle Bertolino agrees about that. Uncle Bertolino says a man can't always give in to a woman either just for peace at any price. He thinks you were right."

"Uncle Bertolino is quite a fellow." Richard was so close now that if she

284

turned she would be in his arms. She didn't turn, and he sighed gently. He made no comment about Vivian's affairs. "How do you feel about it? . . . I'm in love with you, darling. Haven't I been punished enough?"

"I wasn't punishing you," she was so indignant that she half turned. "I just couldn't make up my mind. I'm not mean. I've had to do a lot of thinking too."

"Yes, darling . . ." She was closer now, almost in his arms. Richard was smiling as he gently drew her closer yet. "About this? And this perhaps?"

"Perhaps," she agreed dreamily. He kissed her gently, and suddenly the months were swept away, and they were back again as in the early days of their engagement. Rita turned to him wholly, and their lips met in a long hard kiss.

"I'll be a good husband, darling."

"I'll try to be a good wife," she promised. "If Uncle Bertolino could live with us I think I might manage to pull it off."

"Uncle Bertolino has his own affairs to see to," Richard told her softly. "Leave us to ours. Darling . . . oh, Rita . . . it's true? You won't throw something at me in a minute?"

She laughed into his collar, a small, happy chuckle that delighted him. "Vivian's getting married tomorrow. Are you coming?"

"Sure. Who's going to look after Johnnie Bertolino?"

She drew away, shocked into reality. "We'd never thought of that. Oh . . ."

"I'll stay with him," he offered. "I'm not keen on weddings in general . . . much prefer my own. When's it to be, Rita?"

"Oh, I can't think . . . you've put me off my stroke. Will you really stay with the baby? That would be the perfect solution . . ."

"I'll stay," he promised sombrely. "But write out a list of what I do in certain eventualities."

"Oh, we'll leave that of course, and the phone numbers, and everything will be ready and he'll be asleep anyway. Oh, thank you, darling, that's wonderful." She threw her arms round him and kissed him again soundly.

"Here," he said. "I like this. Could do with any amount of it. Gee . . . life's wonderful . . . It rained every blessed day of last week in Scotland."

"The sun's shining here," she told him blithely, before he swept her back into his arms.

"Thank you, darling."

He left without seeing anyone else. Uncle Bertolino was sleeping in the kitchen.

"At his post . . ." Rita thought, making sure that the pram was still in the yard. Her eyes were dreamy, and she was still glowing from Richard's arms. "Oh, I'm happy."

Vivian came in despondently. "I've just met Benet . . . He's bringing his father and mother round this evening. I think I'll go to the North Pole."

"They'd still be here when you got back. Better face it," Rita advised. "It may not be too bad. After all, what can they do?"

Vivian could not be comforted, and she dressed for the coming interview in apprehension.

Rita helped to put Johnnie Bertolino to bed. Luckily he went off with the minimum of fuss.

"Whatever they say he's not going to be wakened just to pass him round," Vivian said with compressed lips. "They can see him some other time."

Rita felt sorry, but knew this formal meeting was necessary, under the difficult circumstances. She herself felt nervous as the hour approached. They were both strung up when Benet finally appeared. He came bounding up the front steps.

"I've got Mother and Dad with me in the car. Can I bring them in?" he asked Rita.

"Of course. We're expecting them." Rita was to receive them, giving Vivian a chance to pull herself together. For some reason known only to himself, Uncle Bertolino had decided to stay out of it.

"For me—I might say too much. Better say too little at this . . . part," he had said. Could it be that he didn't wish to meet them, Rita wondered, as she stood ready to receive Benet's parents.

His mother was helped out first, a tall, handsome woman of middle age, beautifully dressed in a fawn summer suit and hat. The father was grey haired, of military appearance, keen looking. Benet followed them to the door.

"Rita . . . my mother and father. Mum, this is Vivian's sister."

"How do you do?" Rita tried to sound cordial but knew she was failing.

"How do you do?" They did not offer to shake hands, and Rita showed them into the lounge. She saw their eyes take in the scene curiously. Benet was nervous, but he talked to help the situation along.

"Won't you sit down?" Rita asked gently. "Vivian won't be long. She's frightened . . ."

"Indeed," Benet's mother sat down near the window, and unbuttoned her suit coat. The room was a pleasant one, with some good, old-fashioned but beautiful pieces of furniture. There was an air of near luxury in the carefully chosen carpets and soft furnishings. Obviously the girls had taste.

Benet's father sat down silently, with no liking for this visit which had been thrust upon him. There were certain things that must be said, and he was the obvious choice for saying them, and he wasn't keen on his job. Benet handed round his cigarette case, and Rita pushed ash trays nearer.

"It's been such a lovely day . . ." she said conversationally.

"Yes, hasn't it?" Benet's mother smiled at her. "Are you all ready for the wedding tomorrow?"

"Yes." Rita spoke through stiff lips. "Yes, we are."

"Ten o'clock," Benet said. "Don't be late. Dad will bring a car round for you."

"Thank you."

Vivian came to the door. She stood framed there for a moment, looking pale and frightened. There had been no thought to make up, or dress in her best clothes. She was as she had come from bathing Johnnie Bertolino. Her bright hair was caught back with a ribbon, and her woollen dress clung to her perfect figure.

There was a short silence, until Benet sprang to his feet and went to her. He took her hand and took her first to his mother. "Mum . . . this is Vivian . . ."

Vivian held out her hand timidly. They shook hands in silence. "How do you do?"

"Dad—" Benet appealed to his father, who came over to meet Vivian.

"You're a very pretty girl . . ." he said kindly.

"Yes, isn't she?" Benet's mother seemed to find release in that statement. "You're so different from what we thought."

"How did you describe her last night?" Benet's father chuckled.

Benet's mother looked scandalized. "It's surprising how different things are when you meet the persons concerned. This is difficult for you, child. It isn't easy for us either but we must make the best we can of it. Sit down by me."

They were kinder words than Vivian had expected from the first frozen greeting. Vivian found her voice, and began to chat to them, answering their questions to the best of her ability.

Benet remained close throughout the interview, guiding it back into safe channels when it threatened to stray out of hand.

"Do you know, dear," his mother smiled at Benet suddenly. "I feel so much happier now I have met Vivian. You are so very different from what we thought."

"Can I make you a meal?" Rita said, hoping to escape for a few minutes.

"No, thank you very much. But if you will ask us again some time we'd love to come then. Benet . . ." His mother stood up, signalling him.

"I say, Vivian—is there a chance that they could see Johnnie Bertolino?"

"Well . . ." She considered the situation in the light of these new developments.

"I'll get him," Rita said. She returned at once, carrying Johnnie Bertolino who was just about to object in no uncertain terms, when he caught sight of his mother. Rita handed him over, and they all crowded round to see the baby. Vivian sat with the child on her knees. She made no effort to parade him, simply let them look.

Benet's father was the first to capitulate. "By jove . . . he's like me . . ."

"He's exactly like Benet when he was a baby. I'll show you a photograph some time, Vivian. You'll be amazed at the likeness."

Johnnie Bertolino saw a finger near him, and reached out for it, chuckling and discussing something in his own language. He was a good-natured child. Benet's father looked pleased as the child tried to pull himself up with the help of that finger.

"Let me have him a minute . . ." He picked the child up from Vivian's lap, and his wife joined him. Together they talked loving baby talk, quite forgetting the others.

Benet bent and looked into Vivian's sad face. "Hey, what's this . . ." He saw the tears running unchecked down her cheeks, and bent to wipe them away with his handkerchief. "No more tears, Vivian."

Rita slipped out, and left them to it. "Amazing what can happen in a day . . ." she said, into the roller towel that hung behind the kitchen door. She hurried up and made coffee and presently took it into the lounge. In the bustle of serving, Vivian picked up the baby and took him back to his cot. She turned at the door, and held him up against her shoulder.

"Say good night, Johnnie Bertolino."

"Goo—goo . . ." said Johnnie Bertolino obediently.

They all laughed, and Vivian went away to put her son to bed.

"What a darling child. And what a

lovely mother . . ." It was Benet's mother who spoke.

Rita looked at her levelly. "My sister *is* a lovely girl," she said.

"I can see that. Really, Benet . . ."

"Save it," Benet told them, and he looked glad of the hot coffee that Rita put into his hand. He was unable to chat as they waited for Vivian to return.

Rita wondered if he were thinking of Butch, the friend who had emigrated. This seemed a happier ending somehow.

Vivian returned, composed, and ready to hear what they had to say. But it was never said. The hard words and reproaches were best left alone. Benet's mother kissed Vivian as they were leaving the flat.

"Good night, child. I feel so happy for you. For us all."

"Thank you." Vivian's voice was almost inaudible. "I was to blame, as much as Benet . . ."

"We can go into that when we're ninety-two . . ." Benet's father said.

9

"WHERE is Benet going to live?" Uncle Bertolino enquired soberly the following morning, after they had told him what had transpired. "Had you thought of that?"

"At home I suppose." Vivian looked crestfallen. "That hadn't occurred to me yet."

"Would you like him to have my flat?" was the next question. "I regret to have to tell you this, on this so happy day, but I must leave at the end of the month."

"Oh, no . . . Oh, Uncle Bertolino . . ."

"But why? Aren't you happy with us?"

The two voices, and the genuine regret, must have satisfied even Uncle Bertolino. "I go—for domestic reasons. You understand, to do with my café, my stepdaughter. I promise."

"Not?" Vivian looked horrified.

"Ah, but I was much wrong there," Uncle Bertolino chuckled affably. "No, the manager, he has absconded, with much money and silver."

"So he won't be marrying Rosa after all?"

"No. I think Rosa die an . . . how you say it? Without husband?"

"You must send her to us," Vivian chuckled. "We'll get her off your hands."

"Perhaps Dominic would have her," Rita said softly. They both looked at her in an electrifying silence. "Yes, Richard persuaded me yesterday. I expect we'll be married in a decade or two . . ."

"And you never said a word." Vivian bent and hugged her sister.

"I didn't get a chance," Rita told her. "But Uncle Bertolino must have known."

"One is never quite sure," he murmured. "Until one hears it from the mouth of the horse."

"Thank you . . ." Rita felt puzzled. "You mean the horse's mouth, of course. Well, that's it. But what about Benet? We are in danger of being sidetracked again."

"I'll mention the flat to him," said Uncle Bertolino, waving a fat hand in the air.

"How will you like having him in the same building?" Rita asked practically.

Vivian shrugged. "It won't make any difference, where he stays. But it would mean we needn't show up the temporary arrangement to the world in general."

Amusement showed fleetingly on Uncle Bertolino's face. "Good. Then it is settled and in the basket."

Benet's father arrived some minutes before ten o'clock with the first taxi. Miss Jane and Miss Letty were introduced, and with Uncle Bertolino they went off happily to the Registry Office. Benet's father had given them all flowers to pin to their coats and they began to look quite festive. Uncle Bertolino was fussing about both ladies as if they were his special charge.

"This really is nice," Miss Letty said, settling into the seat. "Now I won't need to wear my great-grandmother's roses."

Uncle Bertolino looked puzzled.

"Until we win a Pool we can't afford magnificent flowers," Miss Jane explained loftily. "These are lovely. So thoughtful of Benet to include us too."

Rita was pleased with her own spray of pink rosebuds. Mrs. Page and Dominic joined them as they stood waiting in the hall for the second taxi.

"We heard all the goings-on," Mrs. Page said. She looked pretty in a grey lace dress and fur coat. She accepted her spray of flowers gracefully. "Dominic's brought his car round if it should be needed. He may have to leave early."

"Come with me now," Dominic said to Rita.

"Oh, I can't. Richard hasn't come yet to look after Johnnie Bertolino. Oh, dear . . ." Rita was trying to write a note, finish off the fresh milk mixture, and talk to everyone. She put the telephone number where he could not fail to find it. "Oh, thank goodness, here he is at last."

Richard joined them. He was panting with the speed of his movement. "I got held up in a traffic jam, and I bolted down the last two blocks. You'd think I was never coming."

He leaned over and kissed Rita in the most natural way possible. She coloured like a peony. Dominic scowled, and moved out to his car.

"Now come into the kitchen, while I show you what to do. There's Johnnie

Bertolino in his pram. Just keep an eye on him. He really should sleep till we get back." Vivian spoke hurriedly. "But they never do the obvious thing, so if he wakes up . . ."

"Which God forbid . . ." Richard said nervelessly. "How will I know when it's hot enough?"

"It's all written down," Rita told him. "Do try to manage. Now we simply must fly. Are you ready, Vivian?" Dominic was waiting on the top step, and she thought he looked decidedly bad tempered. Oh, dear, that would be because Richard kissed her, perhaps.

"You look lovely," Benet's father smiled charmingly, before turning to Vivian.

Vivian's vivacity was under a cloud this morning. Her serious air was appealing. Her violet dress hung in rich folds of silk velvet, clinging to her lovely figure. She wore no jewellery, relying on her youth and beauty to offset the rich colour. She stood her future father-in-law's scrutiny as long as she could.

Defiantly she lifted her head. "Well?"

"Forgive me, Vivian. You look stunning. This is all such a surprise. I begin to think Benet is luckier than he deserved to be."

Vivian took his arm. "Thank you. We had an Italian mother, you know." They all left the building together, laughing light-heartedly.

"Benet is in a complete spin this morning. He left the house half an hour before I did."

Rita got in beside Dominic, with Mrs. Page in the back seat. The others took the taxi. Rita leaned back, wondering if she had overlooked anything. After all, Richard was a grown man and should be able to cope with Johnnie Bertolino for an hour.

Under cover of Mrs. Page's bright chatter, Dominic muttered: "That fellow kissed you just now. What's it mean?"

"Let's talk of it later," she whispered.

"Is he back in favour?" he was driving rapidly, outstripping the taxi behind.

"Yes," she admitted hesitantly. "I was going to explain . . ."

They entered the Registry Office quietly a few minutes later. They were ushered into a small room where the ceremony began. Rita glanced about her, smiling at the assembled guests. Flowers decorated the room rather profusely, and it was close with the heavy perfume. Benet's mother was there, magnificently gowned, with a rich fur stole about her shoulders. She smiled at Rita warmly, and went forward to kiss the young bride. That's nice of her, Rita thought. But of course she is to be Benet's wife and that makes a difference.

They were invited to go closer to the table. They changed places, Benet standing beside Vivian. Rita stepped forward a pace to stand on the other side. She stared straight ahead, hearing the words, but feeling apart and strange.

This wasn't the way it should have been for Vivian. What were her innermost thoughts as she stood so passively beside Benet during the short ceremony? Benet's mother looked serious but kindly, and a little bewildered. They're all so different when you really know them, Rita thought. They react every way but the one you expect. I think she'll be kind to Vivian. Probably they will do their best because they love Benet.

There was a low murmur of sound. Miss Letty's bracelets jingled and she subdued them quickly. Uncle Bertolino coughed discreetly. Vivian was invited to sign her name in the register. Her usual cheerful manner was overcast. It was the guests who helped to keep the moment high.

"I'm not helping very much," Rita thought. "Wonder how Richard is faring?"

Vivian laughed when the Registrar was the first to congratulate her. Benet took her hand and drew it through his arm. There was nothing stiff about him any more. He looked happy and relieved and young and a bit shy.

Rita watched them, unable to do anything but stand stiffly, a permanent smile on her frozen face. She met Vivian's quick, bright glance and tried to respond.

"Hullo, darling . . ."

Benet's mother came forward to kiss her new daughter-in-law. "God bless you, dear. You are a lovely bride. Bless you too, Benet. I hope you will both be very happy." She held Vivian away for a moment. "I've arranged that we shall all go to church for I wanted God's blessing on this marriage. Is it right to you?"

For only a fraction of a minute Vivian

appeared to hesitate. "Yes, of course. What a perfect idea."

Benet glanced over Vivian's head, to meet Rita's eyes. "I'd no idea this was in the air."

"But it's simply lovely. I adore weddings, don't you?" Mrs. Page saved the awkward moment from lengthening. "Can I kiss your handsome husband too, dear?"

Miss Jane and Miss Letty crowded round, and the laughing group opened to include Uncle Bertolino. Benet's father was busy paying fees, calling forth the waiting taxis, marshalling them out to the street.

They broke up into the three cars again, and Rita managed to travel with Miss Letty and Miss Jane. Uncle Bertolino obediently slipped into her place beside Dominic.

At the church door the vicar came forward to greet them. This had been arranged without their knowledge but they all welcomed it. Rita stood quietly beside Dominic, and they all grouped themselves about the young bride and groom.

The sun was striking through the

stained glass windows, outside the birds were chirping sleepily, the scene was peaceful.

The quiet voice of the vicar rose in welcome, their small movements died away. For a moment Rita was unable to appreciate the beauty of what was happening. They were witnessing the man of God as he gave God's blessing to the happy couple, now and for ever, world without end. It was as simple as that.

She recalled the other evening, when she had come to this church with Miss Letty, so worried over what was happening to Vivian, that she could not even join in the prayer. For Miss Letty too a great change had come. Where there had been only darkness, now there was light. On that evening they had both received comfort— and it was so again today. A gladness filled her. This was right and fitting. It was a rounding off of the marriage that had taken place in the Registrar's office. How kind of Benet's mother to plan it this way. How wonderful that she had understood that this would be what they would all remember, not the civil ceremony.

Rita glanced up, feeling herself drawn

by Dominic's concentration. He did not smile, seeming too engrossed in listening to the quiet words that lapped peacefully round them. He was not seeing her. His mind too had taken a far flight.

Vivian stood, young and vulnerable, quietly accepting what was happening. Her hand was in Benet's. Then it was over. The taut group broke up into component parts again. They surged towards the door.

Benet's father began to portion them off to the three cars. "You all know that we are expected at the hotel for lunch? Please come . . ."

"And eat as much as you can," Vivian said, laughing under a barrage of confetti that someone had thoughtfully provided. Uncle Bertolino was unusually smart this morning in his dark suit, pale grey raincoat, and grey hat. The carnation in his buttonhole exactly matched his handkerchief, and he carried a cane and gloves.

Outwardly it was like any other wedding, Rita thought. Conventional, running to a pattern, and rightly so. The young couple looked happy and would make something of the future together.

The meal was a success, with the guests relaxed and happy. Benet and his father made speeches. Everyone seemed to be in a gay mood. Vivian cut the wedding cake, and it was handed round.

"I've got to sleep with some of this under my pillow," Miss Jane said, laughing at the ridiculous thought. Vivian had a small piece wrapped in a paper serviette sent round specially for her. Miss Jane tucked it in her bag, without comment.

"She takes the cake home?" Uncle Bertolino said, missing nothing. "That is excellent, no?"

Rita shook her head at him. "That's something else I'll have to explain later . . ."

Uncle Bertolino made a mental note of the promise and did not insist now.

Benet's mother toasted the happy pair. "You haven't yet told us where you are going for your honeymoon—or are you being modern and not having one?"

"Too many commitments," Benet said.

The moment passed. The talk continued. Dominic said he must go, but continued to sit at the table. Rita was glad when finally a move was made to end the meal.

The taxis were still waiting, Dominic's car between them. The small group spilled out on the pavement.

"I'll return with Dominic," Mrs. Page said. "Coming, Rita?"

Uncle Bertolino was already helping Miss Jane and Miss Letty into a taxi.

"Well, no . . . or could you wait?" Rita wanted to speak to Benet's mother and she hurried round the back of Dominic's car. Uncle Bertolino slammed the door of the next taxi. Rita was not sure how it happened, but suddenly Dominic must have backed his car, she felt the vehicle strike her shoulder, before Uncle Bertolino pushed her savagely into the road. It was over in a flash. Rita sat down in the road with such force that her leg doubled under her. Uncle Bertolino was lying between the back wheels of the car, untouched.

The pavement was alive with people, all talking at once. A policeman emerged from somewhere. Rita was helped up, but she could not bear her weight on her left leg. An excruciating pain made her hop on one leg.

"What's the matter with Uncle Bertolino?" she asked, almost crying.

Vivian was supporting his head. She looked up thankfully. "He—fainted . . . he's coming round. Oh, I thought you were dead, Uncle Bertolino."

"No." Uncle Bertolino recovered himself quickly, but his face was sallow and drawn. "I am not hurt—just shock, you understand."

Dominic and Mrs. Page were standing near. "What a terrible thing," Dominic said. "It was a sheer accident. I was trying to back out between the taxis . . ."

"Oh, Dominic, you might have killed her. Thank God it's no worse." Mrs. Page wrung her hands.

Miss Letty and Miss Jane stood quietly on one side, trying not to add to the confusion.

"Are you all right, carissima?" Uncle Bertolino rose and came towards Rita. His voice was gentle and yet rough. He looked strained.

The policeman had sent for an ambulance. "She has broken her leg, if nothing worse. Better go to hospital."

"I'll go with her," Dominic said. "Oh,

God . . . I'd give anything if this hadn't happened."

"So would I," Uncle Bertolino said.

Benet was only just realizing that something was wrong. He pressed forward and lifted Rita in his arms. "You'll want to go inside until the ambulance comes, won't you?"

Rita scarcely knew what was happening. Shock held her numb as Benet and Vivian went into the hotel again with her. Benet put her down on a chair.

Benet's father got the others away in taxis. The ambulance arrived and Rita and Vivian and Benet went to the hospital. Uncle Bertolino would not accompany them, saying that he was perfectly all right.

"But you can't be," Vivian was almost weeping. "Didn't the car go over you?"

"No. Fortunately not. But it would have gone over Rita . . ." he said strangely. "My build—you understand?"

"A dreadful accident," Dominic was shaking as he gave the policeman particulars. "I've never had an accident in all the years I've been driving."

"Couldn't be that you've been celebrating too well?" he was asked.

"No, not that. I'm sober—have to be
because I've a rehearsal in an hour."

Rita was shut into the ambulance and
did not hear any more. She leaned back
and fainted.

10

"I'LL have to go home," Vivian said uneasily. "Think of Johnnie Bertolino."

"And poor Richard." Rita was feeling better, her leg had been X-rayed and she was awaiting the plaster cast. "This is the oddest wedding I've ever been to. Benet, do sit down."

Benet was still wandering about after telephoning the news that Rita suffered nothing worse than a broken leg. Richard was coping to the best of his ability, and Miss Jane, Miss Letty, Uncle Bertolino were all assisting but . . . "I think you'd better go," Benet said. "I'll stay and bring Rita home, if they let her come."

"They're letting me come all right," Rita answered. "I'm fine really. Uncle Bertolino saved me the worst of the accident. I hope he's all right. Get her a taxi, Benet. That child is on my mind too."

Vivian kissed her warmly, smoothed down her beautiful velvet gown, and vanished behind Benet's tall figure. When he returned a few minutes later Rita was being prepared for the plaster cast in which her leg would be encased for at least a month. The department in which he waited was quiet, orderly, with a strong smell of antiseptics. Benet had time to reflect on the strangeness of life in general. He felt considerably older when finally Rita was returned to his safe keeping.

"I'm not having the ambulance again— a taxi will do . . ." Rita looked wan and tired but her spirit was good. Benet vanished again and presently Rita was wheeled out and transferred to the taxi. As Benet put her down safely on the prepared seat, she smiled into his face. "Thank you. You're a darling."

He was touched by the spontaneous words. "Just a question of strength . . ." he boasted. "Now—home James . . ."

Home is where the heart is, Rita thought soberly. She was still so completely disorganized that she was unable to gain any very clear impression of the next quarter of an hour.

Uncle Bertolino, apparently completely recovered, fussed around, while Benet transferred her from taxi to flat. Miss Jane and Miss Letty made strong black coffee in their own flat and brought it along at once.

"Yes, I am well," Uncle Bertolino said to Rita, as she passed him. "You are the casualty."

When Vivian returned to the flat earlier, Johnnie Bertolino was tucked under Richard's arm, while he tried to do several things at once. Miss Jane had coaxed the baby on to her knee for a few minutes, but the resulting pandemonium scared all concerned. Johnnie Bertolino decided that the only familiar face there was Richard's and he kept as close to it as he reasonably could in the circumstances. After that, Richard did all that must be done, with one hand permanently incapacitated. He was so white when he heard the news about Rita that Uncle Bertolino mixed him a stiff drink.

The first lightening of the gloom came with Benet's telephone message.

"Good." They all sighed with relief. "I don't think Vivian will be long now."

Vivian came in a quarter of an hour later, and scooped up her small son and hugged him. Richard sank nervelessly into a chair.

"I never knew—that babies could be so —possessive."

"Has it been bad?" Vivian asked sympathetically.

"The first hour was all right. By the way, I gave him bread and butter, and he's been sucking a bacon rind, and I mixed him another milk drink, and the juice of an orange, and that's the fixings for another milk shake . . ." Richard sounded exhausted. "Is it all right?"

Vivian looked at Johnnie Bertolino dubiously. "I suppose so. If he didn't choke it must be all right."

Richard drank what Uncle Bertolino gave him, and felt much better. "Actually the little beggar took to me," he boasted. "Right from the first minute he wouldn't leave me."

Johnnie Bertolino hid his face shyly against his mother, and prepared to go to sleep.

"Now if he'd only done that a couple of hours ago . . ." Richard spoke in an injured voice.

"They never do the obvious thing."

Vivian lifted him and took him back to his cot. She could see the pram in the yard, and it looked as if a hurricane had been there.

When Rita and Benet arrived later, they all crowded round. The coffee was excellent and Miss Jane looked gratified, although it was Letty who had thought of it.

"A month?" Richard was kneeling beside Rita, holding her hand closely. "Darling, I'm glad you're all right. You might have been killed." He shuddered.

"You look white yourself," she told him. "Has it been very bad—with Johnnie Bertolino?"

Mrs. Page was not of the group, and presently Uncle Bertolino decided to run up to her flat and tell her that Rita was safely home.

"I go . . ." he said grandly.

"Are *you* all right?" Rita asked tiredly. "One of these days I'm going to tell you what a wonderful Uncle you are."

He smiled benignly and vanished. Miss Jane and Miss Letty withdrew with equal speed.

"We can fetch the cups later, dear . . ."

Uncle Bertolino knocked on Mrs. Page's door. She admitted him at once. He noticed that she had been crying, and her snow white hair was disarranged.

"Do sit down." She indicated a fairly solid chair.

Uncle Bertolino sat down, wondering where to begin. "Rita is home—safe, but she has her leg in plaster. It is broken. Doubtless I pushed her too hard? . . ."

"Thank God you did push her," Mrs. Page said quietly.

"You saw his face too?" Uncle Bertolino's voice was as quiet as hers.

She nodded, unable to answer.

"Then I was not mistaken. He meant to hurt her."

"But why?" She cried, roused out of the misery of her feelings. "Why, when he loves her?"

"The motive is not far to seek. Rita is now engaged to someone else. Something of this she must have told Dominic on the way to the ceremony." He sat stroking his knees thoughtfully.

They considered his words in silence for some time.

"What do I do?" Mrs. Page asked

brokenly. "His father had sadistic tendencies, but so far Dominic has been so kind. My daughter couldn't live with her husband . . . it broke their marriage . . . I told you?"

Uncle Bertolino nodded briefly. "Nothing good will come of telling him these things. The same set of circumstances will never arise again. It would be a pity to send him down into the pit of such knowledge. I would not do anything. It was an accident."

"Could he have drunk too much?" she asked pitifully.

"I don't think so. Could be that a few drinks might excite him, but he was not drunk. No, we must think that it was an accident. Your knowledge has made you afraid. You must put it from your mind eh? Dominic must stand on his own feet. He is not his father. You were wrong to think it anything but an accident." He was so persuasive that she began to smile.

"I just couldn't think that he would try to kill her . . ."

"No. Possibly a temporary mood of deep anger, but he would not have killed her." Uncle Bertolino heard Dominic

317

running up the stairs, and stood up to go. "I believe he only meant to hurt her, perhaps."

"Wait," she whispered. "Hear what he has to say."

Dominic entered, breathing quickly. "I've just seen Rita. God, I don't know how it happened—or what really happened. It was an accident. I've convinced the police but I'll never forgive myself as long as I live. Have you seen her, Gran? Leg's in plaster right up to the knee." He sank into a chair nervelessly. His pallor was accentuated by his emotion. "I measured up later—if there had been another three inches I wouldn't have touched her."

Mrs. Page looked at Uncle Bertolino. Tears were streaming down her face.

Dominic looked at him too. Restlessly he got on to his feet again. "But for you she might have been killed . . ." he said. He thrust a hand through his dark, glossy hair. "I'll never forgive myself."

"Just be thankful it's no worse," Mrs. Page said gently. She herself was so thankful that Dominic was taking it this way. Any other attitude would have condemned him utterly in Uncle Bertolino's eyes . . . and her own. Their knowledge had led them into wrong thinking. She had been wrong to confide in Uncle Bertolino. She had broken the promise made all those years ago. Dominic had not tried to hurt Rita. She was certain of it.

"Queer," Dominic muttered presently. "When I looked in at the office just now I found an offer waiting for me. They want me to go to America—right away—certainly before Christmas."

"You will go?" Uncle Bertolino was drumming ceaselessly on the chair arm with his fingers.

"Haven't got round to it yet. This other business drove it out of my head. I'm inclined to accept. How about it Gran?" Dominic looked at his grandmother.

"Accept. I'm longing to get back to the Lakes. When you return I'll come down here again to keep house for you, if necessary."

"You may find it not necessary, eh?" Uncle Bertolino was smiling affably. "You may meet the girl you will marry."

Dominic laughed wildly. He was in no mood to consider that side of the affair at the moment. "Girls are the deuce. I think I'll stick to music for a bit."

"Ah—the music." Uncle Bertolino nodded approvingly. "The young of this generation are so wise, eh? Now—not to worry any more. This accident has turned out not bad. Good. I go soon to my home in Italy too."

"Changes are in the air, aren't they?" Mrs. Page said. She looked exhausted, but a happier expression was replacing the desperation of a few minutes ago. "When have you to be back at the studio, Dominic? I'll get you a meal."

Uncle Bertolino took the hint. Dominic accompanied him to the door. There they shook hands. Uncle Bertolino had so much to think about for the rest of the day that he did not leave his own flat again.

Vivian nursed Johnnie Bertolino for half an hour after his bath. It was the part of the day that Johnnie Bertolino enjoyed most of all.

"Can you blame him?" Benet said, before he left the flat. He had stayed to see the child bathed, and was lost in wonder at the love and prowess displayed. "By the way, Uncle Bertolino mentioned about his flat—I'm digging in there tomorrow, and will stay on when he leaves. That right to you, Vivian?"

"It's for you to plan it the way you want it," Vivian told him equably.

"I'll bring my tackle along tomorrow then." Benet sighed. "Good night, for now." He kissed Johnnie Bertolino, and after a brief hesitation, kissed Vivian too. "May as well begin the way we mean to go on . . ." he murmured, before leaving them.

"You gave us a scare," Vivian told her sister, after the child was safely in his cot. "My goodness, what a wedding day. None of us are likely to forget it, are we?"

Rita wished her head would clear. The shock had left her, but she knew that she needed a good night's sleep before she would feel back to normal. "Benet has been very kind, hasn't he? It's surprising how many parts there are to a person."

"Yes, indeed it is." The flat was full of flowers. Richard must have called at the florist when he left, and taken their whole remaining stock. Vivian laughed. "That man is trying to show you by every means in his power that he loves you. Gosh, Rita, he nearly fainted when the others came back here without you. Miss Letty was telling me . . ."

Rita was staring at the flowers, feasting her tired vision on their colourful beauty.

"How kind everyone has been. One has to come through a trial before one knows . . ." The words were comforting, and within their essential truth lay something they both treasured. "Has anyone else been?"

"Dominic of course. He wouldn't come in, but he seemed terribly relieved when we didn't blame him. Benet says it could have happened to either of the cars. Dominic just misjudged the distance somehow."

"Poor Dominic." Rita mused over the accident. "It could have been worse. We didn't expect this, did we?"

On Sunday afternoon Rita had her fair share of visitors. She was able to hobble into the lounge and lie on a settee with her leg up. She felt much more composed. Miss Letty and Miss Jane arrived first.

"Sure you're not wanting to take a nap?" When assured that she never slept in the daylight they sat down to gossip happily about the wedding, the weather, Uncle Bertolino, the baby and lastly the accident itself.

"Is your uncle all right?" Miss Letty asked presently. "I only ask, because he doesn't seem quite himself these days."

"Why, I think so." Rita was startled. "You mean the accident?"

"Oh, no. He recovered from that at once. He says he just fainted. Queer, wasn't it? No, it's something else again. Doesn't seem quite natural with us. I wondered if we'd hurt his feelings in some way."

"I don't think so." Vivian was listening to the conversation. "He just seems to have something on his mind. His manager has decamped with some money and he's probably wondering what action to take. You know he's going back at this end of this month?"

Miss Jane nodded vigorously. "Yes, he did tell us that yesterday."

"We'll all miss him," Miss Letty sighed.

"We certainly will." Rita sighed too. "But maybe I'll get back to my normal weight again."

Uncle Bertolino came in while they were discussing him. "Talking of angels," Vivian said affectionately. "Do sit down . . ."

Miss Letty bobbed up. "No . . . I go . . ." She turned pink with embarrassment for that was a saying of Uncle Bertolino's which they all took off on occasion. "I mean, we go."

"Too many guests would be bad for Rita just yet," Miss Jane explained volubly. "We'll come tomorrow, Rita. Glad you are so much better. You'll just have to put up with the leg and try to forget about it as much as you can."

Uncle Bertolino bowed from the waist as he showed them out. He closed the door after them decisively. Vivian glanced at him. Uncle Bertolino was simmering, like a pan with the lid ready to fly off.

"I have news from my stepdaughter," he told them without preamble. "If I do not return this week, she will come here."

"Really? She's a bit of a Tartar, isn't she?" Rita asked him. "Let her come."

"I think—no. I must cut short my holiday eh? That is bad—not good."

"Very bad," Rita was keenly disappointed. "I'd planned for you to be at my wedding. I can't bear it if you aren't."

"Why not fly over for a few days?" Vivian suggested.

A light seemed to break over Uncle Bertolino's dark mood. "That is it. It is what I will do. So much to do here . . . but I could fly home, yes." He snapped his fingers excitedly. "Why didn't I think of that myself. That way I could make all my plans . . ." He stopped dead.

"What plans, darling?"

"Many of them. I wish you and Benet and the baby to come to me for a long holiday when you are happy eh?" He turned back to Rita, and his smile was enveloping and genial. "Then you, my carissima . . . you will come when your leg is healed?"

"I might," she said cautiously. "But Richard has agreed that we could go up to the Lakes for our honeymoon. Maybe we could do both . . ." At the thought Uncle Bertolino brightened.

"Going to have quite a spate of visitors, Uncle Bertolino?" Vivian lounged to her feet. "I must get on with the baby's washing. Now that Rita can't help me I'm terribly busy." She dropped a kiss on Uncle Bertolino's dark head. "Perfume? Uncle Bertolino? . . ." She looked at him disparagingly. "Oh, no . . ."

"Hair oil . . . Benet's . . ." he explained, but his manner was not quite natural. "He tell me I can use his bottle."

"You get on with Benet, don't you, darling?" Vivian was diverted. "How are you managing?"

"Good, very good. I do the cooking, you understand."

"Just as well," Rita put in. "I don't imagine you'd get very far on Benet's cooking." She shifted her leg slowly to ease the weight of the plaster.

Vivian wandered into the kitchen while Rita and Uncle Bertolino continued talking. When Mrs. Page arrived Dominic followed her into the lounge. Rita had scarcely expected that he would come, but she was pleased to see him. She shook hands with them both.

"It's very nearly goodbye in every sense of the word," Mrs. Page began. "How are you, dear?"

"Much better. But what is this? News?" She looked from one to the other.

"I go—to help Vivian," Uncle Bertolino sidled to the door.

Dominic sat down. "Yes, I've had an urgent offer to go to the States and I'm off at the week-end. Have to leave Gran to tidy up here. I may be away months."

"I shan't mind that. I'm just longing to get back to my own home, and I've started packing already. Your Uncle Bertolino has been helping me—did you know?"

Rita looked startled. "No, he didn't mention it. What a complete surprise. I'm glad for you, Dominic. I suppose it may lead to wonderful things."

"We hope it will," he told her, but his young face was bleak. "I'd have been glad to turn it down—if things had been different here."

"I know." Sudden tears stung her eyes, but she tried to be bright. "I'm sorry about that Dominic, but you can't love just to order. You'll know that one day. My fault was that I didn't convince you soon enough—I simply didn't know. I thought I hated Richard. You *can* hate someone you love very much. I wouldn't have hated him so much had I loved him less, I suppose," she added reflectively. "Well, what a change it will be. Uncle Bertolino is flying back to Italy for a few days too . . . but thank goodness he will be coming back."

"I won't be coming back—for a long time," Dominic said.

"You may, dear." Mrs. Page turned to Rita. "I feel quite sad now we're leaving. It's been a wonderful year really."

They bid her farewell a few minutes later. "We'll look in again before we leave, but you can imagine how busy we are . . ."

Rita waved to them, and lay back thinking. Mrs. Page had called it a wonderful year. Had it been that?

Uncle Bertolino flew back to Italy two days later. He refused to say goodbye to anyone. "I come back in five days," he said definitely. "Then I resume this . . . so fascinating holiday."

Rita had to return to hospital at the end of the week, and she was away three days. "Thank goodness that's over," she told Vivian on her return. "I'd no idea they would keep me. How are you getting on with Benet?"

Vivian laughed reminiscently. "Oh, yes, Benet . . . Without you and Uncle Berto-lino to chaperon us we felt quite bereft. He behaved with exemplary fortitude and good manners. In fact, Rita, he's a complete darling. I like him more than I thought I would. Odd, but true . . . Listen . . ."

Benet was lounging in one of the big easy chairs. His huge frame filled it. He was smoking quickly as he watched Vivian making the coffee and serving the supper from a trolley.

"I don't think you should smoke so much, specially before a meal," Vivian said edgily.

"Then I won't." He stubbed out the cigarette with exaggerated haste.

Vivian smiled. "You don't have to obey me as if I had a whip. I only thought you would spoil your appetite for the mixed grill I'd prepared."

Benet nodded. He was thoughtful as he watched her put his plate on the small table by his side.

"You certainly know how to feed a man, Vivian."

"I remembered what Daddy used to enjoy." Vivian took her own plate and sat down. "Mixed grill was always one of his favourites. It's easy to do too—and since Rita had the accident I've concentrated on easy dishes."

Benet ate the food rapidly, and she saw that he enjoyed it. Every evening he came to her and she made him a meal of some kind before he returned to his own flat at the top of the building. She poured him another cup of coffee, and handed him the brown sugar.

"That was good," he said, and he was smiling. "You know something, Vivian—I'm coming to think of myself as the luckiest man in the world."

"That's nice of you, Benet."

"I could be even nicer if you'd let me," he hinted.

Vivian laughed at his sudden seriousness. "You are quite nice enough, as you are, Benet."

"Seriously, though, Vivian—don't you think it's all a waste of time? . . ."

"What is?" Her blue eyes widened in sudden apprehension. He saw the look and softened what he had been going to say.

"Oh—our staying apart like this for three months? After all, I think you like me . . ."

"Yes, I do," she admitted thoughtfully.

"Then . . ." He left the chair and came nearer to her. Vivian put her cup down with a hand that shook suddenly.

"No, Benet . . . please . . . you promised."

"I know I did, but this is something else again. You admit you like me . . ."

"You know I'm always honest." She sounded troubled. Had she been too frank.

"That's the thing I like about you. It's more than liking now on my side. I'm in love with you Vivian. Maybe I always was —I don't know. But I love you now all right. What are you going to do about it?"

The sudden challenge altered the tempo of feeling in the room. Vivian drew a long, slow breath. A glint of temper showed for a moment in her eyes.

"Just a minute, Benet. That's all very fine for you to throw out a statement like that. What are *you* going to do about it?"

He watched her, trying to gauge her reaction, and failing. "What do you mean?"

"You know the situation. You made certain promises. I expect you to abide by them."

"And if I don't?" He glanced away from the sudden change in her face.

"If you don't?" Her voice was soft and slow and impelling. "If you don't, Benet —then I'll hate you all the rest of my life."

Sudden silence engulfed them. When he did not answer, she continued in the same quiet way: "You say you love me . . . then prove it to me. Show me that you think more of me than of your own desires."

"I could have you in my arms in five minutes . . ." he said slowly.

"Yes, I believe you could," she agreed, and he was mystified by her seeming agreement. "But I don't think you will. If the future counts with you . . . as it does with me . . . then you'll keep to our agreement."

"Then the future *does* count with you?" he asked, and there was a triumphant note in his deep carrying voice.

"Yes. It does." She let the admission stand by itself, unable to add to it.

"Then you love me?" He came towards

her swiftly, but something in her expression held him.

"I shall know the answer to that—sometime," she told him honestly.

"I see." He moved away from her quickly, to stand by the open window. She spoke to his broad back, appealing to him because she wanted to help him, out of her new found knowledge of them both.

"I want our future to be a happy one," she said. "Unless we can base it on mutual trust and confidence it can't be. The way you act now has a bearing on all that. I think you are probably right—you could sway me, against my better judgment too, because it all seems so futile at the moment. But we did promise each other . . . and if you help me now, I'll be grateful to you whatever the future holds for us both. Don't let's rush our fences, Benet."

He nodded moodily. Vivian waited. She was not sure that her appeal would sway him. Benet was still very much of an unknown quantity. His youngness was still untried.

He stood apart, his dark hair brushed straight back from his brow. He had a good profile, she thought, and suddenly her heart ached for both of them. She longed to be able to put her arms about his neck, and comfort him, but that way was not for her. If they were ever to find happiness, he must face the future just as she did. Without his goodwill she could not fight alone. Only he could decide.

There was complete silence in the room for a while. Vivian could hear a fly buzzing somewhere, but strained her eyes in vain to find it. Rita hated flies about the place.

Finally Benet turned from the window, grinning at her. "You're right, you know. Where's that coffee? Let's go to the flicks, shall we? Miss Jane will listen for Johnnie Bertolino."

Vivian agreed with relief. She wheeled the trolley into the kitchen and left it. As she put on her hat and coat her hands were trembling with strain. She gave Benet her key with which to lock the flat door after them. He bent swiftly in the gloom, and before she was aware of his intention, he kissed her full on the mouth.

"That's on account," he told her cheerfully, handing back the key. "I quite like you, you know, darling."

She took his arm, and they sailed along the hall.

"So you see, Rita, he's really quite human."

"I think you're probably going to be very happy," Rita said. She had listened without comment while Vivian talked. "You love him, don't you?"

Vivian nodded. "Yes. I love him. Ten days ago I wasn't sure; I just wanted to make it uncomfortable for him, sort of be revenged on him, oh, I couldn't really sort out how I felt. But the way he acts now makes me care for him very much. He's not the type we thought he was. He's quite gentle really and yes . . . I like him terrifically . . ."

"It's quite amazing how things sort themselves out," Rita agreed. Suddenly she began to laugh derisively. She laughed so hard that Vivian joined in shame-facedly. "There was I, worrying about you, thinking Uncle Bertolino and I had let you down badly, quite sure you couldn't manage without us to shore you up . . . when all the time you were taking care of things with the wisdom of an angel."

Vivian hugged her gaily. "Not to worry any more. I won't either if it comes to that." Vivian was happy.

11

MISS JANE was standing outside their door, and her normally pale complexion was suffused with colour. Rita raised herself up and called her to enter.

"Good morning. Do come in. I'm only just settled for the day." She patted the chair beside her invitingly. The room was full of sunshine, for Vivian had already been round with the duster and had thrown the window wide open. Uncle Bertolino was expected later in the day and had promised to come direct to them.

"I know. But I can't stay. I've been before but couldn't make anyone hear. I think Vivian was busy with Johnnie Bertolino . . ." Miss Jane sounded breathless. Although she couldn't stay she sat down. "I wondered—Letty did, anyway— would it be possible for you to come along to our flat? Could you make it, do you think?"

337

"With your help I'm sure I could," Rita swung her legs on to the floor obediently.

"You see, if someone doesn't come soon, I fear Letty will blow up or something."

"You don't seem to be very far from that happy state yourself." Vivian came into the room, with Johnnie Bertolino on one arm. "What *is* it? Come, Rita, I'll help you. Take it steady."

"Are you sure you'll be safe?" Miss Jane was running in advance, making sure no obstacles were in the way.

"Of course. They told me at the hospital I must keep on my feet, so long as I don't over-tire myself, of course. Really, Miss Jane, I never knew anything so intriguing as this." They rather hurried along the corridor, infected by Miss Jane's excitement.

Miss Letty was reading something through her new glasses. She also looked very pink, her apple blossom complexion brushed with colour. She placed a chair for Rita, and put the letter down on the table in front of her.

"Vivian, dear, sit here . . ." She smiled at them. "Oh, I'm glad you're here. We've had the most astounding news in this morning's post, and not a soul to share it with. Jane has gone positively berserk. She went along to find you . . ."

"She told us," Vivian pointed out.

"What *is* it?" Rita asked.

"Even Mrs. Page is out, arranging for her bits and pieces to be taken by rail," Miss Jane chattered on in a conversational way that threatened to send Vivian's blood pressure soaring. Neither lady seemed able to come to the point, and it was completely maddening.

"Well now . . . you tell them, Letty . . ." Miss Jane sobered down.

"No, you. It makes me feel quite weak somehow . . ."

"All right. It's here, in this letter. We're really wondering if it's a hoax or something. Nothing like this has ever happened to us before. At least, it's happened to Letty really."

"Oh, Miss Jane . . ." Vivian cried in despair.

"No, I'm sure it isn't a hoax," Miss Letty put in vaguely. "We don't really think so. But Jane thought we ought to consult someone."

"I've known stranger things happen, but surely no one would be so cruel?" Miss Jane picked up the letter again. "We've read and re-read it and still can't memorize it . . ."

"Wait . . ." Vivian stood up and thrust Johnnie Bertolino into Rita's arms. "Take him before something happens to me. Listen . . . we insist on being told what has happened. Has someone left you a fortune?"

Both ladies laughed delightedly. "You could be further from the truth . . ."

Johnnie Bertolino crowed, and that made them all laugh again. "Bless him . . ."

"Then someone has . . ." Vivian insisted. "Tell me, someone."

"I'll tell them," Miss Jane drew a long breath. "Yes, dear, we've just won a fortune. At least Letty has really. It must be a mistake of course. But it is a fortune really. You know we've been doing the Pools for years? The most we have ever won was five pounds once although we very nearly won forty pounds if Letty hadn't made me change the line . . . But let that go. Well, this morning, this letter came, telling us that we'd won . . . wait for it . . . we'd won . . . I'll quote the exact figure—we'd won two thousand four hundred pounds one shilling and elevenpence . . ."

The silence satisfied even Miss Letty. She nodded approvingly as the four women stared at one another, spellbound. Johnnie Bertolino crowed at the shadow that flickered on the wall as the sun moved round to the back of the house.

"Why the one and elevenpence?" Rita asked feebly.

The sudden question made them all laugh shakily. "It's unbelievable," Miss Jane said. "That's the way we felt—just like you look now. After all this time too . . . Really . . ."

"How many years have we slaved at those things?" Letty asked. "Practically ever since we learned how to do them. Last week . . . no the week before . . . I decided to do them for a change. Jane is really very good at them, but we weren't getting anywhere. So I had a go."

"Whizzo." Rita shook her own hands with gusto. "Oh, I'm glad. You deserve it. It's thrilling news. No wonder you were so excited. I couldn't be more glad if I'd won it myself . . . I think."

The dubious ending made them all gasp. Miss Jane ran sturdy fingers through her hair, making it stand on end.

Vivian was reading the letter hastily. "Of course it's perfectly true. No one would write this if there was the least doubt. Subject to scrutiny etc. etc . . . Oh, it's practically in the bank, girls." She hugged the two ladies with extreme goodwill. "Now I'll ask Benet what are the best securities these days. His father should be able to help too. He knows everything about those things. You met him, didn't you? He'll help you manage . . ."

Miss Jane held up both hands. Miss Letty looked shocked. "Yes, we met him and he's a very nice man dear . . . but we absolutely refuse to be managed. At our time of life we mean to enjoy this windfall. It's unexpected, very welcome, and we'll spend every penny of it if we get the chance."

"I couldn't agree more," Rita said, watching them.

"Good for you." Vivian picked Johnnie Bertolino off Rita's lap and settled him on the table, with one hand on his back. "You mean business."

"You wouldn't like to live anywhere else now, would you?" Rita said dreamily.

"Oh, dear no, I just can't visualize us anywhere else," Miss Letty said.

Uncle Bertolino rapped smartly on the door with his cane. He stood beaming at them as they regarded him somewhat gravely. "I startle you? I just return. My nieces are out. I come here because I hear much laughter . . ." He was beaming at them harder than ever.

Vivian sprang to him, and drew him lovingly into the room.

"Oh, darling . . . of course we're glad to see you. We're just stunned, that's all. Take off your coat . . ."

He shook hands with Miss Jane and Miss Letty, and tickled Johnnie Bertolino under the chin. "And you, my poppet?" he said, turning to Rita.

"Soon be out of plaster, darling . . . Oh, it's nice to see you again. How's everything?"

He blew a kiss into the air. "Poof. Everything just fine. Fine . . ." It was a word he had enjoyed using for some time. "Under the thumb again . . ."

"Completely under control again? How is your daughter?" Rita asked.

"Thank you." Uncle Bertolino accepted the cup of tea that appeared miraculously at his elbow. "Now I know I am back." He took a long drink as if he had been thirsty for many hours. "This is so very pleasant—to find you all together like this."

"Tell him . . ." Vivian said. "It'll kill him . . ."

Uncle Bertolino looked at her reprovingly, but listened while Miss Letty told him of her good fortune. Uncle Bertolino sprang up and embraced her, kissing her on both cheeks. The apple blossom complexion turned to ripe peach.

"You forgive?" he said quickly. "I so much regard you . . ."

He didn't offer to kiss Miss Jane, Rita saw, and wondered why. Of course Miss Jane hadn't won a fortune.

"Now you will come with me to Italy and stay many months, eh? Now you take the holiday we speak about eh?" He was so excited that they all forgave him. His cane rattled on to the floor and Johnnie Bertolino cried.

"Yes, my lambkin you should be asleep." Vivian rose. "Sorry folks, carry on. I'll put him in his pram in the yard. Uncle Bertolino, you're an angel . . ."

Uncle Bertolino opened the door for her, and closed it after her. Miss Jane poured him another cup of tea, and as he drank it, they talked about his trip.

"I go up to the flat now," he said finally. "Soon I come back, eh?"

Mrs. Page came into the building while they were still talking. When she heard their news she congratulated them sincerely. "It's the best news for such a long time. Will you remain in the flats?" Mrs. Page looked tired and depressed, and slightly dishevelled. Her white, wispy hair fell unbecomingly from under her hat brim.

"Oh, definitely—we're so happy here with you all."

"Well, I'm going tomorrow. Uncle Bertolino won't be here very much longer. By the way, Dominic is flying the Atlantic tonight. I said goodbye to him just now."

They all looked at her sympathetically. Her small round body looked defeated.

They had not heard Dominic or Mrs. Page leave the building earlier, but he had said his goodbyes the previous night.

"You'll miss him terribly," Miss Letty spoke gently. "You've got on so well."

"Yes, and Dominic was so kind always," Miss Jane added. "I think we'll miss him too for he always offered the use of his car so willingly."

"Yes, he *is* good, isn't he?" Mrs. Page spoke gratefully, pleased at their praise. "It's worried him about the accident to Rita . . ."

"But it *was* an accident," Vivian chimed in. "So he wants to stop worrying about it. After all it could have happened to anyone."

"I suppose with it being Rita it would make a special impression on him . . ." Miss Letty mused.

Mrs. Page brightened. "Why, yes, I'd not thought of that. Of course, that's it. He was so fond of Rita. If only she could have loved him, instead of Richard, all would have been so happy for Dominic."

"It hadn't to be, evidently," Miss Jane

said sympathetically. They were grouped about Mrs. Page seeing her grief with fresh eyes. "Some people are just luckier than others."

"And we'll be leaving sooner or later," Vivian said. "My in-laws have found us a bungalow."

"Oh, dear—we'll soon be the only ones left. Letty, I don't much like this."

"I wouldn't worry about *that*," Vivian was laughing. "Well, we've had a good natter and I must fly. I'll see you again before you go, Mrs. Page."

Mrs. Page looked at the sisters blankly. They bent forward and kissed her. "Don't worry so much. Dominic will find his feet in America and probably bring home a wonderful girl . . ."

Mrs. Page left them, too full to be able to answer.

"This is what I'd call a nice, friendly block of flats," Miss Jane said pensively.

Richard was waiting for Rita when she returned. He took her into his arms without speaking for a moment. Gently he lifted her face and smiled into her eyes.

"I've been hearing about the excitement. You get around, don't you?"

She leaned against him, putting her arms about his waist. "Oh, Richard . . ."

"You're tired, darling."

She nodded. "Tired all the time, with dragging this leg around. I'll be glad when the plaster can come off. Come in and talk to the others."

"I brought you this . . ." He brought out a ring case. "Remember it?"

She watched as he put the engagement ring back on her finger. It flashed there with all the old fire. Richard bent his proud head and kissed it.

"Some day," he said gently, "when you've got all these other matters off your mind you and I will slip out and get married. We'll have a honeymoon too . . . Where would you like to go?"

"The Lake District, Richard. You remember—where you kicked my poor little pile of weeds in all directions?" She stood on tiptoe to kiss him, for Richard was a tall man. His thin, clever face flushed slightly. "Shall we go back there together?"

"Nothing I'd like better." His consideration helped her to remain strong. "But your Uncle Bertolino has been talking seriously to me. He insists that I bring you out to Italy to stay with them . . ."

"Them?" She was puzzled. "Oh, he must mean his stepdaughter, of course."

"Sooner or later we'll go, darling?" Richard was stroking her hair with quiet fingers.

"Yes. Dear old Uncle Bertolino . . ." She spoke the name with tenderness.

"He's awfully fond of you . . ." Richard continued.

"I know. I feel he is. I love him too."

"You love me, don't you?" Richard spoke very softly into her small ear.

"Yes. I do." They stood close together, so engrossed that they did not hear Benet come to the door and rattle the handle noisily.

"Hey, you two . . . break it up. Sorry and all that—but could you come a minute, Rita? Johnnie Bertolino is playing steam, and Vivian says he won't let anyone but you undress him." He nodded to Richard, and offered him a cigarette.

"I'll go." She smiled back at Richard. "Never a dull moment around here. Can you two entertain each other for a while?"

"Will you and Richard stay on here

when I leave?" Vivian asked presently, when Johnnie Bertolino was sleeping peacefully in his cot.

"We hadn't discussed it, but I scarcely think so. I intend to travel about with Richard. I just hate to think of all those long separations. Months ago he said he'd want me with him; I couldn't see it then, but now I can."

"How the mighty are fallen," Vivian scoffed. "It does make a difference when you love someone, doesn't it? Benet's parents are settling on that bungalow. He's seen it again and it's just what we need. So that's settled. I thought I'd tell you. Good night, Benet . . ." She called out hastily, when he pushed his head round the door.

"Richard's gone to answer the telephone," Benet said. "I'll hang on a minute till we see who it's for."

They all waited curiously, wondering who could be ringing up at this hour. They heard Richard returning down the hall, and some urgency in his speeding feet communicated itself to them. He came to the open door.

"Benet . . . Rita . . . it's for Mrs. Page

. . . and it's bad news. What on earth can we do? She's gone to Euston, hasn't she?" Richard looked strained as his gaze came to Rita's.

Rita stood up, holding on the back of her chair with nerveless fingers. "What is it?"

"Dominic's plane . . ."

"Oh, no." Vivian buried her face in both hands. "No, not that . . ."

Rita waited limply. It took a moment for Richard to tell them. "It's missing. Apparently they've tried to contact Mrs. Page before."

"We must go to the station. There's still time?" Rita looked at the dainty clock on Vivian's dressing table. "Oh, she might hear of it casually. She might see it in the evening papers. Richard . . . get me there somehow." Her words came on a wild ring of pain.

"I'll dash out and get a taxi." Benet was gone with the words. He hailed a passing taxi and it was at the door before Rita was ready. Her hands were so cold that she could scarcely put on her outdoor coat. Richard found her gloves. Together they hastened to the door.

"Shall I come with you?" Benet asked, white-faced in the gloom.

"No. Look after the flat until we return." Rita touched his hand gently, finding it as cold as her own. "Oh, Richard . . ." She turned to him in the darkness, and he put his arm about her waist.

"We'll be in time, poor old soul . . ." Richard's pity sounded in his deep voice.

"The last thing any of us expected. Tell me what else they said?"

In a few minutes they were at Euston station. Rita remained in the taxi, while Richard ran to the platform where Mrs. Page would be waiting for her train. He found her almost at once. She was sitting on a form, her luggage beside her, watching the other passengers who were walking up and down. He reached her, trying to subdue his agitation.

"Could you come to speak to Rita? She wants to see you. She can't get out of the taxi very easily." He gathered up her smaller articles and led the way.

"But why?" she asked, smiling curiously. "Luckily the train isn't in yet. I've just time." They hurried along the platform and back through the barrier. Richard led her to the taxi.

"Get in a minute," Rita whispered, leaning forward in the gloom.

Mrs. Page entered, panting a little with the speed at which Richard had led the way.

Rita told her.

"Is he dead?" Mrs. Page asked, and her small, round body seemed to wither with the shock.

"We don't know yet." Richard spoke, for Rita couldn't. "Apparently they have been trying to contact you all day. The plane was notified as missing at breakfast time."

"I've been out most of the day," Mrs. Page spoke dully.

"We were afraid you'd hear it casually."

"Yes. That would have hurt me even more." Mrs. Page was the more composed of the three. She took Rita's hand in both hers, and they sat so for a while. They heard the shrill whistle of the train coming into the platform. There was no hurry now. She could go north at any time.

"You mustn't go tonight," Rita told her

tenderly. "Stay with us a little while so that we can help you."

Richard looked to her for confirmation before getting out to fetch the remainder of her bags. He got a porter, and together they stowed the luggage into the taxi. Richard told the driver something of what had occurred, and there was sympathy established even in this small matter.

Mrs. Page stayed with Rita's hand in hers for the return journey. Together they got out and entered the building quietly. Benet had been along to tell Miss Jane and Miss Letty so that they also were ready to help.

"Mrs. Page could sleep in our flat," Miss Jane offered. Her own was dismantled and cold. They could not let her return there, to spend the hours in silent agony.

"Would you like to do that?" Rita asked the old woman. "I think it would be wise."

She nodded, sighing, and went with Miss Jane into the warm little room.

"Thank you for doing so much for us, Richard." Rita was exhausted. Suddenly she began to cry, the tears running down her white face helplessly. She stood just as she was, defenceless before their sympathy, her hands covering her face.

"Darling." Richard went to her. Benet muttered:

"I'll get up to my own flat now . . ." He kissed Vivian silently. "Good night, dear."

They all parted a few minutes later. Richard said: "Take care of yourself, darling. You're precious. Try not to worry about what's happened."

"I just can't understand it," she said to Vivian when they were alone. "Oh, dear . . ."

"It's not given to us to understand most things that happen in life." Vivian was lying back against the pillows. "But you know, I can't help noticing—both Benet and Richard sprang to it." There was a strange comfort in the knowledge. Whatever came in life they were not alone. "Richard looked . . . did you see him when Mrs. Page left us?"

"Yes," Rita whispered. She had seen Richard's face. The sympathy there must have comforted the old woman, as much as it did them now. "I hope she'll be all right."

Thinking of her, helped her own grief. Tiredly she rose from the chair.

"You must be exhausted," Vivian said.

"It's dragging this plaster around that's so tiring," Rita told her. "Oh, what a day this has been. How do you feel?"

"Fine. Benet's a darling really. We've come to understand each other."

"I'm glad." Rita trailed off out of the room to make them a hot drink. "Awfully glad dear."

The day was not yet over. Presently they heard Uncle Bertolino returning from the opera and Rita called him in.

"But this is terrible," he said, blinking when she told him about Dominic. He wiped his eyes in sudden uncontrollable sympathy. "Terrible. The last thing . . . Where is she now?"

"Mrs. Page? Oh, she's sleeping with Miss Jane and Miss Letty tonight," Rita explained. "None of us wanted her to go back to that flat alone."

"No." He brightened, and presently went up to the flat he shared with Benet, treading on tiptoe in case he wakened

anyone. "But that is kind . . . kind . . ."
he said to the air.

Mrs. Page drew strength from their help.
In the morning's papers they knew that
the delayed plane had not survived the
storm that wrecked it. Official confirmation came during the day, that Dominic
was not among the survivors.

They all went to the station two days
later to see Mrs. Page off for her long
journey north.

"You'll come?" She spoke to Rita
urgently.

"I promise," Rita told her, and the wind
stung her eyes so that they watered. They
waved silently as the train drew out, and
presently turned away.

12

FOR the next week or two life appeared to be running down in the flats. Uncle Bertolino spent two days touring the south coast. He went alone because not one of them could be spared from the duties that still held them.

"Just wait till I get out of plaster," Rita threatened. "There won't be any stopping me then." Impatiently she longed for the day of release.

"We'll be married the day after . . ." Richard said, listening intently.

"All right." She agreed instantly, and he was pleased.

"Then you'd better get your trousseau together, because you'll be out in another week . . ." He grinned cheerfully. "I checked up with the hospital last time you were there, and they said the tenth . . ."

He drew her to him. "It can't be too soon, my littlest love."

All week, Vivian seemed to be packing things as if preparing for removal at some future date. Even Johnnie Bertolino's wardrobe was scrutinized with loving zeal. She discarded her own garments, when necessary, mended others, placing all ready in trunk or suitcase.

Rita watched her silently.

"I needn't take everything to Benet's flat, need I? Gradually I can take most things as I want them from the trunk; it won't be in your way here, Rita?" Vivian enquired.

"Not a bit. Just plan it the way you want it. It's going to feel queer without you. I'm quite glad I'm going away for a few days just so that I'll get used to it."

"Mm . . . yes." Vivian was pulling silk stockings over her hand, scrutinizing them calmly, and putting them into pairs. "I wonder how one comes to have so many pairs?"

On Friday she was quiet most of the morning, and Rita wondered if she were regretting anything. Benet had been in the evening before, as was his custom, but Rita was not present when he took his leave.

When she came in from shopping at tea-time on Friday, Vivian had her room tidy, the meal ready and she was dressed in one of her best suits.

"Going anywhere special?" Rita asked, sitting down with a sigh of relief, for she was tired.

"Maybe I am. I won't know until I see Benet. We may go out somewhere tonight to celebrate." Vivian gave her a queer look. "Uncle Bertolino is turning that flat over to Benet, you know, until we can get into the bungalow. Did he tell you?"

"No. I'll wash up if you want to go up; he should be home now," Rita suggested.

"He is. I heard him come in a quarter of an hour ago. You know, Rita, now that it's all coming to a head I feel a bit—odd."

"Not regretting?"

"Oh, no, not really." Vivian seemed in an uncommunicative mood. She accepted Rita's offer and presently she left the flat and ran up the stairs to Benet's top floor flat.

She tapped lightly on the door. The blue suit exactly matched her eyes, and her hair was shining with the care and attention she had given it. She was as neat and clean as if she had prepared for a party.

Benet's eyes narrowed as he saw her

standing there. "Hullo. This is the first time you've called on me. Coming in?"

She stepped over the threshold. Suddenly she was breathless and gauche. "I wondered—would you like to go out somewhere tonight, Benet? A show . . . I thought . . ."

"Could be. That wasn't what you came to say though?"

"No. No, it wasn't." She smiled at him, seeing the apron tied round his waist, his air of flurry like any housewife caught out at his daily chores. "What are you doing?"

"Getting the flat tidied up for when you come tomorrow," he told her bluntly.

"It looks very nice."

"I'd just about finished; did most of it last night."

"Oh." Her gaze flickered away. "I wondered—should I come today, Benet?"

"Now?" He strode behind her and shut the door with sudden decision. In that action he shut out their world. "Now Vivian?"

"Would you like that?" she whispered.

"You know the answer to that. But why?" He was holding her at arms length, his dark gaze raking her flushed face.

"I thought—suddenly I knew that I loved you so much—I wanted you to be right. You said that time—you remember —that I'd have been in your arms . . . only your goodwill kept us apart. It was to please me . . . but I wanted you to—not have to wait, the whole time. So I came now . . ."

Tears were suddenly running down her flushed cheeks. For a moment longer Benet held her apart, before sweeping her into his arms.

"Oh, darling . . . darling . . ."

She was laughing now, through the tears. Her soft mouth quivered under the hard pressure of his lips. Suddenly he picked her up and carried her to his big chair, where he sat with her cradled across his knees.

"You needn't explain another thing if you don't want to," he told her. "I guess I understand. Does Rita know?"

"Not unless she's already read the note I left for her. I've been packing up all week but she thought I was leaving tomorrow. Benet . . . it . . . it feels lovely that you understand. I was scared in case you might not." She put her head close to

362

his, and kissed him shyly. "You've been so patient and kind and good and I adore you."

"Hey . . ." he scowled. "I've been none of those things. You don't know me. I've wanted to kidnap you for weeks."

Vivian's dimples came out entrancingly. "Really? I'm glad I didn't know—because I've been wishing you—would . . ."

Benet laughed then, a long, deep laugh of complete happiness. "Methinks I've got me a honey of a wife."

"Listen, darling," she ignored that resolutely. "I may seem frivolous to you, but I'm not really. I'm quite firm inside now about some things. My career for instance . . ."

"Yeah . . ." he drawled. "Your career. May as well have it now as later."

"My career is secondary to my life with you. I want to be a good wife first of all."

He swept her back into his arms. "Go on. You intrigue me."

"I'd like to continue singing from time to time, but it isn't the be-all and end-all as it was—before." She struggled hard to retain her dignity in spite of his laughter. Happiness simplified so much in life.

"Maybe I could help financially now and again, and sort of keep my hand in . . ."

"I understand completely," he told her, and suddenly he stood up and carried her up and down the room. He was laughing delightedly. "I'm first . . . and foremost . . . and that's the way you are with me. You funny little woman . . . don't you know I'm head over heels in love with you? I don't care what you do so long as you are happy and content with me. We'll live a good life . . . we'll have fun . . . and we'll go places. But we'll always be together, and do it together, and live it together, until death do us part. That the way you want it too?"

Suddenly he was sober again, and he put her down on her own feet. Vivian swayed a moment before meeting the mounting passion in his deep-set eyes.

"That's the way I want it too," she told him steadily.

At ten o'clock Rita found the note that Vivian had left for her. Standing with it in her hand she read it carefully a second time. Forgiving and forgetting . . . that was the way of life, the careful pattern that ran through all living. Vivian had made it very clear what her life was to be. Had she realized that until her happiness was complete Rita could not find her own? Was that the message to be read behind the lines of that loving little note of explanation? Rita folded it carefully and placed it in her drawer.

Uncle Bertolino came in about eleven o'clock. Rita said brightly: "You're sleeping in Mrs. Page's flat tonight—do you mind? You're turned out of yours, and I haven't had time to get Vivian's room ready for you."

"Did she take Johnnie Bertolino with her?" he asked, with considerable interest.

"No, she's fetching him tomorrow. Funny, isn't it?"

Uncle Bertolino evidently thought it was. He kissed Rita soundly on both cheeks.

"I go home next week—for good . . ." he told her presently, his voice a little sad.

She sighed. There was nothing to say to that for he must go one day, but she would miss him more than any of them.

"Your Richard will take care of you," he told her gently. "Now, there is a man . . ."

"You like him, don't you?" she asked, sparkling.

The following morning when Rita went up to waken Uncle Bertolino he was not to be found in Mrs. Page's former flat. The mystery was solved when she passed Miss Jane and Miss Letty's door, for Uncle Bertolino was having breakfast with them.

In his usual inimitable style, he had tied an apron about his waist and was cooking a large frying pan full of bacon, eggs, kidneys, sausages and tomatoes.

"But we never eat cooked breakfasts," Miss Letty told him, as he set the plate before her.

"This is different, yes? You eat this one, yes?" Uncle Bertolino bent and looked into her exasperated face. Miss Letty was not used to being pushed around, and she had a strong feeling that was exactly what was happening.

"I'll eat it," she promised.

Replete, they sat chatting in front of the fire. Presently Miss Letty went out to shop leaving Uncle Bertolino washing the breakfast dishes. Miss Letty could never get enough action these days. As she banged the back door he skipped back to speak to Miss Jane. His hands were damp from the water.

"Miss Letty would come to Italy now, eh?"

"She might," Jane answered blankly. "Why?"

"She would come with you, no?"

"I suppose so." Miss Jane was mystified. She sat down—duster in hand while Uncle Bertolino stood brandishing the egg ladle.

"Will *you* come?" he asked softly.

She glanced up at him. His face was unsmiling now. For the first time she saw the beauty of the grave, dark eyes, their leaping intelligence, the sensitive lips, the nobility of the broad face. When she could not answer he continued in the same gentle voice.

"I want you to come, Jane. First for a holiday if you wish it that way . . . but later to stay as my wife. I have come to like you so much. Perhaps you like me a little eh?"

"Like you?" She paused. "Yes, I like you. We all do. No, but wait—don't think that I haven't noticed how you have 'managed' everyone in these flats since you came . . . You've changed the face of the summer, I believe. Or is it even more than that? Those two girls were frightened, but now they have found their true happiness. You've given them something real, something they were in danger of forgetting . . ."

He looked astounded. "But Jane . . . you are not suggesting that I . . . manage you?"

She gave him a keen look. "I wouldn't put it past you."

"No, no." He denied it strenuously. "This I cannot permit."

"Then why did you have breakfast with us?"

"Because so soon I go . . . and we cannot have breakfast together."

"Why have you sent all those flowers . . ." she continued inexorably.

"There were more than Rita and Vivian could take."

"I don't believe it. They like flowers—as much as we do."

Uncle Bertolino turned from the argument with dignity. "These things can all be explained when the heart is right eh? Jane, you like me a little eh?"

She nodded, a little frightened of what it might do for her.

He brightened at once, put the ladle down on the table, and came to stand in front of her.

"You would like to be my wife?" he questioned tenderly. "Once I was married before, Jane. That time I was the happiest of men. Such kindness is rare, but I think I find it again in you, Jane. I love to think it is so. I love your kindness. I love you, my Jane. Do you wonder that I try to keep such kindness always for my own? Is this selfish? Not so. I can make you happy, I think. In my country the sun is always shining. I have wealth . . . I can give you most things."

"Wealth has never counted with me," Jane told him loftily. "Besides, Letty has this money now. We don't *need* anything like that."

Uncle Bertolino stood rebuffed. Puzzled he looked humbly down into her face. "You not like me enough, eh?"

"Oh, yes, I do . . ." Jane gazed over his head dreamily.

"Ah—the English are so different. This I like. I like it very much," Uncle Bertolino was grasping her meaning. "This— you would not marry me if I had all the wealth . . . only if you liked me enough? This I understand now. This is so wise. Jane . . . Jane . . . I could give you much love. I could make you happy. If only you will come, Jane . . ."

He knelt beside her, hesitating for a moment before he took her hand. Jane looked shy and slightly ill at ease for a moment, until she remembered that he was a foreigner. All foreigners showed their feelings, didn't they? She met the look in his beautiful, deep-set eyes, and forgot everything else, even herself.

"I have always liked the red hair . . ." he told her reverently. "I like you. Jane . . . my love, we could be happy." He began to tell her again about his home in Italy, drawing pictures in the air of their joint future there. "If only you will come, Jane." All that had been seemed to have been coming towards this moment of perfect understanding.

They thought they could hear Letty returning, and neither of them was ready.

The matter assumed an urgency it had not previously held.

"I'll come," Jane promised breathlessly.

It was not Letty after all. As they waited they could hear Rita hobbling down the yard to pay the milkman. She closed the gate after him, seeing the four dustbins, the hydrangea, the galvanized coal bins. She felt a sense of shock. Apparently she had not noticed them since that morning in the spring when life was miserable and burdened; the morning that Uncle Bertolino came into their lives! She gazed at them reflectively. Who would use them next?

Uncle Bertolino kissed Miss Jane soundly in Italian, and she liked it very much. Uncle Bertolino was too overcome to speak in English.

We hope this Large Print edition gives you the pleasure and enjoyment we ourselves experienced in its publication.

There are now more than 2,000 titles available in this ULVERSCROFT Large print Series. Ask to see a Selection at your nearest library.

The Publisher will be delighted to send you, free of charge, upon request a complete and up-to-date list of all titles available.

Ulverscroft Large Print Books Ltd.
The Green, Bradgate Road
Anstey
Leicestershire
LE7 7FU
England

GUIDE
TO THE COLOUR CODING
OF
ULVERSCROFT BOOKS

Many of our readers have written to us expressing their appreciation for the way in which our colour coding has assisted them in selecting the Ulverscroft books of their choice.

To remind everyone of our colour coding—this is as follows:

BLACK COVERS
Mysteries

★

BLUE COVERS
Romances

★

RED COVERS
Adventure Suspense and General Fiction

★

ORANGE COVERS
Westerns

★

GREEN COVERS
Non-Fiction

ROMANCE TITLES
in the
Ulverscroft Large Print Series